Ravi Abhiramnew's job is simple: hunt down and neutralize supernatural threats. That is until he meets Cayenne, a charismatic time traveler who claims to know everything about him—even his most closely guarded secrets.

Going to dinner with Cayenne is probably a bad idea, and a romantic island getaway definitely is.

When a monster picks their resort as its hunting ground, Ravi's combat skills and Cayenne's time magic should make it a breeze to kill the monster and get their vacation back on track. But it turns out the real danger lurks much, much closer…

STOLEN FROM

TOMORROW

TRUST TRILOGY, BOOK ONE

FOX BECKMAN

A NineStar Press Publication
www.ninestarpress.com

Stolen from Tomorrow

First Edition, April 2023

ISBN: 978-1-64890-648-0

Also available in eBook, ISBN: 978-1-64890-647-3

CONTENT WARNING:
This book contains sexually explicit content, which may only be suitable for mature readers. Depictions of guns and death.

Prologue

"WHAT WOULD IT take for you to go on a date with me, handsome?"

Ravi, startled mid-jog, spun around and pulled out his single earbud. He raised his hands.

"*Mince alors*, you're a jumpy one! Let's try that again. Hello, I am Cayenne, they/them pronouns, *s'il vous plaît*, absolutely a *pleasure* to meet you." The redhead flashed a wide grin from an exceptionally attractive, fine-boned face, and stuck out a sideways hand.

Ravi glanced warily up and down the trail that, five seconds ago, he would have bet on his life had been devoid of anyone else. It was possible this stranger had been obscured by one of the many moss-clad oaks dotting the trail, but they'd have to be pretty damn obscured for Ravi's keen eyes to have missed them. He took a step back. "Where did you come from?"

Cayenne sighed, resting their unshaken hand on their hip. "*Very* long story. Look, darling, I've got a narrow window, here. So can we just skip the foreplay and get down to business?"

Ravi squared up, shoulders firming. "Who the fuck are you and what do you want?"

Cayenne's green eyes flashed with undisguised delight. "Ooh, tough guy! I thought I was pretty clear from the get-go: I want to know what would convince you to go on a date with me."

This time, when Ravi checked his peripheral vision, it wasn't for a trap or an ambush, but for eavesdroppers. "Is this how you usually pick up dates? Accosting them in parks at five in the morning?"

"No, no," they laughed, "this is just—what do you call—*reconnaissance*. Don't worry about it, darling, you can tell me the unvarnished truth. Pretend it's a dream, if that helps. None of this"—Cayenne tossed a vague gesture encompassing the trail, the two of them, perhaps the whole world entire—"none of this is going to count."

Ravi took another step back. "You're crazy," he said,

automatically sizing up the stranger for hidden weapons, but stopped still as his own words sank in. "Do you need help?"

Cayenne made a little sound of pleased surprise, hand going to their chest. "Aren't you a *sweetheart*?"

"I can call someone for you," Ravi offered.

Cayenne tapped a slender finger to their chin, eyeing Ravi from head to toe. The little hairs on the back of his neck all stood on end, his heart rate skipping. "Guarded, but altruistic. This actually *has* been illuminating, darling, despite your best efforts to deflect." They stepped closer, tilting up a sharp, suggestive smile. "I'll be seeing you, Ravi."

Ravi's pulse froze, every limb tensing in preparation for a fight. "How do you know my name?"

Cayenne grinned wide, winked, then Ravi was again alone on the trail, earbud back in with his workout playlist thrumming up a beat that matched his ground-eating stride. He continued his morning run as if nothing had happened, because for him, nothing had.

Chapter One

CAREFULLY PEERING DOWN the sights of his 9mm, Ravi squeezes off a shot. It strikes true, lodging deep into the monster's exposed heart. The creature doesn't falter in the slightest, snarling in his direction as if he were a particularly irritating gnat. A perfect shot, and it isn't good enough. Typical, really.

In all his years hunting monsters, Ravi has never seen anything quite like this before. Strips of flesh hang off grayed bones between swathes of icy-white fur, a looming eight-foot-tall humanoid crowned with twisted icicle horns, baring a mouthful of jagged fangs while the freezing air steams with its breath. The heart seems to be the obvious target, a stark knot of dark ice threading around exposed ribs into the monster's chest, but nothing the team has thrown at it has had any effect. Val's giant double-handed maul would surely put a crack in it, if they can get her close enough for a hit, but any time they try, the giant beast summons up a swarm of ice serpents from the surrounding snow, keeping the hunters at bay. Because being a giant, slavering behemoth with no obvious weaknesses wasn't enough; it's got magic too. Again, typical.

Ravi curses and ducks back to rejoin the rest of the group as the monster lets loose another bellowing roar, snaking out a many-jointed arm to rip up a huge chunk of earth and fling it at Ravi and his team. Val, eyes burning blue-white behind mirrored sunglasses, calmly steps forward and deflects the projectile with a blow of her maul. It shatters into a shower of snow and icy dirt.

"Little cover, Constance?" Harry suggests. She lowers her gun after Ravi's shot hit dead center to zero effect, looking supremely annoyed. "Also, if you've got any idea what this thing is, that would be really useful."

Constance steps forward, hands working feverishly as she pulls a tangle of thorns from her satchel and slaps it together with a handful of hastily procured dust from another pocket. A thick wall of thorns rises from the ground, cutting them off from the monster and granting a momentary reprieve. "I hast ne'er beheld such a beast 'ere, mine niece."

"Getting a little ye olde there, Constance," Harry tells her ancestress.

Dropping her hands, Constance turns toward the rest contritely. "Ah, yes, my apologies. I have no knowledge of this creature. Hey, nonny-nonny," she adds with a flash of mischief.

"I think it's a chenoo?" Nate pokes his head out from behind one of the torn-up tree trunks, still intrepidly wielding his hockey stick. He slaps one of the ice serpents away as it gets too close. "Fuck! These things are quick."

"What's a chenoo?" Ravi asks, eyes darting from the thorn wall and scanning the snow for more serpents. "How do we kill it?"

Nate winces. "I'm pretty sure it's like an Algonquian version of a wendigo."

Everyone groans. Wendigos are the *worst*. Harry shakes her dark hair, gun hand gesturing to the chenoo. "Okay, Professor, so how do we take it down?"

"Is it not the heart?" Val asks, peering up on her toes over the thorn wall. She's so tall she barely needs to stretch. "It is on the outside of its body." She ducks back down as the chenoo tears another skeletal tree right up by the roots and sends it crashing against the thorn wall.

Constance grimaces, rocking on her heels as if she'd been dealt the blow. "I cannot keep this wall up for much longer, my comrades."

"Noted," says Harry, forehead furrowed.

"A direct hit to the heart did nothing," Ravi reminds her. "You'd think fire would do it, but Constance's first spell did nothing except melt some snakes."

Nate shakes his head. "I'm not sure what will kill it. Usually, you get the Ojibwe version of these things here in the Midwest, and the heart shot would have killed one of those. I'd have to do some research. Would have been nice if the client gave us this info before sending us here, don't you think?"

"Take cover!" Val bellows as a massive tree trunk flies their way. Ravi grabs the person closest to him. He drags Harry out of the way while Val snatches up Nate and Constance and teleports them out of sight just as earth and bark crash down through the thorn wall onto the churned-up snow where they had all been standing.

Ravi helps Harry to her feet as they take cover behind a tangle of fallen oaks. "I guess it would have been too easy if this ice monster was vulnerable to fire, huh," she says wryly, kicking at an errant ice snake. "If I could talk to it, I might be able to figure out what it wants. We've talked down monsters from a fight once or twice before."

"If it's like a wendigo, it just wants to eat people. I could set up a sniper nest," Ravi offers. "There are decent vantage points there"—he points up at a pair of snowy hills—"and there."

Harry gives him an incredulous look. "Is that what you have in that big bag, a friggin' sniper rifle? Where'd you learn to snipe?"

"Israel," he answers shortly.

Her eyebrows lift. "What were you doing in Israel?"

Mourning. "Training," he says. "The Trust has a few consultants in Mossad."

Harry rolls her eyes. "Of course you do. I bet all you covert agent types get together for regular potlucks and barbeques." She scans their surroundings. "No rifles. Let's try to keep any more gunplay to a minimum," she says with regret. Ravi knows how she feels. The two of them are the marksmen of the group, and sometimes it's not easy being overshadowed by an Amazonian angel warrior with a big magic hammer and a spell-slinging sorceress. At least the new guy just has a hockey stick.

Ravi watches her face, sees where she's looking, thinks he can intuit her plan. "You want to give Val an opening?" It's standard ops to get a team's main damage dealer where they'll do the most harm, and Harry has surprisingly good instincts for team dynamics, considering she operated as a lone PI before all this supernatural shit entered her life. She nods decisively, and he holsters his gun. "Good plan. I'll back your play."

"Okay. Let's do it." She breathes out, then they both burst into motion. Harry grabs a couple of branches, hands one to Ravi, and, wielding them like clubs, they wade out into the open. The ice snakes are quick and agile, but only take a hit or two before they shatter. The pair fan out in different directions, smashing and stomping, creating a pie slice toward the others. "Constance!" Harry cries out. "Distract it!"

Constance runs forward into the cleared space, bright energy already swirling around her hands. While she gathers up her magic, Harry nods at Ravi. He nods back and moves to cover their witch, stomping an approaching ice snake's head under his oxfords before it can get too close to her. "Where's Nate?"

"He went down the embankment," Val intones. "He claimed he had an idea."

Constance finishes her spell, speaking an unfamiliar word and pulling her hands up into twin claws. Fire spreads up from cracks in the ground in front of the chenoo. It reels back, roaring with fury, and turns toward the fire, leaving its back open and unguarded.

"Let's hope the Professor is right," Harry mutters,

thwacking a pair of ice snakes. "Val, got your wings on?"

"Always." Val's sunglasses reflect the blaze, and white, feathered wings appear from nowhere, unfurling behind her. With a flash, she teleports behind the creature, raises her war hammer, and slams it down onto the monster. A solid hit. The pained screech of the thing is so piercing and terrible it raises the hairs on everybody's arms. All the ice snakes stop their advance and writhe in place.

Ravi takes the opportunity to stomp a few more of the snakes before they recover as Constance throws open her satchel. "To battle, my familiar!" Her cat, Griswold, leaps from the bag and pounces on the nearest ice snake with a bold, strident battle cry.

"Take that, loathsome serpent! Have at thee, villains!"

The cat sinks his fangs into the back of the snake's head and shakes fiercely.

It's a weird team, Ravi admits, but it works.

Chapter Two

A FEW HOURS earlier, and one year in the future, Ravi's wrapping up practice at the gun range when Harry's group text comes through.

> Hey team, I got us a job. Paying crazy well. We're going to Chicago first thing in the morning to meet with the client. The brief says to wear warm clothes. Also, we can't take pictures of the client, and Constance and her cat have to stay two yards away from the client at all times.

Constance eventually texts back.

> What did'st I do to earn this ire?

Though first, she sends a series of random letters and symbols. Modern technology is likely always going to be tricky for her.

Harry sends back a shrug emoji.

> *So pack up your guns, swords, magic potions, or whatever the fuck. No idea what's going to be waiting for us, let's be ready for anything. New guy, you ready for this?*

Nate's text back is just a series of exclamation marks and cheering emojis. Val tersely chimes in with her confirmation; like Constance, she's not much of a texter.

Ravi dials the secure line to his superior.

"Ravi," his handler answers smoothly, and even though she can't see if he is slouching or not, his spine straightens automatically at the sound of her gunpowder voice.

"Ma'am. McAllister got a lead on a job in Chicago." She is not a fan of small talk. Better he jump straight to the matter at hand.

"Ah, yes. The network just delivered this potential issue to my desk five minutes ago. Someone on your end must be very well informed to get it before The Trust did. Interesting." She sniffs, an expressive sound that manages to fully convey her displeasure.

Very interesting. The Trust's network operates via a

combination of intelligence agents, data mining, and seers, so they are usually extremely well-informed. "We've got no specifics on the threat. Any relevant details from the network?"

She breathes an irritated sigh. "None. Only that the event is to occur in Chicago, but there's some confusion from the seers on *when* this is supposed to occur. It's possible some lines have been crossed."

It's rare, but it happens. "I'll keep my eyes open, ma'am."

"Ravi," she says, her voice lowering with what he *knows* is going to be some sort of chastisement. She always finds something. "Your reports have been light on details lately. Especially after the incident with the young somamancer. You convinced me that we shouldn't recruit the young woman for a few years, despite my better judgment. She could easily become a danger to others."

"Constance has been very successful in teaching Lucy to control her abilities."

"The girl made blood monsters, agent."

"By accident. Lucy is twelve—" he begins, but his handler's voice goes cold and unassailable. He falls silent as she speaks over him.

"That is quite enough."

He takes a slow breath. "Sorry, Aunt Padme."

"I expect a certain standard from you, Ravi. You are not a common field agent. You're an Abhiramnew. We've placed a great deal of faith in you to handle these independent contractors in whatever way you see best. See that we don't have cause to regret that decision."

Long practice keeps his voice calm as a stone. "Of course, ma'am."

He can almost hear her firm nod of approval. "Very good. Maintain the appraisal on McAllister's team. If they keep doing so well against these supernatural threats, we might be interested in offering them a full contract within the Atlanta branch. As always, if you find any useful artifacts, do be sure to retrieve them."

"Yes, ma'am."

"And I expect your next report to be *thorough*."

"Yes, ma'am."

She hangs up. His spine finally loosens.

Ravi checks the group text. A lot of crosstalk about when and how to use emojis, jokes and affection flying back and forth between the rest of the team. He considers this for a time before sending a simple, *I'll be there*.

*

THE FIRST THING Ravi thinks when he sees the client is, *This one is going to be trouble.*

"Bonjour and *enchanté,* I am Cayenne!" A young man in an expensive summer outfit waves at them enthusiastically, French accent ringing clearly through the park. He wears small round sunglasses and a wide, inviting smile, and is surrounded by blankets, picnic baskets, and over to the side, a chalk dust circle decorated with candles and pocket watches. It's an unusual scene, to say the least.

His name is *Cayenne.* Ravi is glad his mirrored shades help hide an uncharitable eye roll. The client is easy to size up: loud, flamboyant, shameless, moving through the world easily and unapologetically. A quick assessment doesn't reveal any obvious weapons. Long-limbed, slim, athletic. Ravi clocks his lithe muscles and is sure he'd be nasty in a fight. If they got in hand-to-hand, he'd watch carefully for tricks; this one looks like he'd go for all the soft spots. Fiery red hair, green eyes like faceted gems, an angular face cut fine. Straddling a tenuous line between handsome and beautiful. Something off about his looks. Like seeing a magazine come to life. There's an artsy tattoo of a clock on the back of his left hand.

Constance tilts her head curiously. "Cayenne. That is a type of pepper, yes?" The gaps in her knowledge are sometimes unexpected, but it makes sense that a fair few spices would be new to her. After all, she came from a time when plain salt was worth its weight in gold.

"*Mais oui!* You don't think the name appropriate? I am a *very* spicy pepper." The client laughs with an artful shake of his hair, sun catching bright coppery highlights. "*Now,* I have gone through considerable effort to procure a *delightful* assortment of picnic baskets for each of you. All of your favorite foods! Shall we enjoy *un petit repas* while we discuss this contract? My dear Constance, if you could just stay on *that* far side of the blankets, it would be most appreciated, thank you, darling." Constance looks baffled but doesn't approach.

"I do not eat," Val states.

Cayenne looks all six-plus feet of Val up and down with open admiration, from her sporty sneakers to her ash-blonde ponytail. "My dear lady, would you be so kind as to step on me?"

Harry coughs sharply in surprise, and even Ravi has to wrangle his eyebrows back down into place. Nate leans over to Constance as if to whisper an explanation, but she holds up a hand with an amused expression. Looks like some things stood the test of time.

Val's pale brows furrow in confusion. "No."

"Such a shame," Cayenne sighs. Ravi bristles, folding his arms across his chest. Abruptly Cayenne looks over at Nate, frowning. "Please, Dr. Corbin, put your phone away. This is the third time you've attempted to take my picture."

Nate blinks and protests, sliding his phone back into his pocket with some embarrassment. "No, it isn't."

"Aha, you merely don't *remember* the previous attempts, because they've never happened. Not for you." Cayenne smiles enigmatically, which is only slightly marred by Harry's exasperated sigh.

"Great, another time traveler," she says. "This is the second time we've met one, now." It's only there for a flash of a second, but Cayenne looks a little put out by Harry's pronouncement. She must have spoiled a planned surprise.

"Third," pipes up Constance mildly. "I only managed it the one time, but still."

"And doth not I count?" Griswold's strident voice rings out from Constance's satchel. "I hath traipsed through the very barrier of time and space itself, mistress!" He pokes his small furry head out from under the leather flap.

"Quite right, my noble prince. Fourth." Constance corrects herself, giving the cat a scratch between the ears.

Cayenne pouts a little before grinning at them all archly. "Oh, believe me when I say that you haven't met a time traveler like *moi* before. And Dr. Corbin has perfectly demonstrated why everyone needs to leave their phones here in this basket before we go any further with this arrangement, *s'il vous plaît*." After Harry nods reluctantly, they all deposit their devices into the basket.

"Do you know James?" Constance asks. "He is a time traveler as well. A nice fellow."

Nate gives her a small friendly shove with his shoulder. "I'm sure all time travelers don't know each other. It's probably offensive to ask. By the way, are we seriously talking about time travel right now? You've met a time traveler before?"

"You missed that one, Doc," Harry says. "Before your time. Tell you about it later."

Cayenne mutters, venomously, "James barely counts," then gives them all another easygoing smile. "I do in fact know James, and while that utter bore uses science to achieve but a small fraction of what *I* can do, *my* talents come naturally. And believe me, I have *many* of them." He grins, broad and flirtatious. "I am a chronomancer, you see."

Ravi shifts impatiently. "What do you want?" he asks, voice flat. "Why are we here?"

"That is *so* like you, Ravi, straight to business." Cayenne rolls his green eyes heavenward, then drops them to flicker over him with appreciation. Each hair on the back of Ravi's neck stands on end. "Though the secret agent mystique *certainly* works on you."

"You know him?" Harry jerks a thumb at Ravi.

He is about to protest that he has never seen this person

before in his life when Cayenne spreads his hands wide, the gesture encompassing all of them.

"I know all of you, in fact! *Well*, your possible future selves, *pour être exact.* We are all quite well acquainted."

"*Ugh*," Harry says with feeling, "this is gonna be some cryptic time travel bullshit, I can already tell."

Cayenne continues as if Harry hadn't interrupted. "You see, I am less a client to you, *per se,* and more of an…accomplice. In fact, I even know dear Lucy as well! Believe me, it can occasionally be difficult traipsing around the timeline with the same face throughout the years. But fortunately, I know the best somamancer around in case things get a little dicey. Do you like her work?" He strikes a pose. Ravi looks away, uncomfortable with the display.

"Thou knowest my young flesh-wizard pupil?" Constance asks.

"Great-Aunt Constance, I'm begging you," Harry says, voice strained, "please never say flesh-wizard again."

Constance clucks her tongue. "In my time, 'tis what we called the rare mage with the innate magical ability to painlessly shape flesh and bone according to her wishes. Why you folk mix Greek and Latin to title things is beyond me."

"It's just the worst name in the history of names. *Flesh-wizard*. Ugh."

Constance leans in toward Cayenne with an appraising

eye. "Little Lucinda did all this? Her power now is still un-reliable. Doubtless why James traveled back through time to warn us she needed our guidance."

If this Cayenne knows Lucy, it means a lot of things. That Lucy was older and more accomplished to have achieved this sort of skillful work. That Cayenne was trusted enough to know about her talents. That they *all* might even trust this Cayenne, to some degree. It was an interesting play, Ravi realizes. A calculated reveal. It also explains why he looks so annoyingly perfect.

As Constance steps closer, Cayenne recoils away as if she were radioactive. "Ah, ah, *non, non.* Sadly, and believe me, it *is* a tragedy, my dear Constance, but you and I cannot ever touch. As I told Miss McAllister in our communique, it would be best if we remain six feet apart at all times at the *very* least. We two are truly star-crossed," he laments, hand to his head in a dramatic swoon. "Your...*brand* of time travel is a blunt instrument, let's say, whereas *mine* has a *bit* more finesse to it. As much as it pains me, you do not want to see what happens when we get in close proximity. And sweet fluffy prince Griswold, you too." This is said with a twiddle of the fingers toward Constance's satchel. Griswold flattens his ears.

"Why. Are. We. Here?" Ravi says again, slamming down every word firmly, like knives into a table.

Cayenne actually looks annoyed for the first time, the first expression shown beside a mask of flirtation. "Very well. There was a monster in this park last year that ended up killing hundreds of people."

They glance at each other cluelessly. "We would know about this occurrence," Val says.

"*Ugh*," Harry groans, even louder than last time. "Time travel bullshit. Let's just skip ahead. So, what, we're here because we prevented it from happening, so now we gotta do it again or there's a time paradox, or whatever the fuck?"

Cayenne smiles, pleased. "Sharp as ever, Angharad! As *clever* as you are enchanting."

"It's Harry," she says flatly. "Only Harry."

Nate breaks in excitedly, "This shit is *wild*. What's the future like? Flying cars? Renewable energy? Do I get tenure?"

"Ah, dear pretty Professor," comes a flirty purr. "Most pop culture is full of misinformation about the reality of time travel, but one thing they *do* get right; the less you know of the future, the better."

Nate looks around at the other hunters. "I know I'm pretty new and this is my first major mish with the training wheels off, but does this kind of thing happen all the time? Is this guy for real or what?"

Val shakes her head and says, "This is a new one. We

have not met him before."

"Ah," Cayenne interjects smoothly, "my pronouns are they/them, *s'il vous plaît*."

Through the safety of his sunglasses, Ravi quickly gauges the group's reactions. Nate is a professor at a liberal college, so as expected he is completely unfazed, and Val's normally impassive face doesn't flicker. He can't tell if she gets it or just doesn't care one way or the other. Harry leans over to her great-great-great etc. grandaunt Constance and gives her an eloquent *later* flip of her hand.

"We have not met them before," Val corrects herself easily.

Nate continues, "But you say you've met another time traveler? Besides you, Constance, I mean."

Cayenne interjects with a little so-so gesture of their expressive hands. "This may merely be semantics, but can one *really* be called a time traveler if they once *accidentally* tripped into the future? 'Traveler' indicates some measure of control."

Constance gives them the evil eye, and for all Ravi knows that might be literal. He once saw her set a monster on fire just by looking at it. "I hath traveled near a thousand years in a single second, with only mine *will*. I will not be disparaged by some rogue claiming to know us."

"She has a point," Ravi adds. "We've got nothing to

confirm any of this."

Cayenne pouts. "So, no one wants to sit and enjoy the picnic I put together?"

Everyone stands awkwardly silent.

Cayenne sighs, then airily waves a hand. "Well, no matter! I have set up a little magic circle, you'll be interested to see, dear Constance. It will take you where you need to go. Or *when* you need to go, more accurately. Now, this is very important: when you are ready, you need to all hold hands, jump into the air at the same time, and shout, '*Cayenne!*'" They hold up jazz hands, and the team all look at each other with varying levels of incredulity. "The jumping is a *very* important part of the spell." Cayenne gestures to the cleared area next to the picnic baskets, where sigils and lines drawn out in chalk dust are surrounded by pocket watches and candles.

They all look around at the beautiful spring day, sun shining on this secluded corner of a Chicago park, the distant sound of children playing. Nate asks nervously, "Are they being serious?"

"I'm assuming this is why we were told to bring warm clothes," Ravi muses, already starting to sweat in the winter wool suit he'd chosen to wear. He hitches his drag bag up to his shoulder, the rifle case disguised as a sports bag. Hopefully, there'll be no need to get out his sniper rifle — his

9mm in its shoulder holster is usually sufficient for these hunts—but better overprepared than dead. "What information do we have about the threat?"

"Yeah, any tips beyond 'monster' and 'kills hundreds'?" Harry asks. "We're going in totally blind." She pulls up her jacket to check the gun on her hip, looking troubled.

Cayenne gives them a careless, Gallic shrug. "All I know is that it's made out of ice. Or has control over ice. Something like that. Oh, and it's *very* hungry. The park has already been cleared, you're welcome, so you don't have to worry about any poor little innocent bystanders getting in the way. I'm sure that'll please you *big* strong *hero* types."

Harry sighs. "Well, it's something."

"One more question. Is shouting 'Cayenne' really necessary?" Nate asks.

"But of course, darling!" Cayenne looks surprised.

"Words of power *can* be used for a spell like this," Constance says dubiously as she inspects the chalk circle. "It seems sound. There are many aspects I do not recognize, but methinks the overarching structure appears fair."

"Such a vote of confidence! I'm honored," Cayenne says, mock-serious, hand over their heart. "Well, if none of you *truly* want to sit together and enjoy the meals I have packed very specifically for each of you..." They wait, eyes roving over each of them expectantly.

Harry shoves her hands in her pockets. "Thanks, but no. Let's just get this party started."

"Now *that's* a sentiment I can appreciate," Cayenne grins. "Whenever you are ready," they say with an airy flip of their hand toward the circle. "And when you are ready to come back, just repeat the process. The circle shows on the other side too. Remember! Hold hands, jump at the same time, and shout *Cayenne*! All those steps in that order, understood, darlings? Happy hunting!"

The hunters step over the chalky grass and into the circle. Ravi frowns. Being involved in magic makes him nervous, having the situation be so far out of his control. But Constance appears at ease, and he trusts her abilities.

Everyone gathers their things, weapons and otherwise. The five clasp hands, with a fair share of eye-rolling, and Harry looks at each of them in turn. "Everybody ready?"

There's a loud pronouncement from inside Constance's satchel. "Aye, the noble Griswold is prepared for anything! Beware, ye fiends of beyond, lest you meet my claws!"

Nate grins widely. "This is so cool. I'm so glad I joined up with you guys."

"On three," Harry says, "one, two, *three*!"

They all jump in the air and, feeling utterly ridiculous, shout "*Cayenne!*" They land in a crunch of snow, and a loud roar rings out in the freezing air.

*

WHILE RAVI AND Harry bash errant ice snakes with makeshift clubs, Val tangles with the giant beast one-on-one, darting around it and slamming her two-handed maul into its ribs. It manages to twist and avoid a direct hit to its ice heart, slamming a meaty fist into her chest. She skids back a few feet, still standing, wings braced wide. Then she dives back in, and the monster is thoroughly distracted. At least for a little while.

Harry hefts the tree branch and calls out in her clear voice, "Okay, on my mark, we move in and give this thin—"

"I got it!" Nate yells from down the hill. "There was a park maintenance station a block away!" He hauls a couple of bright-yellow bags up the incline. Fortunately, he's unusually buff for a professor type, because each of them must weigh over fifty pounds. Ravi runs over to grab one, kicking snakes as he goes. Nate gives him a grateful nod.

"What's in these?" Ravi asks, settling one bag on his shoulder. White powder trickles out of the bag from a rip, and he spares a tiny part of his brain to bemoan the state of his suit.

"Road salt!" With a broad grin, Nate trots up to where Harry, Constance, and Griswold are keeping the area clear of ice serpents with a combination of branches, boots, and claws.

"Aye, a fine plan!" Constance exclaims. "Do we bind this beast in a circle of salt?"

"Nope," says Nate, "we get Val to smash one of these bags straight into its heart." They all stare at him. "Trust me, I'm half Canadian. I know how to deal with ice."

Harry shrugs. "Worth a shot. You two swing one of the bags over to Val when I give her the heads-up."

Ravi and Nate heft a bag by either end, Griswold twining gracefully around their legs, biting approaching serpents with loud cries of, "Thou shall not prevail, knaves, for you face the mighty Griswold!"

"Constance?" Harry asks, and without further discussion Constance darts forward, braids flying. She goes to her knees and jabs both arms deep into the snow. A low rumble sounds, and from beneath the chenoo two thick vines curl up from the hard-packed snow and wrap around the monster's arms, holding them fast. It roars, cords of its exposed muscles bulging against the restraint. The vines creak alarmingly.

Harry calls, "That won't hold long. Val! Batter up!"

Val looks over from her battle and quirks her head to one side. Harry groans, and mutters, "I have got to get you and Constance more caught up on cultural references." She cups her hands around her mouth and shouts, "Hit the bag into its heart!" She slices a hand down toward Ravi and Nate, and in unison, they heave the bag at the chenoo.

Val spins her arms out in a perfect arc and slams her maul into the bag of salt, propelling it directly into the icy heart of the chenoo with astounding force. The bag shatters on impact, a cloud of coarse rock salt temporarily blocking the action from view.

The chenoo snaps through Constance's vines and staggers forward. Water runs down its torn body in thick rivulets as its heart melts, steaming as it hits the snow. All the serpents writhe in on themselves in a tangled knot and shatter into icy shrapnel.

"Fuck!" Harry shouts as they all get pelted by the little shards. Ravi grits his teeth as a few slice into his ankles. He ignores the sting as he approaches the fallen monster with gun drawn. He positions himself at a 45-degree angle to Val and sets his sights on the creature just in case it tries anything.

But its strength is rapidly waning. The icy block of its heart has dissolved into a lump the size of an apple, and the chenoo snarls feebly. Val rears back, maul raised overhead, and slams it down into its chest.

After that, it's over.

Ravi holsters his gun, drags over the other bag of salt,

and upends it onto the monster's dissolving body for good measure. The snow steams unnaturally for a few seconds, but then all is still. The only sign of what has happened is a patch of reddish slush. That, several trees torn up by the roots, a couple of huge craters scooped out of the ground, and five monster hunters (plus a talking cat) still standing and panting with exertion.

"Holy fuck. I can't believe that worked. Nice job, new guy," Harry tells Nate with a smile.

He waves a hand modestly. "That's what I'm here for, mythological know-how and winter survival skills."

Val puts her wings away in whatever pocket of reality they disappear to when she's not using them.

Constance picks up Griswold and gives him a peck between his fluffy ears. "Thou did'st well! A valiant melee." Griswold squinches his eyes shut with pleasure and purrs. "Are any of us injured? I made sure to bring herbs and poultices."

They sit on a fallen tree trunk while Constance patches them up. Val has taken the brunt of the injuries, but they know from experience that she is a fast healer. Some herbal remedies are slapped on the team's various snake bites, abrasions, and shrapnel wounds. Really, it could have been a lot worse. Now he's out of the heat of battle, the weather strikes Ravi as excessively cold. He shivers, his South Asian blood poorly suited for this kind of climate. Next time, maybe a jacket. Even though it meant he'd be kept under closer watch by The Trust, being assigned to Atlanta had been a decided improvement over his last posting in London, weather-wise. He counts himself lucky he hadn't been sent here to the Chicago branch if this is how the winters feel. His fingers are rapidly going numb.

"Not bad," remarks Harry. "You know, seems like that sassy time traveler could have told us a *little* more information about this beforehand, doesn't it?"

Constance shakes her head, wrapping some gauze around Harry's snake-bitten ankle. "One can rarely trust the motives of those with inborn magical abilities. Their powers often keep them separate and strange. Apart."

"Ooh, that reminds me," Nate says, brushing snow out of his short blond hair, "we're back a year in the past, right? Should we go put some bets down for the World Series, or whatever real quick?"

"We have wealth enough," Val reminds him, "from that corpse that turned into diamonds." *That* had been a weird day.

"Oh, yeah, fair point. Well, I wouldn't mind calling my past self and warning me off a disastrous rebound fling with an ex," muses Nate. He looks completely unbothered by the cold.

Val frowns. "The chenoo and its thralls are dead, and this park is once again safe. Hundreds of lives have been saved. Surely that is our main concern, a worthy use of our time. We are not here for personal gain."

Nate holds up his hands. "Granted, yeah. Sorry, it's my first time traveling a year into the past. I'm just excited about it."

Ravi brushes salt off his jacket and jerks a thumb to the magic circle over the next hillock. "We're done here. Let's get back to our own time." The winter wind howls around them, and it's quickly agreed that everyone just wants to get back home as soon as possible.

The circle on this side of the timeline is spray paint instead of chalk, purple lines laid over the snow. Constance gives it a quick check before stepping inside and holding her hands out with an approving nod. Ravi takes one, Val the other, and soon enough they all stand in a ring. "No one left anything, right?" Harry asks. "Gonna be a bitch to get it back." After a quick cursory check, they run through another countdown.

With a jump and a joint shout of "*Cayenne!*" their feet land in soft springy grass, the cessation of cold an immediate relief. And just like that, they've traveled back and forth an entire year in the span of an hour.

Chapter Three

WHEN THEY RETURN, Cayenne is stretched out on a blanket, leaning back on their elbows, head tilted back to enjoy the sunshine. They appear utterly at ease, greeting everyone with a cheery wave. "Ah, the conquering heroes return, no?" The picnic baskets are all gone save for the one holding their phones. By the angle of the sun, it appears as if only an hour has passed here since they'd left.

Harry stalks up to them, scratches on her face and her leather jacket torn. She grabs the basket and fishes out her phone. "Just, 'it's made out of ice or something', huh? You didn't think that warranted any other information?"

Cayenne flips a hand in the air. "It all worked out, did

it not, darling? Here you all are, whole and healthy. That's very good. I don't even have to rewind us all for a second try! See, this is why *you* are the professionals." They smile brightly up at the bedraggled group.

"I have snow melting in places I would'st rather not speak of," grumbles Constance, passing phones back to their owners. Val, covered in a thin coating of salt dust, glitters in the sun like a particularly muscley marble sculpture.

"That was awesome," Nate says, throwing a friendly bro punch into Ravi's arm. "Thanks for the help with the salt, my guy."

Ravi blinks in bemusement. He'd just done what he'd been told. "It was your idea."

"I still wish we could have talked to it," Harry complains. "I'm *so* good at talking monsters out of killing people. When they actually listen."

Constance leans down to pluck some dandelions and stuffs them into her satchel for later. "Next time, my niece, I shall cast a spell of speaking betwixt us and the aggressor. Perhaps you will get the chance to apply that silver tongue."

"Oh, that's *too* easy," Cayenne chimes in with a wicked grin. Harry narrows her eyes. "Ooh, so fierce. Would you like to scold me? Shame to let that silver tongue go to waste." They waggle their eyebrows lasciviously.

"I'd like to ship you off to a mandatory sexual

harassment training seminar, is what I'd like to do to you. Are we done here?"

Cayenne sighs as if truly brokenhearted, rising gracefully to their feet. "May I say it has been a *true* pleasure to meet you all. Or rather, it's been a pleasure for you to meet *moi*." They grin, tousled red locks tumbling over one green eye. "I *do* hope to work with you again *very* soon. Oh!" They lay a hand to their chest as if remembering something important. "Before you go, I do want to say—and believe *moi* it is with some chagrin—that I have to apologize for the fiasco at the airport in August." They do appear genuinely contrite, which alarms Ravi even more than the words they speak. Cayenne doesn't seem the type to waste time on regrets.

"Which August, next August?" Harry asks suspiciously. "The one coming in a few months, that August?"

"*Oui*, my dear Harry, *that* August."

"What's going to happen in August?" Ravi demands, more of a bark than speech.

"Oh, you'll see." They flip a hand dismissively. "Let's just say I am *not* at my best. In fact, that's why I arranged that *lovely* picnic for you all—which none of you even touched, *quel dommage*—to make something of a good first impression."

Harry snorts. "I'm guessing you won't tell us anything

more? More paradox bullshit?"

"See?" Cayenne winks at her. "I *did* say you were clever. As the old song goes, *que será, será*, my darlings. All shall be revealed in time."

Val steps up, maul held casually at her side. "Another question, chronomage. Answer truthfully. Was it truly necessary to yell your name while we jumped in the air?"

Cayenne's grin broadens, a fox in the henhouse look. "Of course not. But it was fun, *oui*?"

Nate claps his hands together briskly. "Well! I don't know about everyone else, but I want to hit up a real deep-dish pizza place while we're here in the Windy City. Grab a few beers?"

"*Fuck*, yes," Harry agrees. Constance and Val join them, and Harry looks back at Ravi and asks, "You joining in this time, agent guy? One drink."

Not quite sure why, he shakes his head wordlessly. He has some vague idea about gathering more information, filling out a thorough report. But that's not the only reason he's staying behind.

She shrugs. "All right. The flight back is in a few hours. See you at the airport." She tosses him a wave, and in another moment the four are away down the path, chatting and laughing. Ravi watches them, their easy camaraderie.

He turns around and immediately takes a step back,

hands twitching for his gun. Cayenne is standing way too close, a handful of steps away. They smile, a sharp thing full of promise. "Alone at last, I'm sure we are both thinking, *n'est-ce pas*? Aren't you just a *delicious* tall glass of chai? Well, sweet thing, you want to get out of here? Go somewhere?" Ravi freezes like an animal caught in a trap, not knowing whether to struggle free or to gnaw off its own leg. Cayenne tilts their head, lips pursed. "Hmm, too much, darling?"

Ravi clears his throat. "I don't even know you." He is definitely not used to anyone looking at him like this, with this wolfish avarice.

"That's not *necessarily* a bad thing, trust me." They smile, the expression slightly hollow. "What about dinner?" they ask brightly. "There's a *fabulous* little place just a few blocks from here, *très chic*."

"Oh, uh. I don't think…I don't think I can." Ravi calculates furiously. The Trust knows he's in Chicago, but the likelihood that they'll alert the Chicago branch to keep an eye on him is slim to none. And some time alone with this time traveler could yield useful intel. The fact that Cayenne is annoyingly gorgeous has nothing to do with it.

Cayenne offers the careless one-shoulder shrug they seem to favor. "*D'accord, pas de soucis.*" Ravi knows mostly tourist French, but this is pretty easy to follow. *No worries.* "Tell you what. I'm going to be in Chicago for the next forty-eight hours." Cayenne crowds in close—Ravi clamps down on his instincts to strike out, to defend—and takes his hand. They grab the pen out of his inside pocket, hand snaking in before he can react, and push up his sleeve to write a number on his wrist.

Ravi can hardly remember the last time someone touched him outside of combat. Goosebumps follow the movement of the pen, his pulse ticking up a degree.

"If you change your mind," they say breezily, "I am but a text or call away." They wink and turn to leave.

"Wait," he calls, then kicks himself. *What the fuck am I doing*?

They turn around, eyebrows raised.

Ravi's schooling was unorthodox, to say the least. Many tutors and weapons instructors, to be sure, and a lot of what he liked to privately think of as Monsters 101; common and uncommon supernatural threats and how to neutralize them. Ghosts, vampires, fairies, werewolves, demons, beings from other dimensions—the list went on and on and got weirder as it did. In those lessons was a fair bit of warning about doorways, portals, and entrances to other lands. People still got led astray through the Veil into the adjacent realms; into Faerie, or the Outside, or Hell itself. Old legends are full of warnings about accepting invitations from strange beings, about accepting boons from old gods, about walking through wardrobes that lead to strange and beautiful lands. There's no telling where those doors might take you, and if you'll ever return.

But the thing about offers like this...they only come once in a lifetime.

"Dinner sounds good," he says, voice rough. Cayenne grins hugely, clapping their hands in delight. Ravi doesn't think anyone has ever looked this pleased to spend time with him before. "One thing," he adds, rubbing the back of his neck.

Cayenne shifts their weight onto one hip, arching their neck invitingly. "*Oui*?"

"I'm... Dinner is on one condition." This had not gone over well with the last guy he'd had this discussion with, and Ravi braces himself for whatever reaction is incoming. "I need everything to be...discreet."

Cayenne doesn't even blink. "You may not believe it to look at me, because *c'est moi*, but I actually do know how to go unnoticed, darling. I'd be a very poor time traveler if I did not. That is not a problem in the *least*." They smile at him reassuringly.

He breathes out, centering himself. "Okay." He steps forward before he can change his mind. "Let's go."

*

THE RESTAURANT IS a secretive, high-class affair in the Gold Coast, modeled after a Prohibition speakeasy, the kind of place Chicago's rich and famous might enjoy for clandestine meets. Or simply to be alone and unmolested in the lowered light.

"I don't think we have to worry about the dress code with *you*, darling," Cayenne purrs, pointedly checking out Ravi's custom suit and leaning over to brush off a bit of salt dust Ravi had missed.

He moves away quickly and picks a table that'll keep his back to the wall. He adjusts his cuffs as he sits down, the only outward sign of his nervousness. He's still not sure why he's here. Why he said yes. Cayenne is not his usual type. Obvious. Careless. An irresponsible flirt; everything he's very much not. But time travel... Now *that* is interesting. James had been around for barely a few minutes, all told, and Ravi knows if his aunt was aware that he has the chance to get some intel on a real, honest chronomancer, she'd expect him to get it.

"So!" Cayenne smiles at him over a rum drink served in a gold-rimmed tumbler. Ravi orders the first craft cocktail on the menu, knowing he's not going to drink it anyway. The menu is prix fixe, so the waiter brings out the appetizer a minute after they are seated. "Isn't this nice."

Ravi raises an eyebrow. "Sure. So what time are you

from?"

Cayenne's grin turns razor-edged, predatory. "Grilling me already for your big, bad Trust, Agent Abhiramnew? And I was thinking this was a date."

Ravi narrows his gaze down into a point. "What is it you think you know about me?" he demands icily.

Cayenne kicks back in their chair, overtly casual, idly tapping a finger to their full lips. "Oh, I know *all* about you, sweetheart. I know every member of your little band of champions, in fact. From your not-too-distant future."

Ravi crosses his arms over his chest, lifting his chin in challenge. "You think you know us?"

"*Mais oui*! I would be *thrilled* to recount all of your fine, *fine* qualities." Cayenne wriggles a little in their seat, as if genuinely pleased to show off, and begins ticking off points on their elegant hands. "First, we have the tall, leggy Valkyrie that is Valiance. By all accounts an *actual literal angel*, which does raise some interesting theological questions, doesn't it? Also, even more interesting questions like, how much pressure *exactly* is required to crush someone's head between her thighs? Inquiring minds want to know." They breeze on so quickly Ravi has no time to react to that.

"Constance Shaw, hedge-witch from the year 1215, of the historically infamous Shaw clan of demon hunters. She's English, but"—here they hold up a hand to their mouth as if telling a secret—"we won't hold that against her. Alas, I can't hold *anything* against her lest the timestream gets very messily fucked. A magical accident sent her, her charming little animal friend, and some big bad demon she was hunting forward in time and space to her nearest living relation, Angharad 'Harry' McAllister—total fox, by the by—and now she's got her very own magic shop, selling crystals and herbal teas to bored housewives. Speaking of Harry. Poor, poor Harry." Cayenne shakes their head sympathetically, red hair catching the low light in interesting ways.

"Harry McAllister, hard-boiled PI, *very* put out that ghosts and ghouls are real. Then she stumbles across an angel, and *then* her eight-hundred-year-old umpteen-great-grand-witch gets dropped in her lap, too. Really, it's enough to drive one back to drink, isn't it?" They take a sip of their cocktail with a wink. Ravi's mouth twitches downward; it's no secret that Harry used to have a problem.

"Your little group's newest member, the very tasty Dr. Nathaniel Corbin, professor of mythological folklore or some such *blah blah blah*, I honestly cannot remember. Who can pay attention to what he's saying when he's got an ass like that, am I right?" They grin widely with another saucy wink. Are they contractually obligated to be this extra? Ravi's almost fascinated by it.

"Then there's sweet little Lucinda, who you should

write a very effusive thank-you letter to for all *this*," they say while gesturing broadly at their physique. "*Such* a lamb. Oh, there's also the damp sponge you know as James, but trust me, darling, he's so dull that if I told you anything more about him you would go into a catatonic state."

Ravi is ready for it when it comes, bracing himself.

"And then there's you! Ravi Abhiramnew." Their lips cut a sultry curve, drawing out his name like it tastes delicious, rolling around on Cayenne's tongue. "*Esteemed* agent of the secretive organization known as The Trust, oh-so-very-hush-hush defenders against supernatural threats. You come from a very wealthy family, are an expert marksman, and a *snappy* dresser, and your late mother was the last Chosen, I believe?"

Ravi's head jerks back before he can clamp down on the reaction. That last fact is *not* common knowledge. It's not even *uncommon* knowledge. Most of The Trust operates to contain and suppress supernatural threats with no knowledge of their ancient origins, that truth reserved only for the handful of old families who make up the inner ring of The Trust's leading consortium.

Expression flat and implacable, Ravi doesn't say a thing. He doesn't ask how Cayenne could possibly know this, know that his mother had been the champion of the demon-slaying goddess Durga, the last in a long line of

Abhiramnews Chosen to battle evil for centuries, generation to generation to generation.

Until Ravi.

Cayenne quirks a copper brow. "Griswold got your tongue, darling?"

Ravi leans back in his chair, eyes locked on Cayenne the way he'd watch a rearing cobra. Still. Calm. Every muscle ready to strike. Outwardly he is a brick wall, but behind it, his mind races. "You have me at a disadvantage," he says dryly.

"Not yet, I don't," Cayenne purrs, running a finger along the rim of their glass.

Ravi blinks. He was expecting...not that. Seems this Cayenne might know all his most closely held secrets. He takes a small sip of his cocktail, to give his hands something to do, his palms clammy. "I told you all this, did I? All these things you know about us, about me, you know from, what? Our future selves trusting you so much?"

"I did say, darling. I'm, hmm, shall we say, a coworker. A compatriot. *Practically* in the inner circle. You know" — here their expression falls a little, to Ravi's surprise — "no matter how many times I've done this, going forward or back, meeting people I've already known, have formed relationships with...*c'est difficile*. Can you imagine it? Being a stranger to someone you...have known for quite some time?" Their eyes hesitantly meet his own.

Some of the steel leaves Ravi's posture. He *can* imagine it. He clears his throat. "Sounds lonely."

Cayenne tilts their head to the side, offering up a sad little smile. "That's okay, *mon chéri*, it just gives us the chance to get to know each other all over again!" They reach out and lightly touch the back of Ravi's hand where it rests around his barely touched drink. Ravi snatches his hand away on instinct, and Cayenne simply takes his drink as if that was what they intended the whole time. They sip it with a coy grin.

Ravi takes a much-needed moment to gather himself. Get back on track. "And where are you from, Cayenne?" He puts a slight skeptical slant on the unlikely name.

"Isn't the French accent a dead giveaway?"

"Not necessarily. People speak French all over. Accents aren't a reliable indicator, anyway. I'm from India, and I don't have an accent." Years of strict tutelage to thank for that.

"Hmm, I'll have to go there someday, if there are more specimens like *you* around." Cayenne glides an appreciative gaze over Ravi, tongue flicking quickly to wet their lips. Ravi looks away, clearing his throat. "How do you find Atlanta? You don't think it's frightfully muggy? *Je déteste quand il fait trop humide.*"

Ravi shrugs. "Sure, but it's less smoggy than Chennai. Atlanta isn't so bad. Pretty diverse city. I hardly ever get folks asking if I'm the dot or feather kind of Indian."

Cayenne laughs loudly before clapping a hand over their mouth. They look as surprised by it as Ravi is. That laugh sounded genuine, not the fake, seductive chuckle they've been using up until now.

"And you're *funny*, too," they say, green eyes twinkling. "Can you blame these yokels for not knowing how to handle you? You are a *very* spicy samosa."

Ravi coughs to hide a laugh and glances away. It's both a tease and a flirt and a self-aware racially insensitive joke all in one, and it's...distressingly charming. "You have a last name?"

Cayenne stops smiling. "Oh, *sweetheart*, you think I'm going to give you anything you can go run and tell The Trust?" They pluck a morsel off their plate and eat it straight from their fingers, licking the sauce off the tips. "I'm sure *you* can understand there are some things it would be better that they *don't* know about. Wouldn't you agree?" Their gaze slides up and locks with Ravi's for a long moment.

Rather than setting him more on edge, Ravi breathes an inward sigh of relief. Now, *this* is familiar ground, at last. Mutually assured destruction. This is a language he speaks well and has spent most of his life navigating around. It means that under their brash, careless exterior, Cayenne is a little afraid of him. Afraid of being exposed. So, they're on equal footing, after all.

He leans on his elbow, softening his posture. "Maybe I would."

The challenge in Cayenne's eyes flickers. Startled, but they hide it well. They mirror Ravi's pose, elbows on the table. "Tell me, do you and your cute little friends have that lake house in the suburbs yet? I don't know what year you procured it."

Ravi blinks at the non sequitur. "Uh, yeah. We have it. As long as we keep the kappa in the lake happy with the occasional cucumber, it protects the whole region from any other monsters."

Cayenne purses their lips in amusement. "Hmm. I suppose that's very important to you, isn't it? Protecting people?"

"Yes."

"Such a hero," they say with a bat of their lashes.

He snorts and looks away, changing the subject. "So, you know me, huh. In the future."

"Indeed, I do, but let me just forestall any awkward questions. I cannot *possibly* tell you details about your future, darling. It could cause all sorts of time paradoxes and anomalies, and besides, there's no guarantee that the past I experienced will be the same future *you* will. We are…crossing paths on a river"—Cayenne motions with both hands, moving smoothly into an X—"and the water is very rarely the same. Unless I get myself tethered to a timeline, which I try my best to avoid. I know it's confusing," they add apologetically.

"I'm following just fine."

"Of course! Forgive me. I'm unused to telling people about my abilities." They tap their fingers on the table idly, eyes darkening. "You are a singularly handsome man."

Ravi's ears immediately go hot, and he fights to keep the blush off his face, thankful for the shield of his dark complexion. He glances around out of habit for any obvious eavesdroppers.

Cayenne gives him a surprisingly sweet smile. "No worries, you skittish thing. If anything happens to risk your discretion, I will simply whisk back in time a few moments and ensure that it doesn't come to pass." They rest their chin in their hand, looking at him with open fascination.

Ravi blinks. He thinks about this for a long moment, eating a bite of food he barely tastes. Finally, he says, "Thanks."

Cayenne waves a hand airily. "Think nothing of it, darling."

A shy smile tries to creep across his face, and Ravi

suppresses it with effort. "Darling, huh?"

Slowly, Cayenne grins, watching him very carefully. "Do the endearments bother you?"

Ravi bites his lip and doesn't answer. After a moment he tries again to change the subject. "Can I ask about today? You can send a bunch of people back into the past. If *you* were to...to 'whisk' back, wouldn't there be two of you?"

"Oh, sweetheart, I did say my talents were *many*. I can go back physically, and with some preparation send others, like with you and your *adorable* little gang of heroes. But I can also" — they hold up their tattooed hand with the finely detailed clock, waggling their fingers playfully — "slip back my consciousness. A little rewind, as it were. Or fast forward, but that's rarely as useful. The way memories fill in later is...*c'est vraiment agaçant*. Very annoying. And sadly, no, there cannot be two of me at once, otherwise I'd never leave my room." This time Ravi doesn't bite down on his laugh quite in time. It manages to escape, and Cayenne's smile widens. "*Anyway*, enough about me, handsome. Would you like to come to my hotel?"

Ravi nearly chokes on a bite of salad. "That's...forward."

Cayenne laughs, not unkindly. "Yes, have you met me?"

"I'm not sure of the answer to that," he says, eyes

skipping over Cayenne's too-attractive features. It's a bad idea. Doesn't matter how long it's been. How intriguing they might be. He can't be stupid about this. "Look, the dinner is...nice." And it really is, strangely. The number of actual dinners he's had with potential romantic partners is vanishingly small. Despite the failed interrogation, and the veiled threats, and the fact that this stranger knows way too much about him for comfort...he's actually enjoying himself. "But I can't."

Cayenne considers Ravi a long time, tapping their tattoo as if in deep thought. "Well," they eventually say with clear regret, "you can't say I didn't try."

*

AFTERWARD, CAYENNE WALKS with him while he goes to meet his ride to the airport, and when they are safely sheltered between a wall and a hedge, Cayenne takes Ravi's hand. Ravi sucks in a breath as Cayenne raises it to their lips, not breaking eye contact, and presses a gentle, courtly kiss to the back of his hand.

Nothing like this has ever happened to Ravi before.

"I'd like to see you again," Cayenne whispers against his knuckles, the warmth of their breath ghosting across sensitized skin. "If discretion is a concern, we can go *anywhere* you like, darling, away from prying eyes. Believe me, money is *no* object. *C'est moi!*"

They release his hand, and it takes the space of a second for him to draw it back. He has to swallow a few times, throat suddenly desert dry, before he can answer.

"I'll think about it."

Chapter Four

A WEEK LATER, after his early morning run, Ravi discovers a candy-red phone in his mailbox. He frowns, scanning his surroundings before taking it out. A sticky note affixed to the phone reads *Call Me Sometime!* with hearts dotting the "*i*" and the exclamation point. Ravi's pulse instantly spikes. His mind has frequently replayed his date—if whatever that was could be called a date—with Cayenne over the last week. It's been exasperating, how often he's thought about it. He tucks the phone in his pocket and heads upstairs.

Once in his Trust-issued apartment, he grabs a protein bar and a bottle of water, then settles in on the minimalist sofa to search through the phone. It has only the standard pre-installed apps, and when he opens the battery case, a cursory inspection doesn't reveal any obvious bugs. He'd need to ask a Trust intelligence agent to make one hundred percent certain it's clean, but...he bites his lip. What could Cayenne have to gain from blackmailing him? It doesn't seem like they need the money, and if they're after valuable information, they shouldn't target a field agent like him.

...Is it possible their interest is genuine?

Shaking off that thought, he debates throwing the phone away when it buzzes in his hand, the screen lighting up with a series of long, emoji-filled texts. With trepidation, he opens it. Instead of a name, the contact info has been pre-programmed with a handful of chili pepper emojis and a winky kissy face. Ravi rolls his eyes. If this *is* an attempt at espionage, he'd think it'd be handled with more profession-alism, and relaxes minutely.

> CAYENNE: *Heard about another NASTY little monster hurting innocents and so of COURSE I thought of my Sexy-Knight-in-Shining-Perfectly-Tailored-Suits!*
>
> *If you agree to go on a TROPICAL GETAWAY with me, I PROMISE to tell you MORE so you can go run off and be a HERO with all of your other CUTE little friends!*
>
> *(I'll even let you have your little adventure BEFORE our*

date and I HATE waiting, so you KNOW I'm being seri-ous!)

OF COURSE, you can text me ANYTIME with no ex-cuse! I have nothing but TIME, my tall, DELICIOUS glass of Chai! (red heart emoji, chili pepper emoji) *XOXOXO*

Ravi snorts. He has never seen so many emojis used in one place before, and the less said about the rampant capitalization, the better. An offer of a tropical vacation with a person he's met once? Not even an offer; a *bargain*. If Ravi agrees, they'll reveal valuable information that could potentially save lives. He shakes his head and texts back a short reply before he can think better of it.

RAVI: *If I don't go, you're going to let a bunch of innocent people get hurt? Did I read that right?*

CAYENNE: *(frowny face emoji) You make ME sound like the MONSTER!* (smiling devil face) *Sweetheart, I only want to make sure you actually ENJOY yourself for ONCE in your LIFE. Would going on a luxurious second date with MOI truly be so TERRIBLE a fate?*

Ravi sighs and rests his head back against the couch, chewing his lip nearly bloody. Several minutes tick by before he decides what he wants to say. He's not great with words, but having the distance of a phone between him and Cayenne helps to keep his mind focused without being derailed by relentless flirtation, scattering his wits to the winds.

> RAVI: *So, last time. That evening I got to live a different life for a few hours. Thank you for that.*

> CAYENNE: *You know I could offer far more than a few HOURS of freedom, darling, if only you'd let yourself down off that cross of yours.*

Let himself down off…ah, right. Christian idiom. He considers for a while before he composes his answer. It takes him a while, likely the longest string of texts he's ever written in his life.

> RAVI: *I don't know anything about you. You deflected anything personal. I don't know who you are. Where you're from. When you're from. Your family. Your values. I don't know you, and you seem to know all of that about me, which I find troubling.*

> *I'm not stupid. I pay attention. If I were you, a chronomage trying to stay off The Trust's radar, I'd do exactly what you're doing right now. I'd find a weakness.*

That's me. And I'd exploit it.

I can't even blame you for it. It's the smart play.

Whatever is going to happen in August must be pretty bad, if you're trying so hard to get me on your side before then.

He waits a few minutes, then a few minutes more. Finally, he stands to pace off some nervous energy when the phone finally buzzes.

CAYENNE: *Look…I can appreciate a soupçon of paranoia (it's how I'm not being DISSECTED in a LAB somewhere) but did you ever think that just MAYBE I'm TRYING to make AMENDS for my past deeds?*

That perhaps I simply even LIKE you?

It's your BOSSES I don't trust, Ravi, not you. I don't talk about myself because I don't want to be a SCIENCE project.

And I do not think you're stupid or anything of the sort. You are NOT weak or anyone's "weakness" save perhaps MINE, darling. You're frustratingly, unflinchingly HEROIC and it is très annoying. You are SO difficult to make HAPPY!

Please do not ask about August. PLEASE just take the gift of this vacation, of getting to live a different life for a little while and ENJOY it. We don't have to talk, you know, if you truly wish to throw away a chance at brief but absolutely perfect HAPPINESS, which I am VERY willing and able to provide. I will just tell you the where and when of the monster business and leave you be, if that is TRULY what you desire.

I've already broken one of my cardinal rules and become tethered to your timeline since last we spoke whether I want to be or not (long story) but if you cannot even IM-AGINE us simply enjoying ourselves together, I'll leave both of us miserable and lonely until that dreadful day in August finally arrives. I just want to make you SMILE. I owe you that much, if not much, much more.

What is it YOU want, Ravi?

That is… It's like all the air has been kicked out of him. He rereads the whole thing a half dozen times before he really absorbs it. This outpouring of vulnerability and sincerity is the last thing Ravi expected. The fervent *familiarity* of it, like Cayenne already knows him, truly *sees* him, hits him like a sudden storm.

He isn't miserable. He has a purpose. He has goals. What he doesn't have is anyone who asks him what *he* wants. That is… He doesn't know how to respond to that in the least. What *does* he want?

RAVI: *You don't owe me anything. I don't want you to do anything because of obligation.*

He agonizes a long time before he sends the next text, palms damp with nerves. He has a hard time believing a time traveler like Cayenne, presumably with the whole world at their feet, could find Ravi the least bit interesting, but…why go through all this effort, for *him* of all people? This isn't just angling for a fuck, which he can wrap his head around. This is something else.

Ravi rubs his face, trying to think clearly. He could get the time off, he'd saved up vacation days, so that wasn't an issue. The issue is… He laughs once to himself, sharply. The sound echoes off his bare walls. The issue is someone handsome said they like him, and now he's a wreck about it. *Pitiful.*

RAVI: *Can we take things slow? You're kind of like a monsoon.*

CAYENNE: *Not something I am USED to, but for you, I could learn to enjoy going slow. Whatever makes you happiest, darling.*

How do a few days relaxing on a lovely beach somewhere sound to you? I'll take care of every arrangement. I could even buy us SEPARATE bungalows and be as much of a gentleman as you WANT me to be the entire time! I'll sit and read a book in complete silence next to you. Or whatever it is normal people do on vacation.

His lips curl into a half-smile. Things normal people do. Probably a foreign concept for them both. He sits a little easier now that he's made his decision, settling back into the couch cushions, trying to remember the last time he's gotten to enjoy a beach.

RAVI: *I have no idea what normal people do on vacations.*

But a beach sounds like it might be nice.

I don't want you to sit in complete silence, c'mon. Who's on the cross now?

CAYENNE: *TOUCHÉ, darling! I'll simply have to check YOU out instead.* (winky face)

PARFAIT! I am so EXCITED! I'll book everything and to the tropics we shall GO!

But, truly, thank you for your trust in me, Ravi. I know that to you, I am merely a bewitching stranger, but I have learned in the course of my FRUSTRATING new goal of making you happy just how RARE and PRECIOUS a coin that trust is.

RAVI: *Look. I don't do this kind of thing often. This is new.*

But then again, I don't meet bewitching strangers often either, so.

At least ones who aren't trying to kill me, I guess.

CAYENNE: *Worry not, I am VERY discreet when I have to be (one must be to avoid popping up in pictures through-out history) and I only plan to kill you with KINDNESS! The only roughing up you need fear is if I spring for a COUPLES massage.*

Merde, I almost forgot! The little monster, yes? Since you've been SO sweet, I may as well give you some info, no? I know how much you ADORE your heroics, after all.

They send a detailed bit of info, fortunately more thorough than the last brief had been. Ravi copies down everything to forward it to Harry and the rest. Nice to get good intel for once.

CAYENNE: *Do be SAFE and give everyone my SECOND best. My BEST is reserved for YOU, darling!*

Ravi furrows his brow. Cayenne seems awfully dismissive of what they call "heroics" for someone who has already helped the team save hundreds of lives, and is now helping them save more.

RAVI: *Thank you.*

If we can help people because of you, you realize that means you're a hero too, right?

It takes so long for the next text to come through that Ravi has assumed there won't be another one and has already started to put the phone down.

CAYENNE: *You're so silly. TTYL darling and best of luck.*

Chapter Five

"MISTRESS! THE WITCH-hunter has arrived!"

Ravi sighs at the loud yowl as he pushes through the magic shop door, a tinkle of bells above ringing a much more pleasant welcome. He only catches a swift glimpse of Griswold's striped tail as the familiar disappears into the back room. The air smells of sage and old books. The shop appears empty, fortunately. Ravi moves up to the counter to wait, eyeing up the back wall, with its display of glass bell jars containing a variety of mushrooms. Some of the fungus is vividly colored, while one is wrinkly black and sweating some kind of orange fluid. He highly doubts any of them are legal.

Constance rounds the corner, wiping a rounded sickle-like blade with the corner of the apron she wears over her usual assortment of skirts, shawls, and bright patterns. Her cat trots close to her side, tail raised high as Constance fixes Ravi with a stern look. "Oh, it's you. Have ye matches? A lighter, anything like that?"

Ravi leans an elbow on the counter, keeping his posture casual and nonthreatening, hands open. "No, Constance, I never do. Do you want me to turn out my pockets?" She had stopped demanding he do just that every time she found herself alone with him a few months prior. It still feels polite to ask.

She waves a hand dismissively, setting her blade down by the cash register. "Of course not. Now, what can I do for you? Have we work again so soon after the last case?" It always strikes Ravi how every time they cross paths, Constance spends the first minute on high alert, wary as a mouse in a room full of hawks. It's as if she expects Ravi to suddenly have a change of heart and try to burn her at the stake, no matter how many times he tells her he is not, in fact, a witch-hunter. Then, after that first moment has passed, she relaxes into the same cheerful camaraderie she shares with all the other hunters of the team.

Griswold jumps up onto a nearby bookshelf, pads over to a pillow placed deliberately in a ray of sunlight, and settles in. The cat keeps one yellow eye slit open, watching him.

"No, no news. Things are quiet for the time being. Can't say I'm disappointed, after the last monster. Tough customer." Cayenne's information had been good, leading to a quick resolution to the scuffle.

"Indeed! A worthy adversary, almost as hearty as the chenoo. Fortunate it was that Harry found it could not bear the sight of its own reflection. Is your wound quite healed?"

"The Kevlar vest took most of it. I'm fine."

Constance's hazel eyes narrow the slightest bit. "Then to what purpose have you come to my shop this day? Be it not hunting and be it not healing."

Ravi attempts a smile. She looks unimpressed. It's unlikely she is ever going to trust him fully. Only to be expected, he supposes. Truth be told, he isn't sure he can trust *her*. The motives of an ancient, powerful hedge-witch displaced into modern times are inscrutable, to say the least. And he had been instructed to keep a careful eye on her, to report any suspicions to his superiors in The Trust, so it is likely a good thing that he doesn't get too close. Obscure his judgement. "I'm heading out of town in a few days, and I wanted to give you all a heads-up. I hoped you could tell the others since everyone hangs out here a lot."

Constance brightens. "Aye, my niece is attempting to

teach Val and me a gambling card game! It is most enjoyable. Nate came to the last one. He said if we took Val to the city of Las Vegas we could make a fortune. She tells opponents exactly what cards she has, but her visage is so fearsome that none believe it. It is quite fun." She gives Ravi a weighted look. "You could join, if you wish, you know."

"That's...a kind offer." He scratches the back of his neck. "So, yeah, I'm going to be out of town for a little while, and if something goes down here, you can get in touch with me on... Hang on." He digs out his phones from his pockets and sets all three of them on the counter.

Constance quirks an eyebrow but says nothing.

Two of the phones are nearly identical, one being the Trust-issued device, and the other he purchased on his own. One of the first purchases he ever made with his own money, come to think of it, thanks to the handful of diamonds Harry gifted him. Also, thanks to the downtown jeweler who agreed to exchange a few for cash without asking too many questions. Every time Ravi accesses his secret, personal bank account, he feels like he's about to get a hearty thwack on the wrist from Aunt Padme. But it's more difficult to move freely here in Atlanta right under the surveillance of his handlers than it had been in London. He needs his own funds and his own phone, neither of which he's allowed to have until he...fulfills the necessary requirements.

The third phone is bright, cherry red.

Ravi swipes through his personal phone to bring up the number he hasn't yet memorized and motions to a stack of receipts. Constance gives him a piece of paper and a pen.

"Here, this number will reach me. If there's trouble, I'll come as soon as I can manage." He holds out the number. As Constance takes it, a loud buzz vibrates the red phone a few inches across the counter. The lock screen brightens with a text.

> CAYENNE: *Hello, my TASTY samosa! I find myself in your enchanting town! Shall we meet to discuss travel plans over coffee? I intend on having a dirty chai. (winky face emoji) I PROMISE no one will see us!*

A kissy winky face follows the text, along with a huge string of red pepper emojis.

Ravi slaps his hand over the phone, ears hot with embarrassment. Figures. Not one peep from Cayenne since he'd agreed to go on the trip two weeks ago, but of course they'd text him *right now*. He doubts Constance can read the screen upside down, as she isn't great with modern lettering, but the pepper emojis are pretty distinctive.

He clears his throat and swiftly puts all the phones back in their respective pockets. "So, yeah. That number. That'll reach me if you need me. Okay." He raps a knuckle on the counter and turns to leave.

"Ravi." To his surprise Constance reaches over the counter and snags his sleeve, her fingers stained with ink and chlorophyll under her nails. "Be not hasty."

He turns back, affecting a casual look. "What's up?"

The witch places both hands flat on the counter, leaning in intently. "Thou should be wary of fae creatures."

That's...what? "What?"

She sighs with exasperation. "Cayenne! The very pretty ginger who hath harnessed the flow of time itself? Or perhaps thou hast forgotten?" She's getting better at sarcasm every day she spends here. Must be Harry's influence.

Ravi hesitates before answering. "Cayenne isn't a fae creature." He is sure of that. Pretty sure. There are usually tells.

Constance brushes him off dismissively. "As good as! The fae come in all shapes and sizes, you know. Both the grotesque and the comely. Perhaps they used some faerie trickery instead of true chronomancy. If I had met such a varlet in my time, I would be painting my lashes with eyebright and putting fern fronds in my boots."

He blinks, unsure if *varlet* is some Olde English word, or just a snippet of vocabulary that has slipped through the cracks of his education. "What for?"

"Eyebright to see truly." Constance glides over to the back shelf. She plucks up a mason jar and waggles it, the dried leaves inside rasping together. "To pierce through illusions and glamour. Even if this Cayenne is pure human, it does not hurt to have an edge against deception." She holds it out to him, offering.

Ravi shakes his head. "Thanks, but, uh. No thanks."

She shrugs and puts the jar back on the shelf. "Fresh ferns, placed in the shoe and walked upon, shall keep you from being led astray."

"Again, no thanks." As much as he doesn't place much stock in the herbcraft, Constance does often possess strange wisdom. He isn't so proud as to dismiss her entirely. "You think I'm likely to be led astray?"

She shrugs and gives him a soft smile. "I think it is always wise to be prepared to become lost." He nods slowly; can't disagree with that sentiment. "This Cayenne... I do not think you should place your trust in them."

"It's not...it's not like that." He forces himself to scoff, fiddling with the cuffs of his suit coat. Almost true. Technically. A half-lie, at best. It rankles to lie to his teammate, but Ravi is well used to that feeling.

Constance is silent for so long that Ravi glances up to check on her. She looks puzzled, and asks, "Ravi. Is all this fuss and fidgeting because you are a catamite?"

"Uh." Ravi is sure he must look like someone smacked him with a fish. "Um." Where to even start. "*Catamite*?"

"Aye." She shrugs while smoothing a braid of her chestnut hair. "I thought it was no remarkable thing these days? In my time, if a fellow got caught with another, they paid off their fees to the church and went about their day. No uncommon thing. Cause for a bit of sneer and gossip, but I thought catamites had an easier time of it now?"

"Uh…some places, they do." He's too stunned to do anything but answer the first thing that comes to mind.

"I have—forgive me, I *had* a big family, you know. I am no stranger to catamites. My little cousin, Pax, went off under the guise of joining the Crusades to hunt a monster and came back with a Saracen soldier in tow. Before long the pair were as good as wed. Oh! And my eldest sister, Verity? She was a…" Constance searches the air for the right words. "Well, a lady catamite. It cannot be—"

"Can you *please* stop saying *catamite*!" Ravi covers his eyes with his hands, spinning around, suppressing hysterical laughter. "Fuck's sake." He takes a deep breath before turning back to face her. "Just…please stop talking."

She tilts her head to the side curiously. "What else should I say? There were much worse words I didn't use."

"Thanks," Ravi laughs, leaning against the counter. He feels a little lightheaded.

"What is the term now?"

Ravi realizes he has one hand up, covering half his face. He scrubs it through his closely shorn beard before gathering enough words to answer. "There…are a lot of them. Definitely *not* catamite, never that one. I, um. I thought people got hanged for that back in your day?"

"Goodness, no! Not unless there were other crimes they wanted to see you hang for too." She peers off into another time, a far-off look he often sees her wearing. "'Twasn't a thing people spoke of much. And of course, if you were a noble you could do as you pleased. There were many rumors and records about lords and kings keeping male bedfellows. None could gainsay the wealthy; I think that has been ever true." She leans over the counter to rest on her elbows. Griswold silently hops up between her arms, and she scratches at his ears absently. "I have been looking into histories, trying to fill in the great gap of my knowledge. I think many, many things change after the Great Plagues. The church saw so many losses to their numbers, they had reason to punish those who wouldn't procreate." Her lip curls with distaste. "Before that, if you *had* to share a bed at a crowded inn, well…" She flashes him a mischievous smile. "Nothing wrong with seeking a little extra warmth on a cold night, yes?"

Ravi huffs a dry laugh. "I didn't realize." This still feels unreal, like the kind of dreams he would wake from abruptly, heart hammering.

"So! How would you prefer I refer to you? My apologies I have not yet learned better." She smiles, and it *is* encouraging, but Ravi doesn't know how to continue, panic tight in his chest.

He's never said it out loud before. To anyone. Not any of the men he's been with, not to Luke, not even to a mirror.

"I, uh. You should ask Harry. There's a lot of factors? And some of it is regional, so. Yeah. Ask Harry." *Coward*, he chides himself.

Constance shrugs. "As you wish. In any case, if you intend to see this Cayenne again, you should take precautions."

Finally, he feels on a little firmer footing here. "I'm pretty certain they are a human, Constance. Not a fae creature."

Constance turns her gaze heavenward. "Thou future folk and all your specific words and little categories for dangerous things! A human who can bend time to their will with such ease is as much risk as demons or the Fair Folk themselves. 'Tis often so with the wild talents. Why think you I have been tutoring young Lucy? Here." She ducks under the counter and rummages around. While she is out of sight, Griswold lifts a paw up to his eyes, then points that paw at Ravi. It takes a confused moment to comprehend the gesture; *I'm watching you.*

Fuck, his life is absurd.

With a triumphant "aha!" Constance springs back up and pushes into Ravi's hands three long iron nails. They look rough-hewn, maybe hand forged. "At the very least, keep these on you. Should you by happenstance find yourself in opposition with the creatures of the Undying Courts, these will help more than any common blade or arrow." She smiles her cheerful apple-cheeked grin.

He gives up. "Okay. I'll take the nails. Thank you, Constance. And about...the other thing." He looks away, biting his lip. "When you ask Harry about it, could you...not mention me? Please."

Her inquiring gaze takes on a tinge of sympathy. "Oh, Ravi. Do you imagine the others do not know? Or at least, suspect?"

There were...hints. That hadn't escaped his notice. But it is hard to hear his suspicions confirmed. He swallows hard, looking down at his oxfords. They could use another polish, he notes distantly.

"Hark." He looks up. Constance watches him with kindness, and her familiar is watching him with...well, it's hard to tell with cats. Probably indifference. "You have been a steadfast and stalwart companion. None of us think any less of you for it. Indeed, as much as I am, by necessity, wary of you and your grand order of witch-hunters, I count myself fortunate that you are on my side. I feel more confident that my demon nemesis shall fall because I know you will be at my back."

He isn't sure how to respond, how to tell her that her words mean a great deal to him. But he has had quite enough of being the center of attention, thank you very much.

He clears his throat. "I should have asked. How are you doing with that? Anything I can help with?"

Constance again grants him a long, considering silence before she sighs, pushing herself up off the counter and scooping Griswold into her arms. "You are a nice person, under there, witch-hunter." She starts walking toward the back, clearly a gentle dismissal. "Enjoy your trip. We shall endeavor not to pry you away from it."

When Ravi leaves the shop, bells again tinkling softly overhead, he stands outside for a long minute. Then he digs out the red phone and swipes into the messages.

Chapter Six

CAYENNE HAS PERFECTED the art of sprawling comfortably and casually in the booth, to all appearances without a care in the world, while at the same time keeping a careful watch on the door. They take a sip of their steaming drink—a dirty chai of course, because what is the point of subtlety?—and wait. Patience isn't something that comes naturally to Cayenne; when you can simply adjust time to whatever suits you best, why would you wait for anything? But they have to admit, there is something delicious about the building anticipation of it. A novelty.

Still, if they have to wait much longer…*ah. There he is.*

They watch as Ravi enters the coffee shop, and they

aren't the only ones who notice him. Dressed as always as if for a magazine photoshoot, he certainly turns a few heads. Everyone likes a sharp-dressed man, after all. Cayenne grins. Oh, but he cuts a fine figure.

Well-groomed, close-cropped beard accentuating a sharp jaw and high, aristocratic cheekbones. Eyes velvety dark and thickly lashed, with a way of looking straight through you, making you feel stripped to the core. A nose with some character. His hair is fashionably swept back, sides shaved close, but it falls into a tumble over his brows that he is always pushing back into place. Some impressive muscle to him, but not the bulky kind gained from hours of vanity in a gym; the lean, athletic form of someone who got their physique from actual work instead of recreation.

Cayenne's mouth waters just to look at him.

They watch as Ravi scans the whole room in one practiced sweep, cataloging bodies and possible hazards. The way his eyes catch on Cayenne's indolent sprawl is quite gratifying. A moment later he slides into the booth across from them.

"A pleasure to see you in one piece, *mon ami*! Nothing to drink? They do a very passable chai." They wink.

Ravi snorts, leaning back. "I doubt that."

Cayenne sways in, head propped on their palm. "Come now, it will look strange if you don't have *something*. What do you normally order?"

Ravi shrugs. "Black coffee. Blonde roast. Cinnamon if they have it. But I don't need—"

But that is enough. With a delicate tweak to the clock tattoo on the back of their hand, it's as easy as breathing to turn back time, like winding thread around a spool. They can do it without touching the tattoo, but it's smoother with it, and helps with precision. For this meeting, they want to be precise.

Alone again, Cayenne goes up to the register. This time, they add the coffee to their drink order, stuff a $50 in the tip jar on a whim, and once drinks are in hand, they sit back down to adopt the careless pose that had seemed to go over well enough before.

They have the pleasure of watching Ravi enter the shop again, turn heads, do his visual check of all the corners and exits, hesitate just that split second when he spies them at the table, and slide back into his seat.

"A pleasure to see you in one piece, *mon ami!* Here, I got you this." They wink as they push it across the table.

Ravi's brows raise in surprise. He sniffs the cup, then looks at Cayenne with mixed astonishment and suspicion. "This is how I take my coffee."

Cayenne adopts an air of innocence. "What a lucky guess! And how did the last adventure go, hmm?"

Ravi takes a hesitant sip of coffee. "It was fine. Little rough in places, but your info was good."

"Of course, it was." Cayenne smiles over the top of their oversized mug, looking up through their lashes.

"You helped a lot of people," Ravi adds softly.

Enough of *that*. "Nonsense! I'm so happy you and your merry little band of heroes enjoyed yourselves. Just as I am over the moon, as the saying goes, that we shall be borne away on the winds to far-off lands in merely two days. I've never been to the Seychelles islands, darling, but it looks *terribly* romantic. I can't *wait* to be alone with you."

Ravi coughs, glancing around for eavesdroppers. There are none; Cayenne had been very, very careful in the choice of venue. But it is still fun to tease him. He's so easy to rile up.

"I have procured a private jet, but *of course*, darling, *c'est moi*. It is a long flight, but no worries, it'll be a luxurious ride. Perhaps we can enjoy some champagne in those little bottles. And a bit of a snuggle, perhaps?" The flight would go quite differently, in fact, but if it makes Ravi blush, it's worth stretching the truth a little.

Ravi shifts uncomfortably in his seat. Perhaps they should ease up a bit on the flirting? They don't want to push him too far; he's a skittish one. Easy enough to rewind time a few moments and try again, as many times as it takes, but maybe there won't be a need. Cayenne decides to enjoy the challenge of getting things right all in one go. It's not something they do very often.

"Sweetheart, I only tease. Do not fear, I will be a perfect gentleman, as long as you wish it. Two bungalows have been procured, so you need not worry about your privacy. And it is a *very* discreet resort, I have been *quite* thorough. No photos of guests are allowed. I am as concerned with not being found out as you are, darling."

Finally, Ravi looks up at them, a worried furrow on his brow. "Two rooms. Good." The words are harsh, but his tone is more distracted than anything.

They sigh, setting down their chai. "You know, my dear, if it is *truly* going to be a hardship for you to be whisked away on a tropical getaway, we need not. I am not going to make you do anything you don't want to do."

A hint of shame crosses Ravi's face. "No, I...I know that. I'm not..." He takes a deep breath and starts over. On the other side of the timeline, the man was so unaffected, stoic; an impenetrable fortress wearing an expensive suit. It's nice to see him now so human, stumbling to find the right words. Ugh, so annoying, that Cayenne now finds things like this *cute*. "I do want to go. With you."

Cayenne smiles broadly. "Glad am I to hear it, darling."

Ravi shuts his eyes for a second. When they open again,

Cayenne notes with interest the new set of determination on his handsome features. "Cayenne."

"Yes?"

"Have you ever been in a monsoon?"

For once, they are taken off guard. "Ah, *quoi*?"

"I said before, over text, that you were kind of like one. A monsoon."

Cayenne pulls their sprawling limbs in and leans forward on their elbows, moving in as close to Ravi as the table will allow. "I do recall that." They had, in fact, nearly swooned over that little tidbit of poetry. *Shall I compare thee to a storm?* Delicious.

"Well," Ravi continues, "I've decided you're actually *exactly* like a monsoon. Have you been in one?"

"I can't say as I have."

"It's the end of the dry season," Ravi says, crossing his arms and squaring his shoulders. "At first, when the first monsoon comes, it's such a relief. The cool rain on the parched ground, it's like...like breathing clean air for the first time." He pauses, and Cayenne is on tenterhooks, waiting for more. "But later, sometimes, there are floods and windstorms, and then nothing but ruin. Sometimes"—he shrugs one shoulder—"but not always. Sometimes it's just a nice rain. But other times it's...devastation."

Cayenne is speechless.

Ravi takes a deep breath. "It would be best if we didn't spend time together."

Their stomach falls to the floor. Immediately they start tallying seconds, figuring how long ago they would need to rewind to fix this, to try again, through a growing ache of rejection. But Ravi is still talking, and...offering them a shy, little half-smile? They quickly tune back in.

"But...I did make a promise, so I guess I'm not going to do what's best for me." And there it is: a real smile, a small and fragile thing, to be sure, but there. Cayenne's spirits rise again to their proper place, always quick to adapt.

"Ravi, I think that might be the most romantic thing anyone has ever said to me."

"Wow," Ravi laughs self-deprecatingly, "kinda sad. A whole lot of it was mostly a complaint. I think it might be the most romantic thing I've ever said?"

Cayenne bites their lower lip, keeping a grin under control. "Aren't we a pair."

Rubbing the back of his neck, Ravi shakes his head. "Aren't we just. Thanks for the coffee." He begins to slide out of the booth. "See you at the airport."

They clasp their hands together in delight, masking a flutter of nerves. "Marvelous! I'll be seeing you, my hero."

Ravi nods, that same delicate smile still on his face as he turns to go. As they watch, Cayenne lays a hand on their chest, relishing the little skip in their pulse. *My, my.* This sweet boy is just chock-full of surprises. They can't wait to unwrap every single one of them.

Chapter Seven

WHAT THE FUCK am I doing here? Ravi strides across the tarmac, the Georgia heat already making the air rise in rippling waves. The private jet ahead is all sleek lines and rounded contours. He's used to being sent around via jet for assignments, sometimes even for non-monster-related things, like family weddings. Always with the weddings. A major affair for any of the old Trust families. But seeing this particular jet makes Ravi's chest tight, his limbs tense.

What the fuck *am I doing here?*

He can't lie to himself that it's only out of obligation. Just fulfilling a bargain. Cayenne is absolutely a gale-force wind of sexuality and promise. Ravi has had years of expertise at clandestine glances, at the careful dropping of coded clues while still being on high alert for any hints of suspicion or aggression. Someone approaching him and just saying, "Hello, you're sexy, let's spend some time together and let's see what happens," bold as you please is… It's not what he's used to. He can't decide what he wants more; to run away from it, or toward it.

Evidently, toward, he muses wryly as he approaches the jet. Whether what he *wants* aligns with what is *wise* remains to be seen.

Halfway up the rolling staircase locked into place at the jet's entrance, Cayenne speaks to a smartly uniformed attendant. Sunlight glints off their tousled red hair, picking out notes of gold and bright copper. Once they spot him, Cayenne grins, jumps down the last two steps, throws their arms around a flustered Ravi, and presses a quick peck to each cheek. The enthusiastic greeting could be taken for a simple European custom, and a little curl of gratitude takes root in Ravi's stomach. So far Cayenne has been very careful to honor Ravi's need for discretion, and even though he knows it has a bit to do with an unspoken agreement for mutually assured destruction should one of them go telling tales to The Trust, it's still nice. He relaxes a fraction.

"*There* he is," purrs Cayenne, "dressed to the nines as always. A suit for an international flight, darling? I suppose the shirt is made of hair, as well?" They give him a teasing wink.

It takes a second for him to place the idiom. Ravi looks down at his clothes, perplexed. "This is a Havana suit. It doesn't wrinkle." It's linen too. Obviously quite suitable for the tropics, and his shoes are Turkish loafers. Very casual. Cayenne is dressed simply in a thin sage-green collarbone-baring T-shirt with a fashionable knot tied at the hip, and what looks to be yoga pants that fit like a second skin. On anyone else, the outfit would look like pajamas; on Cayenne, it looks like it just came off the Parisian runway.

Cayenne rolls their eyes hugely, very green with the color of their shirt complimenting them. "*Désolé,* of course. And is this all you've packed?" They motion to the canvas and vegan-leather duffel held at his side. Their smile is wound a little too tight, their stance a little too stiff. Instead of answering, Ravi furrows his brow and leans in closer.

"Are you okay?" he asks. He's never seen anything other than utter confidence from them before. When Cayenne hesitates to answer instead of launching immediately into some coy flirtation meant to distract him (which often worked, annoyingly), Ravi's focus narrows down like a laser. "What's wrong?"

"Ah. I..." Cayenne clears their throat, glancing up at the stairway. "Can we talk on the plane?"

Do they look paler than usual? "Sure," he says, motioning for them to go first and hefting his duffel over his shoulder. On the way up he tries not to ogle. Yoga pants are fighting dirty.

The staff greet the pair warmly as they board. The pilot, an older woman in a sharp suit, tips her hat before disappearing into the cockpit. Ravi turns down an attendant's offer to take his bag, explaining that it has his reading materials and personal effects, and he would prefer to keep it on him. The real reason is because he has his gun in there, but he keeps that snippet of information to himself. There are offers to fetch them refreshments, though Cayenne demurs and leads Ravi straight back into the main area.

The jet's interior is similar to others he's been in, designed for luxury and comfort. Maybe a little more spacious than most. A long L-shaped sofa along one side, tables and recliners on the other, and a full-service bar in the back. Ample sunlight pours through the windows. Ravi slings his bag onto a recliner before following Cayenne to the sofa, where they perch on the edge of the cushions, face tight and wan.

"Okay. We're on the plane. You going to tell me what's up?" Ravi settles on one end of the sofa.

Cayenne nods, restlessly smoothing invisible wrinkles from the thin fabric over their thighs. "Yes, my dear, you have been...yes. Thank you." They take a deep breath, eyes skating past Ravi. "I hate flying."

"Oh. That's okay. Not a big deal. I've flown with other agents who are nervous on planes. They usually just get really, really drunk."

"It is not merely nerves, *et tu vois*." They swallow hard, looking out of the window for a long second. Their eyes lock back onto Ravi's with the air of having come to a difficult decision. "Nor is it a matter of preference. It is…" They take a deep breath before continuing. "I am going to share something with you that I have not told anyone before. Something of a weakness of mine. I need you to promise me that you won't…" They bite their lip. "That you won't tell anyone."

Ravi hears what they don't say. *That you won't tell The Trust. That you won't use this weapon I'm giving you against me.*

"I won't."

This brings out a small smile, Cayenne relaxing a few degrees. "I believe you." They ease back into the cushions, stretching out. "My abilities don't work reliably if I am moving very fast. Planes, fast cars, and suchlike. They are all very uncomfortable for me."

"So…speed makes a difference to time travel?"

Cayenne offers up a cocky grin, their confidence inching back to the forefront. "I know I make it look effortless, darling, but traveling through time is in truth a difficult art.

The Earth is always moving. Someone like *moi*, or even to a lesser degree someone like James, *ugh*, has to account for that at all times. Add the extra velocity of, say, a rented luxury *jet*, and it becomes nearly impossible. A jet can move *quite* a distance in a single second. If I get my calculations wrong at *this* height, well. It would be very inconvenient for me, to be sure, but only for as long as it takes to hit the ground. So—" they pull out a satchel from under the sofa and remove a small tin, shaking it so it rattles. "I deeply apologize, my tall glass of chai, but I shall be a complete and utter *bore* during this flight. I intend to sleep the whole way through."

Ravi hadn't really taken the time to think about the physics involved in time travel, but it makes sense. "You could just not do any time jumping while we're flying."

"Aha, yes. Well. Let us say the *knowledge* that I cannot use my abilities is the worst part, shall we?" Cayenne taps idly on the tin of sleeping pills. Ravi considers this, imagining how it must be for a carefree, consequence-averse time traveler to be fixed in only one place and time. It's not the same, but he knows something about feeling trapped. Being unable to move freely. Having your choices winnowed away to nothing.

He offers Cayenne a crooked smile. "I get it. Not a problem. I've brought stuff I can do. Reports to finish. I'm sure

I'll sleep too at some point, it's a thirteen-hour flight."

Cayenne fixes him with an intense, searching stare. Like a sunrise it breaks into their usual dazzling smile. "Thank you, Ravi. If I may ask one more favor? *S'il vous plaît*...do not take my picture while I am asleep." Another flash of apprehension.

Ravi senses this is the most important issue for Cayenne, that a great deal of trust is being placed in him. He nods firmly, sincerity ringing in the words, "I won't."

*

CAYENNE SLEEPS SPRAWLED on the sofa like a baroque muse being painted. Meanwhile, Ravi occupies himself with first work, then a game on his handheld console, occasionally taking breaks just to look over at Cayenne. He's never gotten the chance to simply *look* at them; at their long, lean form. Their too-perfect face that even in slumber holds a hint of self-satisfaction. They look like an aristocratic libertine from another era. Like they haven't a care in the world, like oceans will part for them if only they would ask.

The attendants are an expert balance of attentive and unobtrusive, bringing Ravi anything he likes but otherwise offering him privacy. One of the attendants looks to be maybe Pakistani, and after a few hours Ravi strikes up a conversation with him. The man notices Ravi eschews the fine wine and cocktails and sticks to bottled water and offers to make up a *real* drink for him. Shortly thereafter Ravi enjoys a traditional savory lassi. He gives the man his thanks in Urdu, offering a tip for the thoughtful gesture. The man refuses to take it, saying they have all been extremely well paid already.

And so, Ravi spends the rest of the flight playing video games, studying Cayenne as they sleep, flipping through the movie selection until he slips into a catnap, reading brochures, looking at Cayenne, eating a little, watching Cayenne, and gazing out at the overhead view of clouds. All in all, it's one of the better flights he's had.

*

WHEN THEY LAND the attendants move quickly, gathering bags that must be Cayenne's luggage off the plane. Cayenne stirs slightly as the wheels touch down but doesn't rouse until Ravi gives their shoulder a gentle shake. A slow blink gives way to a charming smile when they see Ravi over them. "Now *this* is a pleasant way to awaken," they rasp, accent a little thickened. "Would you be a *lamb* and see if the car is waiting for us? I will be but a moment behind you."

"Sure." Ravi shrugs. They probably have a dire need for the bathroom. He scoops up his bag, shares a friendly nod with the desi attendant, and descends onto the runway. The weather is predictably perfect; probably even a few degrees cooler than Atlanta had been and considerably less humid. The salt of the ocean is redolent on the breeze, and Ravi takes a deep lungful.

The driver waits for him with the car door held open, so he slides right into the back. Cayenne stretches luxuriantly as they step onto the stairs before joining him in the backseat. They regard Ravi with a strange expression, cheeks and lips lifting and smoothing as if they are incredibly pleased but attempting to hide it.

"Everything okay?" He digs out his sunglasses and puts them on.

"What could be wrong, darling?" Cayenne answers with a wink. "Shall we?"

Chapter Eight

"GENTLEMEN," CHIRPS THE lady at the concierge desk in barely accented English, dressed neatly with a colorful silk scarf tied around her neck and her dark hair wound into a tight bun. The lobby mirrors the aesthetic of the whole resort; high luxury emphasized by charmingly rustic accents as if to say, *if you're here you are so rich that you don't need to be reminded of how rich you are,* the sort of unpretentiousness only achieved by the truly financially secure. "We are very happy to welcome you to the Seychelles!"

Ravi lets Cayenne deal with the check-in. They lay the charm on pretty thick, he notes, as the concierge laughs at something they tell her in rapid-fire French. Ravi's eyes are busy behind his shades, checking corners and assessing details. Aside from the three of them, there are no other people in the lobby, and no visible security cameras.

"Sir?" The concierge smiles at him politely, and Cayenne crooks a finger to call him over.

"Sorry." He moves up and takes the stapled pages the lady hands him.

"The NDA, sir."

Cayenne lays a hand on his shoulder. "This charming *mademoiselle* was just explaining about the resort's privacy policies."

"That's right," she says, seemingly happy to repeat herself. "We pride ourselves on providing the gold standard in privacy for our guests, and we take this responsibility very seriously. All guests must sign the nondisclosure agreement, stating that they will never share the names or occupations of other guests, or take any pictures that have faces in them, aside from your own. Any deviation from these rules will warrant the strictest prosecution possible. You may rest easy with us knowing that your confidence will be kept."

Ravi's brows climb up. He's impressed. This resort must see a lot of dignitaries, high-ranking officials, maybe even royalty. Admittedly money is a bit of an abstract concept for Ravi, but he wonders how much of a fortune

Cayenne is spending on this trip. "Won't be a problem." He signs the contract.

She hands him another with an apologetic smile. "This one is in case of a medical emergency. Sorry, new policy."

Ravi fills it out obligingly, glancing up at her over the top of his sunglasses. "New policy?"

"Oh, yes." She smiles very brightly, and for the first time, it feels a little false. "Nothing to worry about. I assure you we take the safety of our guests as seriously as their privacy."

"I am certain you do, miss." Cayenne leans in, pulling at Ravi's shoulders impatiently. "And here we are *wasting* the *lovely* day while we could be enjoying the amenities! Shall we go see our bungalows, *mon ami*? Thank you very much, miss, goodbye!"

Somewhat bemused, Ravi allows himself to be led away. Once they are out, heading toward the more secluded side of the resort that boasts an array of beachside bungalows, he asks, "What was that about?"

"Whatever do you mean, darling?"

Ravi gives them an unimpressed look. "You know what I mean."

Cayenne sighs dramatically. "It was about to get frightfully dull, is all. I did you a favor. You would have stayed there asking about boring medical waivers for *five minutes*.

Trust me, you wouldn't have missed anything interesting." Ravi stops abruptly, and it takes a couple of steps for Cayenne to realize he isn't at their side. "What is it, darling?"

"Did you...did you time travel us? Or whatever you call it?"

"Just a *teeny* bit, sweetheart. A little skip. Think of it like fast-forwarding through the boring parts of a movie." Cayenne flips their hand in a careless gesture. "And I didn't rewind you, my dear. Just myself. If I do the both of us, you'd remember the possible future too." Then they gasp as if a new concept has just occurred to them. They take Ravi's hands, looking up at him with enormous puppy-dog eyes. "You aren't mad, are you? I just want our time together to be *perfect*, darling." They nibble at their lower lip and bat their lashes. It's a transparent attempt to charm him. Aggravatingly, it still works.

"It's...weird, sure, but no. I'm not mad. I wouldn't call it a surprise that patience isn't one of your virtues."

They give him a meaningful once-over from head to toe. "Mm. I don't know about that. I can be *very* patient if I know it's going to be worth the wait. Now come, let's get out of this beastly sun before I freckle."

*

THE BUNGALOWS ARE set across from one another on

docks directly over the shallow water; thatched roof, the walls facing the open sea almost entirely glass, white curtains wafting in the ocean air. The view is something else, the sea painted deep turquoise with the white sands of the islands on the horizon shining like scattered jewels in the sun.

When Cayenne moves to open a door, Ravi stills them with a hand to their breastbone. "Wait," he says, securing his duffel across his chest and unzipping it just enough to have his weapon easily accessible. He moves inside, first checking the space behind the door and in the corners. There's not much space to hide. A simple open-plan layout with an understated living area in rattans and bamboo, a small sleek kitchenette, a sliding door to the bathroom, and most predominantly the bed. A four-poster king surrounded by mosquito netting and fairy lights. Ravi tries not to look at it.

Once he's sure the place is clear of hidden inhabitants, he starts a sweep for surveillance bugs, hidden cameras, and signs of hexes or curses. The whole while Cayenne leans against the doorframe and watches him with undisguised amusement.

"You don't do this when you travel?" Ravi asks them incredulously, toeing open the bathroom door before clearing that space next.

Cayenne laughs. "Not typically, darling. But by all means, *enjoy* yourself. I *do* like watching you work. The word 'strapping' comes to mind."

Ravi shakes his head, suppressing a smile. "Looks clear. I'll go check the other one too. This one's yours, unless you have objections."

Cayenne shrugs, walking into the bungalow as if they own it. "It's all the same to me, my dear. I expect they'll be bringing my bags any minute. Go on, do your secret agent routine." They shoo him out with a smile, then stand in the doorway with both hands propped against the frame. "Afterwards, what's the first thing you want to do? This is *your* tropical getaway, after all. Anything you like."

Ravi hardly has to think about it. "Beach. I haven't swum in the ocean in months."

"Then a lovely afternoon on the beach you shall have." Cobra quick, Cayenne lands a kiss on the tip of Ravi's nose.

His ears go hot, and he clears his throat. "Okay. I'll see you in a few?"

"Are you sticking with that outfit," they ask with wide-eyed innocence, "or do you have a bespoke three-piece wetsuit you intend to wear instead?"

Ravi rolls his eyes and turns away, while Cayenne chuckles behind him.

*

FOR THE FIRST time in recent history, Ravi lets his muscles completely unknot one by one, the sun soaking him through, sand under the beach blanket conforming to his body like memory foam. It's a different ocean than the one he'd grown up close to, but the angle of the sun here is almost right. Yeah. This is all right.

An arms-length away, Cayenne slathers on practically half a bottle of high SPF sunscreen. They have a lot of displayed skin to cover. They brought a floral tote and a luridly printed kimono-style robe down to the beach, but under it are clad only in fitted shorts that are very short indeed. Aqua with little pink flamingos. Ravi tries not to stare.

"You're *sure* you don't need any, my dear? I know you are a big strong hero and all, but melanoma is a foe you can't exactly punch into submission. I would be *more* than happy to help you with the hard-to-reach areas."

Ravi tips up a lazy smile, feeling pleasantly like a lizard on a hot rock. "Nah, thanks. My daily moisturizer has SPF5 built in." Plus, the summery cotton-linen shirt he wears adds a bit of extra protection, even if it is so thin as to be nearly see-through.

Cayenne gives him a rueful smile. "*Five*? Mine here is"—they check the label—"SPF80. And I'm *still* going to get a burn, I just know it."

Ravi props himself up on his elbows. "I've got to ask. If you don't like the sun, and you don't like to fly, why did you invite me here?"

Cayenne says nothing for a long second, capping the sunscreen with a snap and dropping it into their bag. Then they pull their knees up close to their chest and rest their head atop them, granting Ravi a rare, honest smile. "You're worth a little inconvenience, sweetheart."

Ravi is grateful for the mirrored surface of his sunglasses, for surely his eyes must be wide as saucers. He looks away out to the shore. No matter how hard he works to prove himself, to be what is expected of him, no one has told Ravi he was worthy of anything for a long time. Not since he was seventeen.

He's saved from finding a response by the sound of laughter and a Frisbee landing right at the edge of their blanket. He automatically tenses before two figures hove into view, a pair of women about his age, both in fashionable one-piece suits.

"Oh, I'm so sorry about that!" exclaims one of them, leaning down to retrieve the Frisbee. She has well-muscled arms that remind Ravi a little of Val, her hair in long Senegalese twists. Her friend joins her, smiling at Ravi and Cayenne. She's white, hair in beachy waves under a wide-brimmed straw hat. "Hi, *bonjour*, you guys speak English, right? So sorry to interrupt. Did you two just arrive today? I don't think we've seen you at the resort before!"

*

AT FIRST ANNOYED at the ladies' approach, Cayenne then notices that the big floppy hat the one girl wears is *exceptionally* fine. They'd look fabulous in it. Still, the sensibilities of their gentleman companion must be taken into consideration; if Ravi doesn't want to risk exposure by talking to other resort-goers, they will of course follow his lead. They give him a questioning lift of an eyebrow.

Ravi nods a tiny fraction and sits up the rest of the way. "Yeah, hi, no, uh. You aren't interrupting."

Cayenne greets them with a twiddle of fingers.

"I'm so glad!" The one with the hat sits cross-legged in the sand and tugs her friend down beside her. "I'm Elissa, this is Taylor."

Taylor smiles at them, a little apologetically. "Hello. Sorry about the Frisbee. I wasn't paying attention to where I was throwing."

Uh-huh. Somehow Cayenne doubts that. They extend a hand, infusing their motions and speech with a little *tra*ness, overtly blurring their gender expression. "Think nothing of it, ladies. I am Cayenne, and it is a *pleasure* to meet you." Elissa shakes their hand, and Taylor leans over her to follow suit.

"I *love* your robe," Elissa gushes, "very Freddie Mercury." Both women have American accents, perhaps with a Californian twist.

"You are too kind!" They glance over at Ravi, but he still seems fairly comfortable. Taylor offers her hand to Ravi, and he shakes it readily enough.

"Ravi," he tells her, to Cayenne's surprise. They would have bet on a fake name. Speaking of bets...

"We were just talking of our first pets," Cayenne informs the girls, ignoring how Ravi glances at them like they have lost their mind. "Mine was an ocelot named Clyde." The way Ravi gapes at them is *très drôle*; they have to look away from him or else they can't keep a straight face. "What about yours, Elissa, your very first pet?"

Elissa blinks in confusion but answers regardless. "Um, my first pet? I had a turtle when I was little. His name was Dash."

"Thank you," Cayenne breezes, immediately laying a hand on their tattoo, winding time back just a hair.

"—Ravi," he is introducing himself to Taylor, then glances over at Cayenne. He seems to notice the way they're touching the back of their hand with curiosity. Cayenne tilts him a careless shrug, smiling guilelessly.

"Are you guys from the States?" Taylor smiles bright white against her skin, directing most of it at Ravi.

"Yeah," he answers, attention dragged away from Cayenne. "Just arrived a bit ago."

Elissa gasps. She seems an easily excitable sort. "Oh, oh! Then you didn't get to see all the drama go down this morning!"

"Liss," Taylor chides her friend. "There's an NDA."

"Um, for names and stuff, Tay, not for like, resort gossip. That's totally different. I didn't sign anything that said I *couldn't* talk about ambulances."

"Still, they just got here, I don't think they're interested—"

"Ambulances? Did someone get hurt?" Ravi interrupts, spine straightening.

Ugh. Predictably concerned, their hero. Doesn't he know how to turn it off and *relax* for once?

Elissa leans in with enthusiasm. "Okay, so this guy got found on the beach around dawn, super fucked up. He had to be wheeled out on a gurney."

"Fucked up how?" Ravi asks, wholly attentive. Cayenne sighs and contemplates the chances of avoiding this entire conversation altogether if they rewind time a little more.

"Well, we've only been here four days, but apparently,

this has been going on all week. People have been getting so drunk or whatever that they're blacking out. Then they're found on the beach in the morning, still all fucked up from whatever they did last night. Some of them have weird marks, but you can get those if you get, like, super drunk and run into things."

Taylor speaks up reluctantly, as if she were being drawn into the conversation against her better judgment. "It's been happening so much that I hear they're starting to make people sign medical waivers at check-in."

"But the *crazy* thing?" Elissa spreads her hands dramatically. "The crazy thing is that all of those people swore up and down they hadn't been drinking or taking any drugs."

"It's probably a jellyfish," Taylor mutters.

Both Cayenne and Ravi turn to look at her, completely perplexed.

"A jellyfish?" Cayenne asks, intrigued despite themself.

"Oh my god, Taylor. Here we go again." Elissa cups her hands around her mouth as if playing a game of telephone, her voice a loud stage whisper. "She had a minor in marine biology."

"I did not," Taylor protests, "it was just two semesters." She shifts in the sands, rearranging long brown legs. The movement inches her a little closer to Ravi, Cayenne notices.

"These people probably went out for a night swim, weren't careful, and swam into a school of jellyfish. That would make marks, and the venom *could* mess you up pretty bad, depending on the species."

Horrified, Cayenne turns to Ravi. "What sort of godforsaken corner of the earth have you dragged me to?"

Ravi's jaw drops. "Wha... *You* dragged *me* here!"

"Whoa, whoa, Taylor, tell them the other thing!" Elissa lightly slaps her friend's shoulder. "You freaked them out! Now they'll never get in the water."

"*Technically*," Taylor continues, gathering her thick twists over her shoulder, "there's no poisonous sea-life in this area. So, we should be safe." They are relieved until she adds, "But with global warming, who knows. Migration patterns are all messed up."

Elissa laughs, and despite themself Cayenne notices she has a nice laugh, loud and unselfconscious. They kind of like her style, though grudgingly. "I am *so* sorry about Tay. She is the *worst* at flirting. Look, the reason we came over here is because we've been hoping to find some guys who like to dance. The resort has an amazing club, but it's mostly couples staying here."

Cayenne has been half expecting something like this the entire time. The old accidental Frisbee toss. A popular ploy in any timeline.

"Oh, uh," starts Ravi.

Taylor winces. "You guys are together, aren't you." She aims this at Ravi, obviously disappointed.

His face goes completely still.

"We are not labeling things just yet." Cayenne swoops in to save the day, then grins at the pair conspiratorially. "You know how these things are."

"Oh, that's cool," Elissa says quickly, "I mean, we could still dance, right?"

Now, as a rule, Cayenne does not do jealousy. A useless emotion meant for *other* people, people who don't have the good fortune to be able to rewind time again and again until they get what they want. And they certainly aren't feeling jealousy now, *c'est ridicule*. However. If reserved, straitlaced Ravi was ever going to loosen up enough to step onto a dance floor, it was *damn well* going to be Cayenne who brought him there. In fact, new goal. Teach Ravi to dance. But first, it's well past time to wrap up this little encounter.

"Tell you what, beautiful. If you can...oh, let's see, guess the name of my first pet, we will dance with you." They grin with calculated encouragement.

Elissa perks up. "Do I get a hint?"

"You get a hint and three guesses," Cayenne offers generously.

"Okay!"

"And if I can guess *your* first pet, I get…hmm." They pretend to consider, lacing their fingers together and resting their chin on them. "Your very fetching hat."

She grins, touching the brim. "This old thing? Okay, deal. You get a hint and three guesses too."

"*C'est parfait*. Your hint is it's a color."

She thinks for a moment. "Is it in French?"

"Ah, ah, ah." They wag a finger at her. "That would be two hints, no? But I shall be generous. English."

Taylor leans over and whispers in Elissa's ear. While the girls confer with each other, Cayenne looks over at Ravi with a sly grin. Ravi's eyes narrow over the top of his sunglasses. *What are you doing?* he mouths soundlessly. Cayenne lays a hand on their chest as if clutching pearls, the picture of innocence.

"Okay, my guesses are Ginger, Violet, and Amber."

Cayenne plays with them a little bit, like a cat with a mouse, eyes going wide as if with shock, before smiling apologetically. "Afraid not, ladies, so sorry. It seems your search for dance partners must continue."

"Aw." Elissa looks crestfallen. "I was really sure about Ginger."

Cayenne tosses their red hair at her and winks. "A good guess, but alas. Now, what's my hint?"

"Oh, right. Um…okay. It means fast." She shares a

smile with her friend, who seems to be quickly losing interest in the whole conversation now she knows Ravi is unavailable. Cayenne is unaccountably pleased.

They tap a finger to their chin, debating how long to draw this out. "Speedy?"

"Nope!"

"Hmm...how about Dash?" The way her mouth falls open is very funny. They suppress a laugh.

"What! No way!"

Feigning sympathy, Cayenne clucks their tongue. "That was it, then? What a stroke of luck!"

"Cayenne," Ravi interjects softly, "c'mon."

"No, no," Elissa says, taking off the hat and handing it to Cayenne. "He won it fair and square. I guess it was a pretty easy hint."

Cayenne accepts the hat gracefully. "Thank you very much. And the pronouns are they/them, *s'il vous plaît*."

They both accept this with barely a blink, which does raise them up a couple of degrees in Cayenne's esteem. "Oh, cool. Sorry."

"Think nothing of it. And we shall keep our eyes peeled for jellyfish."

The two ladies get up, brush off any sand, and say goodbye. Ravi waves wordlessly. Once they are out of earshot, he turns a disapproving frown on Cayenne.

"Did you steal that girl's hat?"

"Not at all, darling, you heard her. I won it fair and square." They plop the hat on, mercifully blocking the sun's harsh rays. A relief, as they were just starting to feel their nose go pink. They carefully arrange the hat so their fabulous mop is highlighted instead of obscured; now *that* would be a crime far worse than theft.

"The power to bend time, and you use it to steal a sun hat?"

Cayenne doesn't know why Ravi looks so reproachful; this is just a little sport. "It's not stealing if she agreed to it. She played the game."

"Uh-huh. And that was a totally random guess?"

It's obvious Ravi isn't going to buy it, no matter what they say or how many tries they take. "What difference does it make, darling? She likely has a dozen others."

"It's cheating."

Cayenne pouts, adjusting the tilt of the hat. "What, you don't think it suits me?" They arrange themself into a winsome pose, like a vintage pinup.

Ravi laughs, and from his expression is surprised by it. "You know it does," he says, voice low. Cayenne's smile goes a little sultry. Ravi lays on his back with a sigh, arm shading his eyes.

Cayenne creeps close. "You know," they drawl,

stretching out alongside Ravi, "those pretty girls liked you."

"And you," Ravi murmurs, surely aware they're nearly touching as they lie next to each other, but he doesn't move away.

"Oh, they were hardly interested in me, you sweet thing." Cayenne smirks. "Even if I am very *flexible* in my tastes, I know how I come across to most people. They were definitely angling for you. And who can blame them?"

"Well," Ravi says slowly, a barely visible smile on his lips, "I'm not here with them, am I?"

Something melts, warm and smooth, in their black little heart. They fiercely wish to kiss him, weighing the cost of going for it and rewinding when he inevitably protests, before they instead settle for a featherlight caress to the corded muscle of his forearm just below the roll of the sleeve.

Ravi shivers, taking his arm off his eyes. "So, what was your first pet's name?"

They wink. "I never had one, darling."

Ravi shakes his head, biting his lip to contain a laugh. "You should come with a warning."

"You aren't wrong." Cayenne draws a finger softly up his arm and across his shoulder, delighted that they are allowed to do this, first try. That Ravi is letting himself be touched. It's a heady sensation. His white shirt is open down to the sternum, showing an alluring amount of collarbone and pectoral muscles. As he shifts, the shirt gapes enough to show off a very interesting set of scars low on the center of his chest. Claws, perhaps?

"Oh my, these look fearsome." They run a hand lightly over the raised lines, pleased by the plainly visible jump of Ravi's pulse in his throat. He is so easy to take apart, this one. "And what daring feats of adventure got you these, my hero?"

"Just a fight."

Cayenne raises a single eyebrow and pouts. "Just a fight? I thought I was going to be treated to an exciting tale of your derring-do. Come now. Tell me!"

Ravi shrugs, almost too casual. "It's a boring story." He pushes himself up and fastens another button of his thin shirt, hiding himself away again. Surely that is a crime somewhere. "I'll get you a drink from the bar. Something in a coconut. How's that sound?"

Thoughtfully, Cayenne watches him pull away. They could drag him back but decide to let him go. Everyone has stories they don't want to tell, after all. "Aren't you sweet! Very well." They flash a cheeky grin up from under the shade of their new hat. "Go on, then. You can save me from this wicked sobriety, hero."

Ravi rolls his eyes, but Cayenne feels quite the thrill seeing that he's biting down on a smile as he does so. It is really quite alarming how much they want to see the real thing.

Chapter Nine

UPON SEEING THAT the resort had multiple options for fine dining, Cayenne had seemed so delighted by the prospect of a dinner for two that Ravi had let them pick which venue.

In retrospect, it might have been a mistake. The restaurant is definitely the most over-the-top romantic place Ravi has ever been in his life. Each table is tucked into corners with velvet curtains affording plenty of privacy, soft mood music evoking an intimate bedroom feel. Truly dangerous amounts of real candles have been scattered around to give the place a warm, lambent glow. This setting makes Ravi more nervous than when he'd been practically spooning on the beach, makes his stomach knot and his palms sweat. *Keep your shit together, kid.*

Cayenne, however, practically has little cartoon hearts in their eyes. "Oh, this is just *lovely*. You look *unbelievably* handsome in this light, my dear. If it weren't against the rules, I would be most tempted to take your picture to preserve it for posterity." They prop their elbow on the crisp tablecloth and rest their head on their palm, smiling flirtatiously.

Ravi scoffs, fidgeting with the salad fork. "Yeah, I know how concerned with rules you are." After the words are out, he realizes they might be taken more harshly than he means them. He rubs his forehead. "Sorry, that's… I'm really nervous."

Cayenne blinks, eyes going wide before their expression gentles. "My dear Ravi," they purr, "as gratifying as it is that I can crack your icy exterior, I don't want you to be uncomfortable. I am just—" they pause to take a deep breath, another small flash of apprehension on their face. "I am unused to this." Their gesture seems to encompass the entirety of their surroundings. "I haven't, ah, taken things slowly with somebody before. And I did say that I would try, for you. If I go too far, too fast for you, you must let me know. *Oui*?"

A few of Ravi's nerves settle as he exhales. "Okay. If it

STOLEN FROM TOMORROW - 117 -

helps, I don't know what I'm doing either. I can count the number of real dates I've had on one hand and still have fingers left over."

Cayenne laughs stridently, and Ravi is taken with the way the candlelight catches in their eyes, by the pink of their lips. He glances away, catching the eye of their waiter as he returns with a bottle of wine. After the wine is poured, they put in their food orders, and Cayenne lifts their glass for a toast.

"To not knowing what we're doing," they say with a grin. Ravi smiles back, clinking glasses. Cayenne takes a long, indulgent sip, then quirks their head to one side. "My dear, do you not drink? I think I've only seen you take a little sip of a cocktail, in Chicago, and not a drop since. If I had known, I would have—"

"Oh, no," Ravi interrupts, waving a hand dismissively, "you know how it is."

Cayenne raises their eyebrows. "No, I don't think that I do."

He picks up his glass, watching the ruby swirl of the Tempranillo as he speaks. "It's habit, mostly. I'll sometimes have a little bit to be social. But I was raised to behave as if my body were a temple. Because..." Well, they already know everything about him anyways, though he knows almost nothing of them. Unfair, but also somehow freeing? It strangely feels like a weight is off his shoulders to tell them this small bit, a tiny shaving from the most painful period in his life. "I was supposed to treat my body like a temple because it was supposed to be one. But...you know. That didn't turn out."

"I treat my body like an amusement park." Cayenne grins wolfishly, and when Ravi laughs, their smile widens even further.

"I'll bet," he chuckles. "The Chosen aren't supposed to have any tattoos, only traditional piercings, and no drugs or alcohol. So, when their body becomes a vessel for Durga's favor, it is *dhaarmik*. Sacred."

"Hmm. So that is why you keep yourself in such fine form? Because your body is a temple?"

"You know what," Ravi says, feeling reckless, "I think it's maybe just a body." And he tilts back his head and takes a big gulp, no doubt very unmannerly and not at all the way wine is supposed to be savored, but it's good regardless.

"A very nice body," Cayenne says, and Ravi nearly chokes as a bare foot runs up over his pant leg to the inside of his thigh. He doesn't drop the wineglass, but it's a close thing.

"Cayenne!" he hisses, a hand gripping the table so hard the cloth is pulling askew. He scoots back out of reach of the exploring toes.

"Oh, I'm sorry," they say with their big green eyes nearly round with innocence, "is this not slow?"

Ravi drops his head into his hands, shoulders shaking with suppressed laughter. The waiter returns with their meals, so they wait a few moments, enjoying the first few bites, before returning to their conversation. "What do you think is up with those people being found on the beach?"

Cayenne makes a face. "Who knows? It is nothing to do with us now, is it?"

"You aren't concerned? What if it's something serious, or even"—he glances around for eavesdroppers, more out of habit than any real suspicion—"something supernatural?"

Cayenne sighs heavily, taking their wineglass between both hands. "I know you are trained to look for dangers wherever you may go, and it is one of the things I truly admire about you, darling, but people get intoxicated. There's likely nothing more supernatural going on in this resort than a bad batch of cocaine."

"You don't think it's some rogue jellyfish?"

At his joke Cayenne snorts a small, surprised laugh into their wine. Being able to catch them off guard is immensely satisfying, pulling forth that genuine smile. "As loath as I am to disregard Taylor's *two whole semesters* of marine biology, I don't think so. Besides, if we *do* run across anything dangerous, I'll just pop back and warn you, like that." They snap their fingers with satisfaction. "There is nothing to worry about beyond how best to *enjoy* yourself, darling."

Ravi considers this while he chews. After a short, companionable silence, he asks the question that has been in the back of his mind for days. "What's the future like?"

Cayenne's expressive face goes blank, a window shuttering. "Do not ask me about August."

"I'm not!" Ravi holds up his hands. "Promise. I mean the future in general. Surely there's something you can let slip without...I don't know. Collapsing the time-space continuum."

Cayenne goes pale, hand at their throat. "How did you know that is what will happen?"

"I...what, *really*?"

"Kidding!" Cayenne's laughter is like bells. "You should see your *face*!"

"Okay, okay." Ravi rolls his eyes. "So, then it won't hurt anything to tell me a little?"

Cayenne shrugs, pulling one knee up onto the chair, wineglass dangling carelessly from their long fingers. "Eh, *comme ci comme ça*. James is always on about timeline integrity and paradoxes and blah blah blah, but I go wherever and whenever I like and do exactly as I please, and the universe hasn't ended yet." They drink their wine with a beatific expression, as though they were truly savoring every second of the taste. "The future in this timeline is as every time is. Some things are better. Some things are worse. Most things remain exactly the same with different advertisements."

"Sort of a bleak outlook."

Cayenne's only answer is to raise up a palm in a wordless gesture as if saying, "what can you do?"

"That's where you know me from? My future, your past?"

Myriad expressions chase one another across Cayenne's face, too swift for Ravi to read. "That is...broadly true, yes. But I assure you, my tall glass of chai, even if I hadn't known you already, I wouldn't have changed a single thing." For once they aren't smiling. They somehow manage to look both deadly serious yet still brimming with promise. "I wanted you from the very instant I saw you in that Chicago park, and that is true no matter what the future holds."

Ravi has to look away, to deflect. "Seemed like you wanted everyone."

"Did it?" they ask archly. "I *do* like to flirt, darling. You could say it's in my nature."

"Can't blame you," Ravi teases, glad to move away from that dangerous sincerity and back into nice, safe banter. "We're an attractive group."

Cayenne laughs. "That you are! How is anyone supposed to resist? I'm surprised the monsters don't all fall at
your feet."

"It's still early days."

The two share a smile, finish their wine and their meal,
enjoy a shared dessert, and it's without a doubt the strangest, most stressful, and nicest date Ravi's ever had.

*

THE LONG, SHARED dock connecting the overwater bungalows curves in graceful arches and circles. It's a pleasant
thing to wander back to their bungalows, watching the
stars. So far from cities, the sky overflows with them, the
pale curl of the Milky Way easily visible above the horizon.
It's been a while since Ravi's had a chance to see it this
clearly. Perhaps it's that breathtaking view, plus a slight
flush from the wine, that makes him not think twice about
leaning into Cayenne as they walk. Their shoulders brush
with every step.

Cayenne is telling an amusing story, carefully edited so
as not to reveal dates or names, but Ravi is distracted by
their expressive hands as they talk, tracing wide gestures in
the air. They have long, delicate fingers; an artist's hands.
Unlike Ravi's. Blunted nails and calloused from weapons-

work. Strong, but nothing of grace in them. Cayenne is practically grace personified, a study in elegance.

Fuck, he's had too much wine.

"Do you want to sit on the edge?" he asks during the next silence. He doesn't know why that's what he suggests. All he knows is they're getting closer and closer to their separate bungalows, to saying goodnight, and that knowledge makes him want to delay the inevitable moment for as long as possible.

"Mm, and dangle our feet in the water? You know what? I think I do." Cayenne wraps a hand around Ravi's arm, and they walk together to the culmination of the open dock. One other human-shaped silhouette sits on the dock nearby, but Ravi doesn't pull away.

In the dim glow of the solar lights, they claim one curve of the dock, toe off their shoes, and sit on the edge with legs dangling into the still sun-warm ocean. Cayenne leans into Ravi as if they intend to rest their head on his shoulder. His heartbeat kicks into a quick rhythm as he realizes that he hopes they will. Casual intimacy is a new thing for him, and it is quite frankly ridiculous that something as simple as someone leaning on him could make him this jittery. He's faced down dozens of snarling monsters with more calm than he feels right now.

"Excuse me," comes a rich baritone behind them, "did

you happen to see a strange shape in the water?"

Turning to look, Ravi berates himself that he didn't sense this guy approaching. Two glasses of wine and he's useless. Fortunately, the man doesn't seem to be much of a threat; a friendly handsome face, long dark hair curling around his shoulders. Shirtless and barefoot, clad only in a pair of loose wrap pants with the hems wet and dripping.

"*Mon Dieu*, what is with the *constant* interruptions to-day?" Cayenne mutters in his ear.

"Be nice," Ravi whispers back, "he's probably our neighbor."

"I'm *always* nice."

"Uh-huh." Ravi looks up at the man in what he hopes is an inoffensive manner. "Sorry, did we what?"

The man smiles apologetically. "I am sorry to disturb you both. But I saw a strange shape in the water around dusk, and I have been keeping watch for it since." He has an odd way of shaping his consonants, a difficult accent for Ravi to place. Maybe German? "I was hoping someone else had seen it too."

"Ooh, a dolphin perhaps? I wouldn't mind seeing one this trip," Cayenne exclaims. Ravi's neck is tired of craning up at this guy, so he motions for the man to join them at the edge.

"Thank you, very kind." He folds down a few feet

away, one foot off the dock in the water. "Unfortunately, what I saw was not a dolphin. Much too large."

Cayenne recoils at his side. "If you say there are sharks here, I am never going into the ocean again."

"They're really rare here," Ravi reassures them. "It was the first thing I looked up." Cayenne gives him a grateful smile. Ravi returns it, then fixes his attention on the newcomer. "You say you saw this at dusk?" Cayenne sighs heavily next to him, but he ignores it.

"I did."

If this is in any way related to the people waking up in the morning with no memories of how they got on the beach, it's worth investigating. "What's your name?" He tries to keep his tone from falling into an interrogation, but this kind of thing isn't exactly in his wheelhouse. He wishes Harry was here to ask the right questions. He doesn't possess the same easy way with people that she does.

"Uwe," the man answers as he extends a hand. Ravi shakes it. Does the man let the contact linger a second too long? Ravi clears his throat and leans back into Cayenne, who reaches over to shake hands too. This time, the contact is *definitely* too long. Cayenne's eyebrows inch up, and they shoot Ravi a quick, barely concealed smirk.

"So, Uwe," he plows ahead, "what exactly did you see?"

Uwe takes a moment to look them both over, just enough to show that the interest is there, but not too much to make things uncomfortable if it wasn't returned. Ravi is almost impressed; it's exactly the kind of unspoken communication with men like himself that he's used to, and this man speaks the dialect very eloquently.

"Two nights in a row, both times at dusk. I saw a large, dark shape, with white patches like an orca. But it was flat, like a manta ray."

"You're sure it's not just a manta ray?"

Uwe smiles and shakes his head. "I am sure. I am very familiar with the sea. This creature I have not seen before."

Ravi and Cayenne share a look. "What was it doing?" Cayenne asks. "Just swimming?"

"Cruising," Uwe states coolly, "like a shark. Looking for something. Hunting."

"Well! This has been *fascinating*, and it is very nice to meet you, Uwe, but we really must get our beauty sleep. Isn't that right, my dear?" Cayenne stands and yanks at Ravi's sleeve.

Uwe looks embarrassed. "I did not mean to alarm you. I just think we all should be careful, with the strange things going on this week."

Ravi doesn't get up right away, despite Cayenne's grasp. He gives Uwe a solemn nod. "I'll keep an eye out."

A smile crosses Uwe's handsome face. "I knew you seemed the type. You know, I did not catch your names."

"Ravi. This is Cayenne."

Cayenne twiddles their fingers in greeting.

Uwe nods, slight smile broadening. "Cayenne and Ravi. It is very nice to meet you both. I hope we will run into each other again."

"It's possible." Cayenne winks while Ravi gets to his feet. They say goodnight and make their way to their bungalows. Once they are alone, Cayenne shakes their head. "You just can't turn it off, can you, *mon beau*?"

"Turn what off?"

Cayenne's only answer is an annoyed cluck of their tongue.

Ravi stops in front of his bungalow and pulls Cayenne to a halt with him. "Wait. What's bothering you?"

Cayenne crosses their arms over their chest. If they were just pouting, Ravi would chalk it up to a little dramatic flair, but there's real hurt in Cayenne's expression. "Are you so desperate to get out of spending time with me you are going to entertain the idea that there is something sinister going on? Some people got too drunk. One guy sees a bit of shadow in the water. And you are only too ready to snap right into monster-hunting mode instead of taking *one day* to enjoy a *tropical paradise*. I wanted to give you an escape from all that. But you're, you're..." Cayenne makes a frustrated noise, fingers pulling at their hair. They drop their hands, then Ravi watches as their expression shifts into a peculiar kind of speculation. They reach for their clock tattoo.

Before he can think better of it, Ravi bends down and kisses them. Under his lips, Cayenne goes completely, utterly still. For a long second, Ravi lets himself...get a little lost.

When he pulls back for breath, Cayenne hangs on to his shoulders like they might fall over without it. "Oh," they say, audibly breathing heavier than a moment ago.

"Now you can't turn back the clock, or that won't have happened," Ravi says, his own hands shaky on Cayenne's hips.

"That is..." Cayenne swallows and steps back. "That is a *very* dirty trick. I am impressed." They look up at Ravi with a slow foxy grin that grows by the second.

"I'm not trying to get out of spending time with you, Cayenne." Ravi pulls his hands back into his pockets. It feels like birds are fluttering in his chest, and the space helps him center. "I just... I want..."

Cayenne sighs, this time with fondness. "Yes, I know. You want to help people."

Ravi shrugs one shoulder. "Yeah."

Cayenne looks down, kicking at the dock a little. "I *suppose* I've been a little silly about this. I just want you all to myself." They look up at him through their lashes. "You realize that fellow wanted us to invite him back to bed with us?"

Ravi coughs, his face growing hot. "I did manage to pick that up, yes."

They laugh, then fall quiet, biting their lip. They look meaningfully at the door to their bungalow. "I did say that I would be a perfect gentleman for as long as you wish it. And I shall hold to that." They give Ravi's chest a gentle push with a regretful sigh. "You had better go before my chivalry runs out."

Ravi nods and rubs the back of his neck. "Yeah. Okay. And you're right. I'm on vacation. I don't get many of those. I'm looking for patterns where there are none. I'll try to be better at turning it off."

Cayenne beams. "And I will try to be more forgiving of your heroic impulses. They are, after all, one of the things I simply *adore* about you, my Double-Oh Sexy." They wink outrageously.

Ravi shakes his head, laughing in disbelief. "Okay, that one is awful. That one's a *no*. Absolutely not."

"But 'my tasty little samosa' is still on, *oui*?"

"Good night."

"Wait! What are your thoughts on 'cupcake'?"

Ravi's door shuts with a click. Cayenne takes a moment to turn their face up to the night sky, to simply look at the bright stars wheeling imperceptibly overhead with a triumphant smile. Then they turn around and go to bed.

Chapter Ten

CAYENNE PUTS THE finishing touches on the careless tousle of their brassy hair when a knock sounds on the bungalow door. It's quite a bit earlier than they expected to meet Ravi to plan out their day. They grin at their reflection.

"Ah, see? He just couldn't bear another moment away," they purr smugly, blowing the mirror a kiss. After a quick check of the fit of their clothes, another knock sounds, this time louder and faster.

"Impatient, are we?" They unlock the door and open it, artfully framing themself in the doorway for full effect. "Why, he*lo*!" They are *very* put out when Ravi merely brushes past them into the bungalow. "Well, good morning to you too, pet," they mutter in affront.

"Cayenne." Ravi whirls around, utterly serious. "I saw it."

They blink at this odd statement and are quickly distracted by the way Ravi is dressed: clad only in running shoes which he quickly kicks off at the door, gray joggers, and an indecently tight V-neck T-shirt. A triangular patch where his shirt has darkened with sweat points down like a neon arrow, and Cayenne has a hard time tearing their eyes away. "Ah. You saw what now, exactly?"

"The thing!" Ravi crosses the room swiftly and checks the ocean through the open windows. "I saw the shape in the water that Uwe told us about."

Cayenne trails behind him, lips pursing in disbelief. "You saw the big manta ray thing."

"Yes!" Ravi turns and takes both of Cayenne's shoulders in his hands. His palms are branding hot. "I was out on my run. Over that way"—he nods westwards—"and while I was looking out over the ocean, I saw a shadow under the waves. Maybe two hundred yards away. I stopped to take a look, and it, you know, *crested*. Like whales do. Right out of the water. And then it went back under. Disappeared." He releases Cayenne and steps back. His eyes are wide with excitement, the early sun turning their shade a warm cinnamon.

Cayenne folds their arms across their chest. "Very well, you saw a manta ray. Good for you. So, *I* was thinking for today, how about a couples' massage?" They turn on their heel, make their way to the countertop, and pick up a brochure. "It says walk-in appointments will be available at any time. They do seaweed wraps too."

There's a huff of disbelief behind them. "Are you being serious?"

Cayenne turns around, arms still crossed, and leans back against the counter. They fix Ravi with their best pout. "I'm never serious. *You* said you'd try to turn it off."

"That was before I *saw* it!" Ravi rakes both hands through his thick hair. It's uncharacteristically unstyled, falling softly over the tips of his ears. "It was definitely not a normal manta ray, before you ask. I looked it up last night. Normal rays can be huge, yes, and they can have white and black patches like Uwe said, but none of them have *tentacles*."

Admittedly odd. "Tentacles?"

Ravi looks pleased with their interest. "Yeah. Two long, thin tentacles on the front of it. Like whips." He waits for Cayenne to speak, and the silence stretches out thin. "Well? What do you think?"

Cayenne looks away, letting their irritation show in the restless tattoo of their fingers over their elbows, in the wrinkle of displeasure between their eyes. "I really don't know what you expect me to say. Do you wish to strap on an oxygen tank and go by yourself to investigate a giant tentacled ocean beast that hasn't even really hurt anybody?"

Ravi steps back, shaking his head. "You're saying what, live and let live?"

"I'm saying I *don't care* about this, you infuriating man." They throw their hands up in the air. "This is not our problem. I'm not even convinced it *is* a problem, full stop. Nobody has died, or lost any limbs, or *anything*."

Ravi's pretty eyes narrow. "So, if it doesn't affect you, it doesn't matter."

"Yes! No. What do you want me to say?"

"I want…" Ravi laughs mirthlessly. "I have no idea."

"Well, it's comforting to know that some things are constant, no matter the timeline," Cayenne mutters loudly enough to be heard. They are just going to rewind this conversation anyway, so they might as well see what Ravi would say to that.

Ravi looks away and nods grimly. "How could I forget? You're only here because you owe me. Or another version of me."

"That's hardly the only reason, darling." They really, really don't want to talk about that. "You're a snack and I want a taste regardless of the calories."

Ravi turns to them incredulously. "You can't flirt your way out of this."

"Oh, can't I? You *kissed* your way out of an argument last night. How can I do any less, sweetheart?" Blushes don't easily show on Ravi, but if you know what to look for, you can observe the tips of his ears darken just a bit. Cayenne congratulates themself on bringing it out.

Ravi rubs his temples. "That was… Okay, I can agree that this monster—"

"If it even is a monster," Cayenne interjects.

"—yes, all right, if it even is a monster, it hasn't killed anybody. But that doesn't mean it won't, or that I'm not going to keep my eyes open. If someone *does* get really hurt, and I didn't act on knowledge that could have helped them, how am I supposed to live with that?"

He looks so earnest, so sincere. Cayenne can't understand how he survives like that, his truth exposed like the soft flesh of a shucked oyster. It makes them unaccountably nervous, aware suddenly of how easy it would be to crush it underfoot.

A sudden wave of exhaustion hits them, and they let their shoulders slump. "Very easily, my dear. You'd be surprised what you can live with." They don't like the way Ravi looks at them; sympathy is barely a step up from pity.

It won't do at all. Cayenne sighs in annoyance and

starts to trace the tattoo with their other hand. The clock tattoo emits a faint glow as Cayenne begins to wind time backward a few minutes.

Whip-quick, Ravi firmly grasps Cayenne's hand. The time spool stops before it can begin. They'd forgotten how fast he can move when he wants to. "Hey," Cayenne begins with a moue, but falls silent at the stricken look on Ravi's face.

"What the hell are— Are you turning back time?" He furrows his thick brows in a rather distractingly attractive fashion.

"Darling, it's nothing. You've seen me do it before." They frown at him and pull back their hand. "I know what I am doing."

"I didn't think you were doing it *every day*! You're telling me that every time I say something you don't like, you rewind time?" Ravi releases them and crosses his arms.

Cayenne flips their hand carelessly as if to brush off the whole affair. "Ravi. Beautiful boy. It's more a tool I use when *I* say something that *you* don't like."

They're somewhat taken aback when Ravi begins to pace around the bungalow like an irate panther. "Let me see if I am understanding this right. Every time something hasn't gone the way you think it should, you skip us back?"

"Not *every* time," Cayenne begins, pushing up from

their indolent lean against the counter with a long, lithe stretch in hopes of perhaps distracting him, but Ravi ignores their rather considerable charms and locks eyes with them. Abruptly Cayenne feels like a bug trapped under a glass.

"How can I know that if I say no to something, you're not just going to rewind us and try again? Until you find the right words that make me say yes?"

Cayenne winces. It is…an uncomfortable thought when phrased that way. They must have sent a dozen failed texts, traveling back and trying again multiple times, before finding the right combination of flirtation and sincerity that made Ravi agree to see them. It was the most effort they've put into something in *forever*, and it's incredibly irksome to know that Ravi wouldn't appreciate the effort; would even be upset with them for it.

Ravi leans in, bottomless brown eyes piercing through Cayenne. "How many times have you already done this to me? How am I supposed to believe that anything you say is true? You'd get to learn all kinds of things about me, good and bad, and you're…you're *stealing* any chance for me to do the same, to learn about you. You get to…to shape every interaction the way you want it to go." Suddenly Ravi breaks his intense gaze with a bitter laugh. "*Ada paave*, I'm an NPC in a video game! With no idea you're just reloading an old save. Fuck, Cay. So, who am I talking to right now?

The real you, or your second try?"

With a sigh, Cayenne poses with one arm folded on the other, hips canted, free hand gesturing airily, trying not to focus on the cute little nickname Ravi let slip. Something they can treasure thinking about later, perhaps. Hopefully, he will say it again sometime under more agreeable circumstances. "See, this is unpleasant. Unnecessarily so, my dear. When two people argue, things can so easily get out of hand. Slammed doors, punched walls, one or both parties leaving forever. So, what's the harm? I have the unique ability to make our time together *perfect*. Why shouldn't I use it?" It was, after all, what they had promised Ravi to begin with. Perfect happiness. Why is it so hard for this absolute *martyr* to accept perfection? It beggars the imagination.

"You're doing this because you want to avoid arguments so badly that you'll *turn back time* to escape one?"

"I'm doing this because I want you to be happy!" Perhaps that was a trifle too loud. Taking a calming breath, Cayenne crosses their arms tight over their ribs and leans back on their heels. "Ravi, it was hard enough getting you to agree to come here with me at all. Why would I want to risk the chance of you..." Cayenne can't find a good place to rest their gaze. "Well. The chance of you changing your mind. Of leaving. What kind of host would I be, after all?" They try for an arch tone that falls flat.

A beat passes. Ravi steps into their space, close enough that they can smell him. He smells good. Sandalwood and sunshine and sweat. "Well. We're arguing right now. And I haven't left." His lips twist in a half-smile, shy at the corners. God, but Cayenne wants to bite that smile. "And I wouldn't punch a wall, or anything else for that matter. Unless it was a monster masquerading as a wall."

A surprised laugh escapes Cayenne's lips. Tension they didn't even realize was building in their shoulders drains right out. How did this man constantly manage to catch them off guard like that? It's *very* frustrating. "Ah, *oui*, those wicked wall-beasts."

The breeze through the open windows sends the gauzy curtains into a lazy swirl. Cayenne is aware from head to toe just how close Ravi stands. He still looks angry, but there is something else there too. A softness, perhaps, at the edges?

"I think... I think I don't want perfect," he says slowly, like he just found the thought buried at the bottom of his mind and is unfolding it for the first time. "Real's better than perfect, isn't it?"

Cayenne blinks at this. What on earth should one say to that sort of madness? Their teeth catch at their lower lip. They sway in even closer, and impulsively say, "I won't do it anymore. If it really bothers you, I truly promise I won't."

A big promise, and they're not at all sure if it is one they can keep.

Ravi rakes both hands through his hair again. "I want to trust you, Cayenne. I do." Another flash of that crooked almost-smile. "You probably haven't noticed, but I've got a hard time trusting anybody. And you...you just require so much more than a normal person."

"Oh, you *absolutely* shouldn't trust me," Cayenne says lightly, as if it's a joke. "I'm the worst sort of liar."

Ravi huffs a low laugh. "If you're promising not to do it again... I'm not saying, don't *ever*. I'm saying...I'm saying, don't leave me behind."

A pang in their breast. "I know what you are saying." They tilt their head to the side. "Do you want me to go? We can cancel—"

"No!" Ravi breaks in forcefully, stepping toward Cayenne. "I don't... Look, if I make you a promise, I'm going to keep it."

Cayenne smiles and spreads their hands wide, an attempt to lighten the mood. "Of course you will, my hero! I would expect nothing less from you. So *noble*, after all. So *honest*." Ravi flinches at that, nearly imperceptibly. "*Mais oui*, I have said I shan't be so cavalier with my abilities, and so the matter is settled, yes? Now we are just going to have to argue all the time like boring normal people, instead of like the incredibly attractive superstars with magical powers that we are."

"Hmm. All the time, huh?"

"If today and yesterday are reliable indicators, I'd wager a guess it's going to be fairly often, yes."

They both are still moving closer and closer to each other, the way two ships at sea will drift together if not anchored in place.

"You know I don't have any magical powers, right?"

"Don't sell yourself short, *mon tigre*." And that does it; they grab his face and pour themself into the kiss, demanding and offering in equal measure. Ravi grasps their waist, easily spanning the breadth of it with his hands. Cayenne greedily drinks in his little gasp of surprise, the testing flick of his tongue. They open to it readily, balancing on one leg while wrapping the other around Ravi's thigh. Maybe the occasional argument isn't so bad if this is what comes of it.

A murmur of surprise as Ravi pushes them back to the counter, setting them up on the ledge and surging in between their thighs in one easy motion. Oh, *all right then*, this is more like it. Cayenne snakes both hands up Ravi's back, over his neck, and into that thick mane of black hair like they've been wanting to do for ages.

Ravi kisses like he's starving, which is probably not far from the truth, Cayenne muses, carding their fingers through the silky strands. They pull back to take a couple of ragged breaths, then move in on the curve of Ravi's neck, nipping with sharp teeth. Ravi's gasp stutters, his strong fingers digging into the meat of their hips, and the whole thing is really rather delicious.

They're disappointed but not terribly surprised when Ravi takes a step back. Leaning back on their hands, Cayenne splays their legs wide in clear invitation should he change his mind. They grin, relishing the way Ravi looks at them like they are both poison and the antidote all in one.

"Sorry," Ravi rasps as he backs away, "I got carried away."

"Anytime you want to carry *me* away, darling, I have no objections," Cayenne purrs.

Ravi's Adam's apple bobs in his throat. "Give me a second," he says, voice interestingly rough as he turns away.

"Sure," Cayenne says with a shrug, completely at ease. They watch Ravi while he gathers himself, the curve of his spine, the broad line of his shoulders, and his assets a little lower down as well. Those sweatpants really don't hide very much. You could bounce a quarter.

"Okay." Ravi turns around. Cayenne doesn't bother disguising where their eyes have been, enjoying the dark flush on Ravi's high cheekbones. "Okay," he tries again, more firmly. "Here's the deal. Atlanta is nine hours behind us. Later today I'm going to call Dr. Corbin and ask if he knows any folklore or legends about this creature. If he gives me the all-clear, I won't launch into a full hunt. Deal?"

Cayenne considers this, humming thoughtfully. "I suppose it will have to do, darling."

"I'm, um. I'm hoping he says it's nothing."

Not following, Cayenne gives him a questioning stare. "I would assume so?"

"No, I'm saying…" He clears his throat before continuing. "I hope it's nothing, because I really, really want to enjoy my time with you." Ravi glances down at his feet, and it is absolutely *pathetic* that Cayenne finds this boyish, awkward sincerity as charming as they do. It's embarrassing, *honestly.*

"And if Professor Dreamy says otherwise?"

Ravi half-smiles at the nickname. "If it turns out this thing is truly dangerous, then I need you with me on this." His beseeching gaze is so arresting Cayenne couldn't look away if they tried. Isn't this how cobras freeze mice in place to devour them, this exact kind of stare?

Cayenne puts on a heavy sigh, swaying their head back and forth as if weighing their options. "I suppose, in the interests of preserving our tropical vacation, I can *maybe* do that. As long as it doesn't take very long. And if it won't demand much of my attention. Or effort."

Smirking, Ravi shakes his head and leans against the countertop just out of arm's reach. "Can't ask for a better pledge than that."

They slide off the countertop to sidle up alongside him, tilting their head up invitingly, almost baring their throat. "Now, lest we forget, this is supposed to be a pleasant little getaway for you, is it not? What is it you would most like to do right now? We can stay cooped up in this little bungalow and continue brooding if that is your idea of fun." Or move things to the bed. That would be a good option.

Ravi rolls his eyes. "I usually only do my brooding around teatime."

Cayenne grins. "You have but to name your pleasure, my dear."

With a pensive stroke of his close-shorn beard, Ravi glances at the brochures on the counter. "We could tour Vallee de Mai? We might get lucky and see an endangered black parrot." He smiles his lopsided smile, as if fully expecting Cayenne to object.

"Nothing would delight me more! Sightseeing sounds just the thing. We'll grab breakfast on the way. Come, I'm sure that lovely young lady at the desk would be overjoyed to assist us."

They slide their arm through the crook of Ravi's elbow, trusting that Ravi's automatic gentility will kick in to escort them. Ravi does in fact lead them both to the door like a movie star with his bit of arm candy. "You just dash on over to your bungalow. I will slather on a *truly* obscene amount of sunscreen and change into something more suited for a jungle excursion. And as much as it is a true affront to all things good in this world, you ought to do the same and put on some real clothes." They turn to face him and run their fingers just under the collar of the V-neck. The heat in Ravi's eyes is like a warm, chocolatey promise. "If we leave now, we can be back in time for your afternoon brood. I'll meet you in the lobby."

With that, they lean up and give him a peck on the cheek, a wink, and usher him out of the door.

Once alone, Cayenne falls back against the door with a groan. They press the heels of their hands against their eyes until they start to see spots. "*Merde.*" After a minute, they pull themself up, plaster on a smile, and go to change.

Chapter Eleven

IT'S AN EASY trek, this trail meant more for couples strolling along to see the sights than for the more avid hikers of the region. The palm trees grow thick and lush, fans lacing overhead and keeping the trail cool and shaded. A panoply of colorful birds flit from perch to perch. Cayenne points out things that clearly can't be a black parrot purely for amusement, occasionally pointing at nothing, and when Ravi turns to look, they cheekily claim it was there but a moment ago, they *swear*.

At the peak, there are many little lookouts carved along the path for tourists to enjoy the excellent view in some privacy. They find one such alcove to claim for their own, and

Cayenne leans over the safety railing to watch the gulls over the sea, the green canopy of the trees swaying gently.

Ravi watches them as they close their eyes to enjoy a deep breath of cooled ocean air, a smile of contentment on their fine-boned features. Ravi wishes he knew how to do that; to live in the moment as they do, to truly relish every second of life the way Cayenne does. He's always either dwelling on what-could-have-been or too preoccupied about the future to ever really enjoy the now. The way Cayenne breezes through life without a care is simultaneously inspiring and maddening. Selfish. Irresponsible. And absolutely *infuriating*.

Ravi can't wait to get their hands back on him.

If a trap were expertly designed to prey on Ravi's weaknesses, it couldn't have bait any better than Cayenne. It's all too easy to forget how dangerous this person is. Both in general and for him specifically. He knows next to nothing about them, not their real age or their real name, nothing but what information they carefully choose to dole out. Obviously, their ability is dangerous, uncontrollable, and would serve The Trust well.

But on the other hand (and he is guilty at the selfishness of the thought), who else but a time traveler could offer him this kind of escape? This kind of freedom from his real life? And even if it's only just for a little while, just a few days, his past encounters have only ever been "just for a little while." Nothing new there. In Ravi's experience, everything has an expiration date.

The talk about "owing a debt" and "making amends" from Cayenne's texts, though. That raises some pretty significant flags. He'd give a great deal to know what's coming in August. What kind of deeds could make the stubbornly unrepentant Cayenne *apologize* for them? And once the debt is repaid in Cayenne's eyes, there's no telling how long they'll remain interested. They come off as the type to relish the chase, perhaps even more than the catch itself. He still has no idea why Cayenne is bothering with him in the first place. Seems like a lot of effort when they could easily have someone who doesn't require so much work.

Add to that the duty Ravi could not abandon: his place in The Trust. His family and their traditions, their expectations; the inevitability of someday having to give up that fight and accede to their demands. He can probably put off marriage for another five years if he's lucky, but he can't avoid it forever. Not with the next Chosen still lost to them.

Ravi only has a handful of pieces to the puzzle that is Cayenne; it's like hearing half of a conversation, like a song with every other note silenced. Fucking time travel.

So, he watches them, and wonders what it must be like to be so free, to live without regrets. Cayenne looks back at him, casting an invitation over their shoulder. He joins them at the railing. When their hands touch, he lets his fingers tangle with theirs, and tries to live in the now.

*

WHEN THE TWO arrive back at the resort, it's just in time to see an ambulance pull up to the main doors. The lights flash, but no siren wails.

"*Merde*," mutters Cayenne as Ravi goes stiff and attentive, like a wolf spotting an antelope. His pace swiftens. Cayenne follows behind with a sigh.

They enter the lobby into a flurry of activity. Two paramedics wheel out a gurney, administering aid to the person strapped on it. Honestly, Cayenne is surprised the resort didn't force the ambulance to pull up to a hidden service entrance or something. This can't be a good look for tourism.

There's a great deal of commotion at the lobby desk. Several staff members try to calm down a young woman as she cries and attempts to follow the paramedics. She looks different with her hair pulled back in a ponytail and her face red and puffy from tears, but it's the hat girl. Cayenne struggles to recall her name. Liss? Ellie? Elissa, that's it.

Ravi grabs Cayenne's shoulder. He indicates the quickly disappearing gurney with a jerk of his chin.

Cayenne tries to catch a glimpse, peering around the paramedics.

Yes, it's definitely the other girl. What's-her-name. Taylor.

Cayenne looks up at Ravi, tightening their grip as his head whips back and forth between the gurney and Elissa, the possible witness. It's obvious he is torn which one to approach.

Cayenne pushes him toward Elissa while taking a step back in the direction of the entrance, where the glass doors are swinging shut. "Go ahead. I'll take a look." They aren't quite sure why they offer, but they have a long and storied history of following every wild impulse that crosses their mind; no reason to stop now.

Ravi shoots them a grateful nod and leaves their side. Cayenne moves quickly, slipping through the doors just as the medics start to slide the gurney into the back of the ambulance.

Slowing time down is particularly difficult, and potentially dangerous to the mage. If not careful, moving around while time is slowed can have disastrous effects. Physics is a harsh mistress. Honestly, most of the time it's not worth the effort, with a few notable exceptions. But so long as they stand still, it shouldn't be a problem. They don't even need to manipulate their tattoo to achieve the feat, simply exert a bit of concentration.

Suddenly the paramedics move at a crawl, all ambient sounds slowed down to create an unsettling, ever-present drone. The world creeps along at a snail's pace, giving Cayenne plenty of time to inspect Taylor. She's breathing, judging by the condensation inside the oxygen mask, but her dark skin has gained an unnatural, clammy pallor. Her eyes are open and rolled back, the whites visible. It could still be drugs, Cayenne hopes. A bad trip.

The sheet belted over her had been haphazardly thrown on and doesn't quite cover her bare legs. Nothing out of the ordinary, apart from pruney toes, but then Cayenne notices the bites. Partially covered by a stack of rose-gold chain ankle bracelets. A strange curve of even punctures, as if she had been bitten twice on the ankle by a mouth filled with needles. Not bleeding, but clearly deep.

Definitely not a jellyfish sting.

Cayenne gives her another once-over while time crawls ahead but can't glean anything more. They release their hold with relief, and the stream of time flows normally again. It only takes a handful of seconds for the medics to secure everything, start up the sirens, and speed away. Cayenne winces at the volume and goes back inside to join the small, localized storm of chaos that is Elissa. Most of the staff have dispersed, leaving only Ravi and the woman working the concierge desk today, a fellow redhead who stands off to the side on a phone call.

Elissa is still nearly frantic. "This is my fault. I couldn't find her all morning, I thought she just hooked up with someone! I should have been looking for her."

Cayenne sidles up at Ravi's side and shares a grim look with him. Ravi purses his lips, obviously wanting details, but that will have to wait.

"Elissa," Cayenne says as they reach out to touch her comfortingly on the wrist, but their awareness is all for Ravi, hoping he'll be at least a *little* impressed with their show of compassion. "Are you all right, dear? What has happened?"

Elissa sobs, hand over her mouth, so Ravi answers, "Taylor was missing this morning. One of the bartenders down on the beach found her unconscious, half in the water."

"What if she had drowned?" Elissa wails. "And they came and got me, and she woke up a little and couldn't remember what she had been doing all night, and they say she's going to be okay, but what if she's not?" She flings herself at Cayenne, to their great surprise.

"Oh, *chérie*. There, there." They give her a little pat on the arm, looking helplessly up at Ravi. What would a good person say in this situation? "It is going to be all right."

"No, it's not!" Elissa sobs against their shoulder,

hopefully not getting snot on their clothes. "She's my best friend, and I don't know what to do!"

"Miriam is going to give you a ride once she clears things with her boss," Ravi cuts in, indicating the ginger concierge with a nod. "You're only going to be a couple of minutes behind the ambulance. Everyone who's been affected like this has pulled through just fine. Taylor is going to be okay."

Elissa sniffs but calms down, releasing Cayenne from her clinging grasp. Cayenne looks over at Ravi, a bit impressed as they straighten their shirt. His calm, matter-of-fact demeanor seems to set her at ease, and she quickly pulls herself together.

"Yeah. Okay." She wipes her cheeks and smooths her clothes. "Okay. Thanks." She smiles wanly, and Cayenne is reminded why they had earlier decided they liked this girl's style. Tenacity is a trait they admire, though one they rarely employ themself.

"Miss, if you're ready, I got the go-ahead from the office," cuts in the concierge, putting away her phone and grabbing a ring of keys from a drawer. "I can drive you to the hospital now."

Elissa springs forward. "Yes, I'm ready! Thank you so much!" She stops and turns around long enough to grab both their hands in a grateful squeeze. "And you two are *so* sweet, thank you so much. Okay, let's go!"

They turn to watch the women leave, and once they're gone, Cayenne turns to Ravi, sighing hugely. "You had better call Dr. Hotstuff."

*

"HEY, RAVI, WHAT'S up?" Dr. Nathan Corbin's deep timbre is friendly and casual as always, a comforting familiarity. "Constance said you were out of state?"

"Yeah, hey. Sorry to bother you, Doc. Look, I need your folklore expertise on something. I've got a weird creature here I need intel on."

"Oh, yeah? Not that I'm complaining, but doesn't The Trust have intelligence agents for that?"

Ravi looks over at his duffel bag, in which a lead-lined bag contains the dismantled pieces of his Trust-issued device, SIM card and battery kept in separate compartments. He isn't going to risk putting that back together unless it's a truly dire emergency. His gaze skids over to the couch, where Cayenne reclines upside down in an insouciant stretch, long legs kicked up over the back of the cushions. As long as they *stay* there; Ravi wouldn't put it past Cayenne to try something indecent while he was on the phone. When their eyes meet, the mischievous glint lets him know that is *exactly* what they have in mind. He shakes his head, frowning forbiddingly, and retreats behind the kitchenette counter. Cayenne rolls their eyes, mimes locking their mouth shut, and lets their arms flop onto the floor dramatically. A character study in boredom.

"You know we like to consult with experts," he says, dragging his attention back to the matter at hand.

"Oh, flattery," Nate laughs. "No need, I'll help. Whatcha got for me?"

"Multiple victims, all survived. Found on the beach in a drug-like stupor. They've all reported memory loss and blackouts with no knowledge of what happened or even the events leading up to it. One had two wounds on her ankle that looked like bites. Needle-like teeth. Not sure of the size of the bite mark. Relatively small, I think. No other side effects evident. Maybe some blood loss, but I'm not sure about that. I don't have access to medical or toxicology records."

"The beach, you say? This is happening in the ocean?" Nate sounds a little surprised.

"Yes. Around the islands on the eastern side of the Indian Ocean. The attacks may be occurring right at the shoreline. All victims were found mostly out of the water, not in it."

"Huh, okay." The sounds of a keyboard clacking. "Are the attacks occurring at a certain time?"

"Seems like sometime during the night. The creature

has been spotted at both dusk and at dawn."

Nate's voice rises with excitement. "Crepuscular sightings, got it. You have a description? That's going to make this much easier."

"I saw it myself."

"Cool!"

Ravi can't help smiling. Nate is new to the bizarre and harrowing nature of their shared reality, but he's always eager to learn everything he can about the supernatural; the professor continually surprises and impresses with his academic enthusiasm.

"I'm ready," Nate prompts, "go ahead with the description."

"Closely resembles a manta ray, about twelve feet wide at the wings, the body maybe six feet long. Black with a few white markings. Two long, whiplike tentacles at the front, by the eyes, I think. I only saw it for a second."

"Pretty detailed for just a second." More keyboard sounds. "And you're sure it wasn't just a regular manta ray? Maybe tangled up in a rope that just looked like tentacles?"

Ravi bites back a sigh. "I'm sure."

"Okay," he says, taking Ravi at his word. "Anything else? Other relevant details?"

"That's everything I've got."

Nate clicks his tongue repeatedly with an idle filler

sound he sometimes exhibits when browsing research. Ravi waits, glancing over at Cayenne. They've shifted over onto their stomach, chin propped up on their elbows, heels kicked up in the air behind them. They watch Ravi as he paces, the way a lazy housecat watches a bird through the window.

"Hmm. This is a little weird." Nate pauses, and over the line Ravi hears him scratching at his ever-present five-o'clock shadow. "Tell you what, can I call you back in a half hour? I've got to cross-reference some stuff."

"Yeah, a half hour is fine. Thanks, Nate."

Nate hangs up without saying goodbye, no doubt already completely absorbed in his research. Ravi sets his phone down, turns, and nearly jumps out of his skin when he finds Cayenne already there, tipping up a smile that is pure trouble.

"A half hour, did I overhear, my delicious samosa?" They drag their fingertips from the center of Ravi's chest down over his abdominal muscles. Ravi's heart rate instantly kicks up into high gear. Everywhere they touch leaves his skin oversensitive and hyperaware. Cayenne presses close, and the electric feel of their lean body against his makes some of his higher brain functions short-circuit.

"I'm *bored*," they purr straight into his ear, and nip at his earlobe. Ravi breathes in sharply, his knees going honest-to-goodness weak. Fuck. He isn't a teenager anymore. He shouldn't be so easy to twirl up like this. "I've been so *good* while you were on your little call, darling. Don't you think I deserve a reward?" Cayenne slips their graceful hands under the hem of his shirt and slides them up.

Swallowing, Ravi shifts a hand over the slim moon-pale column of their throat and down to the intriguing jut of their clavicle. He wants very badly to set his teeth there, to taste the salt of their skin. He wants... He can't even begin to parse through all the things he wants.

When he speaks his voice is sandpaper rough. "You bored sounds like a recipe for disaster."

Chuckling low in their throat, Cayenne inches their fingers up Ravi's chest. "Truer than you know." Their nail grazes a nipple, and Ravi has to brace himself against the fridge or risk losing his balance. Cayenne keeps in lockstep, surging forward as Ravi leans back, pinching once sharply. Ravi arches up into the sensation, mind emptying. He licks his lips, mouth suddenly dry.

"What do you want," he breathes, "for a reward?" Fuck, right now he would do anything Cayenne wants. He's rapidly forgetting any reasons he has to keep a distance between them. Right now, it doesn't matter how dangerous they are; all he wants is to unwrap Cayenne like a present and see if he can even the odds a little, make Cayenne gasp and flutter like they so easily do to him. He wants to see Cayenne completely undone, insensible, unable to remember their own name.

"Mm, what a *delightful* offer." Cayenne brings their mouth close to Ravi's, almost but not quite touching. A bare inch away from a kiss, and Ravi wants it like he would want water after days in a desert. They pull their hands from his shirt and set their palms flat against the fridge on either side of his head. "I think I know *exactly* what I want." They lick a wet stripe up Ravi's neck, and for a split-second Ravi forgets any English. *That* hasn't happened since he was a little kid. Fuck.

"Ask," he manages, because it's better than saying "fuck yes, anything, I'll give you everything you ask for, please, *kripaya*…"

"I want," Cayenne says a millimeter from his lips, "I want you to go dancing with me."

"Not…what I expected," Ravi croaks. He cups the back of Cayenne's head and licks his way into their mouth. Cayenne makes a little sound of pleased surprise and drops their arms to tighten around his neck. Hand at the small of their back, Ravi urges Cayenne to close that last tiny inch of space between them and pushes his hips up into a lazy grind. Sparks flash behind his eyes at the sensation, at

Cayenne's heady moan.

The phone buzzes on the countertop. Cayenne breaks away and glares at it. "That was *not* a half hour," they snarl. Ravi's inclined to agree, but reluctantly pushes Cayenne away and adjusts the front of his pants. Cayenne looks similarly affected, their face flushed and eyes glassy. They look *beautiful*.

The phone buzzes again, and Ravi fumbles for it, trying to get his breathing even before answering. When he gets himself under control, he swipes open the call. "Dr. Corbin," he says in what he's pretty sure is a normal tone of voice.

"It's just Nate, for the millionth time, Ravi. Okay, buckle up, this is a lot." Ravi hastily pulls over the nearest stack of paper, some brochures that were left on the counter. "There are a handful of sea-dwelling things that could maybe prey on people the way you describe, but they're mostly from European fairy tales. You got sea hags, kelpies, nixies, grindylows. Some of them are known to bite, but traditionally all of those definitely kill their victims, not leave them alive."

He glances around for a pen, and Cayenne holds one out to him as if anticipating his need. He takes it and mouths *thanks*. Cayenne smiles, arranging themself in a comfortable lean over the counter.

"I've found a lot of things that it's probably *not*. The only remotely close creature in African legends is a jengu, but that's a benevolent mermaid type thing that brings good fortune. It's probably not Jenny Greenteeth unless you're in Lancashire. You've met a kappa, so you'd know if it's that. The Slavic peoples say the vodyanoy likes to drown people, but they stick to lakes only. Nix or nixies are malicious shapeshifters in some stories, but harmless in others. You also get a lot of variations on the pretty lady sitting in bodies of water myths, with undines and nereids and such. Don't think that's particularly relevant here, but I do like to be thorough."

Ravi blinks, trying to jot down notes on the back of a brochure. "That *is* pretty thorough."

Nate continues as if he hadn't said anything, clearly in a professorial groove. "The part I'm having trouble nailing down is the whole manta ray thing. Most folklore portray them as benevolent protectors, able to move from one plane of existence into the other. They are often regarded as guardians of the next world."

"The next world?" At his question, Cayenne tilts their head curiously at him, and he shrugs.

"Eh, it differs from culture to culture. Tonga says the land of the dead, and Māori say the world of monsters. But once I started looking *way* back, I found there *were* old

Polynesian legends of huge rays sinking ships and pulling people down to drown. At some point the public perception changed, but those old myths are still there. There was a long period where people were afraid of them. And dawn and dusk make sense; they're supposed to be liminal beings, there when the veils between this world and others are thinner. Or maybe it just likes hunting at night." Nate's shrug is nearly audible.

Ravi chews on this. "Pulling people down to drown, huh?"

"Yeah, it doesn't quite fit the MO, does it? You said all the victims were found on the land, definitely undrowned, with bite marks. Some of the details don't fit, but maybe it's a regional thing? I don't have any salient legends from your area of the world."

A disturbing thought, that the creature could be from anywhere. It isn't the first time he's faced something that had been summoned or displaced from where it was supposed to be. Nate's comment about "the world of monsters" is unsettling too. "You think the creature might not be local?"

Nate chuckles. "I mean, we found a Japanese kappa in the middle of the Georgian suburbs, so yeah. Anything's possible."

"So, we've got nothing." Ravi's shoulders slump.

"Not so fast, tough guy, I absolutely have something."

"That's a relief. Tell me."

Satisfaction rings in Nate's voice. "I've got a Polynesian warding sigil. Or glyph, whatever you wanna call it. They used to carve it onto their boats or etch it into the sand to ward them off. I can text you a picture."

Ravi shoots a pleased look at Cayenne, giving them a thumbs-up. "A warding sigil? You think that'll work?"

"Look," says Nate, "I don't have a lot to work with, here. There's next to nothing about this kind of creature. But by all accounts, if you draw this sigil in the sand above the tideline, maybe each sigil a half-mile apart, you can secure the coast. Probably."

"Hmm," Ravi grunts. "I had hoped for a more long-term solution."

"Sorry I don't have a silver bullet for bitey, tentacled, manta ray monsters."

Ravi barks out a laugh. "Okay, fair. This is really useful, Nate. Thank you. As long as it stops attacking people, that's really the only goal. I appreciate you taking the time."

"Hey, happy to help, my guy. I'll send those pics over as soon as we hang up." He pauses. "Hey…Ravi. Is it a real bad scene there? Do you need us all to hop on a plane and help out?"

Whatever expression his face is making must be

interesting, judging by the way Cayenne is looking at him. "No, no," he says quickly, "that's not necessary. But thanks. If we can keep it away from the beach, that'll be good enough."

"*We*? Who's we? Are you with someone?" Nate sounds delighted.

Fuck. "Bye." He hangs up.

The picture comes through via text a second later. He looks it over. A few graceful curves with a set of diagonal slashes. Should be easy enough to replicate. He texts back a quick thanks.

"Good news," he tells Cayenne. "We've got a way to repel it."

"Yes, yes, I did overhear some of that. The dear professor's voice does tend to carry. We have to go draw this thing in the sand? But that'll take *hours*." They pout, casting doe eyes up through their lashes.

Ravi gives them a look. "It will not. The resort beach is only five miles long. It'll take *maybe* forty-five minutes."

"That's forty-five minutes that would be better spent bending me over this counter, don't you think, darling?" Cayenne stretches easily out across the countertop, ass wriggling, arms reaching ahead to grip the edge. Ravi actually forgets how to speak. For a few seconds, he can only gape stupidly as Cayenne smirks up at him. "You know, sweetheart, if you weren't so easy to shock, I wouldn't have *nearly* as much fun doing it. You've really only got yourself to blame." They prop their head up on one hand, still draped suggestively across the counter. "Are you *truly* going to claim you don't want to stay here and do just that?"

He wants to. Yeah, he definitely wants to. "What I want to do to you can't be done in only forty-five minutes."

Cayenne's eyes glitter with delight. "Oho! You have teeth after all, *mon tigre. Very* interesting. Why don't you show me?"

Ravi bites his lip so hard he's surprised he doesn't taste blood. "If you go with me to set these wards, I'll go dancing with you."

Cayenne stands up, excited. "You will?"

"Yeah." Ravi offers a smile.

Cayenne makes a show of pretending to consider. "You drive a hard bargain, my dear. But very well, I accept! We will finish your oh-so-heroic *art project*, how thrilling, and then we shall hit the clubs, as I believe they say now."

"Okay. Good."

"And then," Cayenne's voice drops low, "we shall perhaps see where the evening takes us, no?" Ravi swallows, and Cayenne hesitates, dropping some of their seductive languor in favor of a more sincere tone. "Though, truly my dear, if you don't wish to do anything more than we've already done, I shan't press. You aren't…you aren't obligated. I do need you to know that." They actually look concerned, and Ravi feels a tremor behind his sternum.

"Thank you for saying that. I…I'm interested." He coughs, looking away from Cayenne's slow, spreading grin. "I'm just not used to… You're fucking terrifying, you know that?"

Cayenne steps back. "Terrifying?"

"Yes," Ravi stresses, "terrifying. I can fire fifteen rounds into a charging monster without missing a shot but being alone in a room with you makes me…makes me tremble like a damned leaf. You're…" He shakes his head. Despite speaking several tongues, Ravi isn't any good with words, and he doesn't have the language for what Cayenne does to him. He places both palms flat on the counter and leans on them heavily, needing the stability.

"I know you've met another version of me, and for all I know, to you, I'm just one in a long line of interchangeable Ravis, but…I've never met *anyone* like you before. Ever."

Cayenne stares at him for what feels like an eternity, hands twitching restlessly at their sides. "How are you so…so *genuine* all the time? Isn't it exhausting?" Their expression slips just a fraction, like a mask shifting out of place.

Ravi can't help the sour twist of his features. "I lie all

the time."

He's surprised by the change that comes over Cayenne's face; they look *furious*. Then in a blink, it's smoothed away, their usual cool nonchalance back in place. "You are *forced* to lie to protect yourself. That's different."

"Is it?" Ravi asks softly. "I'm not so sure."

"Well!" Cayenne says brightly, forcibly shaking off the somber mood. *"Regardless"* —that one word and single flip of their palm doing a lot of work to both encompass and subsequently dismiss any unpleasantness—"I am *quite* thrilled at the idea of getting you on the dance floor. Let's get the busy work done first, shall we? And then afterward, I can *really* show you some moves." They flash a dazzling smile.

Ravi takes a deep breath and releases it slowly as if he were taking aim on a distant target. His heart rate slows to normal, his nerves calm, long years of practice serving him well. When he's able, he stands up to his full height, raking his hair back into place. "Okay. Let's go."

Chapter Twelve

IT TAKES CLOSER to an hour to tromp the entire length of the beachfront since Ravi insists on looking for spots that will be hidden, or at least hard to find, in hopes of keeping the beach protected for as long as possible. They draw the runes at the base of a cluster of palms, under an elevated dock, beside a locked utility shed, places that won't be easily walked on. Easily bored, Cayenne occasionally amuses themself by trying to distract Ravi into skipping the rest of the glyphs. After the fourth time this happens, Ravi crowds Cayenne against the nearest palm tree and kisses them until they shut up.

"The sooner we finish this," he growls in their ear, "the

sooner we can enjoy our vacation."

Cayenne gives a victorious grin, hands drifting down from his shoulders to rest on his backside. "That is what I'm trying to do, darling, to speed things along. Surely this is enough scratching around in the dirt, yes?"

"Are you in a rush?" Ravi scrapes his teeth along the tensed line of Cayenne's neck, then gentles into light kisses along the arch of their shoulder. Cayenne shivers.

"Yes," they hiss, just that one word, craning their neck back to give him better access.

"Well, maybe I like to take my time. Savor the moment." He doesn't get to have many moments like this. It would be a crime to miss any of them.

Cayenne clucks their tongue, hands going a little grabby in Ravi's back pockets. "Of course, you do, you don't have any other options. It's *quelle tragique*."

Ravi can't help but laugh a little at their arrogant tone as he pushes away. If he keeps finding that kind of thing charming, he's in *real* trouble. "Come on. It's getting close to dusk. Just two more to go." Cayenne puts on an aggrieved sigh but allows Ravi to lead them away. They don't let go of his hand for a good while.

They lay the last glyph near their bungalow, and on the way, they spot Uwe in his usual place on the dock, dabbling his feet in the water and apparently getting ready to enjoy the sunset. Uwe waves as he spots the pair, and they wave back. Ravi stands a little straighter after they walk on by. Cayenne looks at him with one brow arched high. "It's just…nice to know that he's not going to be the next victim," he says, feeling compelled to explain. "I might be able to arrange a better solution here after we leave, but for now, well…" He shrugs. "It's nice to know we've helped people here."

Cayenne rolls their eyes. "How noble, keeping a bunch of vacationing millionaires from getting their ankles nibbled by a fish. What rewarding work you do, my dear!"

Ravi laughs. "Hey, there's no telling if the fish would have stuck with just nibbling. And besides, you're one of those vacationing millionaires. Have some class solidarity," he jokes.

Cayenne looks away, their laugh a touch harsher than normal. "Spoken like true old money." They throw him a sly glance, twining an arm around his. "I have held up my end of the bargain, my sexy *tigre*. And here we are, victorious against the forces of evil! What*ever* shall we do now, hmm?"

As they step onto the bungalow dock, Ravi crooks his elbow, as if escorting a lady to a ball. "Well, *I'm* going to change into something I can dance in. Come get me in ten minutes?"

Cayenne doesn't answer, but they squeeze their fingers tightly into his bicep and flash him a grin that could give the sunset a run for its money.

*

IN TRUTH, IT takes Cayenne closer to an hour before they're ready. Perfection takes work, after all.

Weeks ago, they had been so inspired by Ravi comparing them to a monsoon that they decided to lean hard into it. After seeing him for coffee, they found a picture of that year's first monsoon, a dark storm arriving inland just at sunset, golden highlights still shining through the clouds. So, they commissioned this outfit; a gold mesh crop-top designed to accentuate every muscle of their lissome frame, painted-on shorts in a violet so dark it's nearly black, and cloud-gray Roman sandals that hug their calves. They've highlighted the ensemble with smokey eyeshadow in shades of stormy purples and grays, metallic gold eyeliner, and lipstick in a glossy plum. Every nail is painted a different color of the rainbow, because fuck subtlety. They admire themself in the mirror, checking the distribution of shimmery gold-toned body glitter.

Not only do they look incredible, naturally, but it's also a challenge; a gauntlet thrown. They're curious to see how Ravi will react, being in public with the most gorgeous and outrageous twink anyone's ever seen in their lives, knowing all eyes will be on them both. They want to mark him, leave violet kisses all over his dark skin, *ruin* him; see him try to hide himself away while covered head to toe in Cayenne's glitter. *Good luck pretending you're straight in* this *monsoon, ravageur.*

A knock on the door. They suppose he has been kept waiting long enough. Time for the reveal. *"Un moment, s'il te plaît,"* they shout, making last-minute adjustments to the artful tousle of their hair, then head out.

As they slip out of the door, Ravi is standing off to the side looking out over the waves, so they're able to catch a glimpse of him before he sees them.

They can't say they're surprised by Ravi's choice of outfit; not too dissimilar from what he believes is appropriate beachwear. The slim black jeans admittedly *do* fit nicely, his height visually lengthened by black ankle boots. Not quite black, now they look closely, with panels of gold brocade on the sides. Understated, but nice. His shirt only has three low buttons, so it shows off a nice amount of chest, and the mandarin collar lends a masculine, exotic appeal. At first, the fabric seems to be just another example of one of his boring white tailored shirts, but as he moves, a subtle pattern picked out in ivory thread shimmers in the light. Not as bad as Cayenne had expected, all things considered.

Then Ravi sees them. They pose contrapposto, like a Renaissance masterpiece with considerably more fashion sense. Ravi doesn't say anything, just stares. Very gratifying. Cayenne smirks, one hand to their hip.

"Constance was right," Ravi manages hoarsely. "There's no way you aren't some otherworldly fae being."

Well. Cayenne preens. "Glinda said that?"

Ravi stalks in close and stops a mere handbreadth away. "I'm paraphrasing. She also said you were going to lead me astray."

"That *does* sound like something I'd do," they say, walking their fingers playfully up Ravi's broad shoulders. He looks so irritatingly put together. They want to see him rumpled and messy, taken completely apart. They want him wild, frantic with need; they want to leave him a disheveled wreck of a man.

Might as well get a head start.

They lean up and plant a kiss on the swell of his cheekbone, pushing hard before leaning back to inspect their work. Very nice; the color will show up beautifully, especially if there are any blacklights. Ravi's stunned expression gradually fades into his usual crooked smile, one side of his mouth hiked higher than the other as if he's trying to hide his pleasure at being so obviously claimed but can't quite help himself. A good start.

"The evening awaits, sweetheart," and they take Ravi's hand and begin to lead him astray.

*

CAYENNE IS WELL versed in the language of nightclubs. Pretty much every time period has an equivalent somewhere to be found, and even before entering, this one is shaping up to be a good one. The atmosphere has a unique, multicultural quality going, live musicians accompanying the DJ's electronic jams. There are bodhrans, djembes, tambourines, and two huge tribal drums that boom their deep throbbing rhythm right through the floor. The resulting sound is a heady melting pot of thrumming bass and tribal melodies, kind of a music festival vibe. The shifting colors of the lights and stage effects add an ethereal quality. It's a pretty cool club for such a bougie resort.

The dance floor is barely visible, already wall-to-wall with dancers. However, when the two of them approach, Cayenne swaying forward with Ravi's hand in his, they do garner their share of eyes. A space opens up around them. Cayenne looks back to check on Ravi. He digs his teeth into his lower lip, visibly nervous. Poor thing. They lean over and shout in his ear over the pounding beat. "Ever been to a nightclub before, darling?"

"Once," he yells back, "in London."

They would love to ask some follow-up questions to that, but it will have to wait. Right now, they want to climb this man like a goddamn tree, show all the onlookers—oh, and there are *definitely* onlookers—that this tasty dish is thoroughly taken. They want Ravi to be all theirs tonight.

They saunter close, hips catching the rhythm, and press another plum-shaded kiss right on the divot at the base of his throat. They move around him, circling like a shark, rubbing their glittered body over every inch they can manage. When they arrive back in front of him, his nervousness has been completely replaced by heat, a fierceness that sends a little thrill through Cayenne. Then they *really* start showing off, hips canting along with every step, limbs liquid with the flow. "Let me show you a few moves, beautiful boy."

A strange smile slowly spreads across Ravi's face and he tilts his head to one side. "You think I don't know how to dance?"

Cayenne pats his cheek. "We're in a club, not a ballroom, precious."

"Have you ever been to an Indian wedding, Cay?"

That little sobriquet sends a frisson up Cayenne's spine. It takes them a second to process the actual question. "*Non?*"

Abruptly Ravi grabs both Cayenne's hands and moves into a cross-body lead that he shifts into a double underarm twirl. Cayenne ends up with their hands trapped in an *X* over their chest, Ravi plastered against their back like a second skin. His breath is hot against their neck. "As much as I hated it, you are literally not allowed to avoid dancing at them. Practically an arrestable offense." He spins Cayenne back out at arm's length, and his hips are…doing something pretty indecent. Cayenne gapes, at a loss for words.

Ravi lets go of Cayenne and launches into a choreographed routine that matches perfectly with the heavy drumbeat. "My tutors insisted dancing builds agility and stamina. So, I learned." It's a rather impressive bit of footwork with lots of grape-vining steps, to Cayenne's eye a melding of different styles; a little hip-hop, a little jazz, and some Eastern styles they aren't familiar with, all accentuated by sweeping, Arabic-looking arm motions that flow smoothly into the next fluid step. It builds into an athletic jump that shows off Ravi's strength and control. He lands with his feet planted wide, shoulders rolling in a masculine shimmy, and he flicks his shirt open to either side like an afterthought.

For the first time, Cayenne gets why some people say that clothes, worn correctly, can be more tantalizing than none at all. He looks *magnificent*. The way his rolled-up sleeves strain against the taut tendons of his forearms only accentuates their strength instead of hiding it. The open shirt frames his defined chest and abs like art in a gallery.

Pausing, Ravi cocks his head to the side and juts out his chin, a clear challenge.

They let out a delighted laugh. So full of surprises, this one. Well, they'll just have to step things up a notch, won't they? Moving in close, they reach out and flick a finger just under that dark beard. His eyes flash, lips shaping a dangerous smirk. The club lighting coruscates over him in strips of color and shadow. He looks like a hungry tiger, and Cayenne is quite keen on being devoured.

Cayenne turns around, lithe muscles of their back and ass taking center stage. They throw a flirtatious look over their shoulder as they drop into a low grind. Languidly, they undulate their way back up, grinding against Ravi's groin, sliding their hands over their own torso and up into Ravi's hair, throwing it into complete disarray with relish.

Time to flip the script a little. They spin into a flurry of modified ballet moves, circling around Ravi as they twirl on toe tips, showing off their flexibility to full advantage. They lift one leg completely parallel to their body and rest it on Ravi's shoulder. He automatically takes their calf in hand, already bracing for Cayenne's lean weight as they press up against him, practically doing an upright split. There are impressed cheers from the other dancers nearby, and Cayenne grins and gives Ravi a wink.

Ravi's eyes are kindling so much heat it's a wonder nothing has caught fire.

Cayenne pirouettes out, then crowds back in close to wrap around Ravi as easily as if he's a strip club pole, encircling his hips with their thighs. They meet Ravi's eyes and bat their lashes, curling their feet around the back of his legs and slinging their arms over his shoulders. Ravi moves to support them, which honestly, they don't need—their thigh muscles aren't simply decorative—but it's still nice to have his hands cupping their ass. His pupils are blown wide, the warm chocolate of the iris barely visible. He glows with sweat, golden all over, and with a little thrill of possession Cayenne notes the bright-violet lip print still highlighting his cheek.

"Has this been enough dancing?" Ravi asks huskily. He squeezes his hands over Cayenne's cheeks. A happy coincidence that they happen to fit there perfectly.

"Oh, you *lovely* thing, we've barely just begun."

And the two dance, exhilarated, synchronous, lost in the rhythm, spotlit in the center of a throbbing mass of dancers while still somehow being the only two people in the world.

Chapter Thirteen

BY THE TIME they get back to the bungalow Ravi has glossy purple all over. He doesn't care that his shirt is ruined. He's not concerned with how exactly he was going to get all this glitter off later. He's not even embarrassed at his brazen display of bhangra (which he had only ever before performed under protest; the stunned delight on Cayenne's face had been more than worth it), not even calculating the risks of having all those eyes watching him with Cayenne. All he is currently concerned with is managing to get the door shut with a ginger octopus clinging onto him and kissing him breathless.

Their lipstick has long since been utterly ruined, most

of it now smudged all over Ravi. The gold around their eyes makes the green look bottomless, unearthly. They both have a light dusting of gold and glitter decorating them from head to toe. They must look like they just stepped out of a Klimt painting.

There is one other concern, a thought that edges itself to the forefront of his mind like an unwelcome guest. He'd been trying so hard all day to suppress it, to just live in the fucking moment for once in his life, but he isn't very practiced at that. As soon as the door shuts behind him, Cayenne pushes him roughly against the door—they're delightfully stronger than they look—and squeezes a hand over the bulge in Ravi's jeans.

He makes a sound like he's been kicked in the chest. The want that swells up is so intense, he's not sure if he's ever been this hard before in his life.

So, when he pushes Cayenne back, he simultaneously wants to run away and smack himself for stopping this.

Cayenne pauses, breathing as heavily as if they had been running. They lean in, lips a bare inch away. "You don't want to?"

The green of those eyes is so sharp it cuts. Flayed, Ravi can only answer in a gasp. "Of course, I want to." He grips Cayenne's shoulders, unsure if he will pull them in closer or do the smart thing and push them away. Stop playing this game.

Cayenne chuckles, deep and throaty and dangerous. "So why don't you, darling?" They skate a slim hand down Ravi's stomach and stop at the waistband. Painted fingers play idly with the button there, and Ravi's head swims like he's drunk too much wine. He rests his forehead against Cayenne's, finally pulling their lips away from that hovering inch and catching a breath.

Cayenne's touch gentles. "Ravi, sweet thing. It isn't your first time, is it?"

He huffs with amusement. "I've had sex before, Cay."

"With a...with someone like me?"

His laugh is a thin, breathy thing, his forehead pressing against the soft fall of Cayenne's fox-red hair. "No one is like you."

"Now *that* is certainly true." Cayenne snakes forward and sinks their teeth into the lobe of Ravi's ear. Their grin is sharp around sharper teeth. He gasps, flexing his hands helplessly on Cayenne's toned arms. Their voice pours into his ear drip by drip. "Then what on earth are you waiting for, handsome? Take me to bed already."

Every reason why he shouldn't feels miles away.

From the very depths of his willpower, he voices a piece of that errant thought, that hesitation niggling at the back of his head. "What, and have you get bored of me?"

He goes for a light, playful tone, trying to match Cayenne's easy sensuality. When they go still and pull back, Ravi wishes he could kick himself. *Keep your shit on lockdown, kid.* Lessons he learned young. He should be stronger than this.

Cayenne moves through life while wearing the whole world the careless way they'd wear a coat. They could have anyone. Not for the first time, Ravi wonders what the hell Cayenne wants with *him*. He knows he's a lot of work. Too much work for anyone else he'd been with to think he was worth the effort. No reason Cayenne shouldn't be the same. No reason Ravi should want them to be different.

Cayenne lays their hands on either side of Ravi's face, elegance at odds with their strength, tilting his head so they are eye to eye. "You truly think I'm going to get bored of you?"

"No," Ravi lies, "I was just… It was supposed to be funny."

Emerald eyes flick over his face, cutting out his secrets. "No, it wasn't." Their touch turns into a soft caress. "Sweetheart. You think I'm going to wake up with *you* in my bed, and the emotion I will be feeling is *boredom*?" They grin wolfishly. "I can *guarantee* you that won't be my reaction."

"Well," Ravi breathes, finally letting his hands free to glide up over the lithely muscled shoulders and sharp collarbones. His thumbs rest naturally in the hollows there.

Cayenne leans into the touch with a purr. "I get the feeling you enjoy a challenge."

A soft laugh, red hair tossed carelessly back from their face. "You certainly qualify, my dear. But I enjoy other things too."

"Do you know why I said yes?" It takes a handful of seconds before Ravi realizes the words are his. He bites his lip, hard, as if to bite the weakness out of them. Too late he sees he's drawing attention to the cracks in his armor, as good as if he has a tattoo that reads *insert knife here*. A mere two days with this person and walls go crumbling. Against any violence, Ravi can hold them defiant forever; but after a dance, a few caresses, and a kind word they fall to dust. Such an easy fucking mark. Pathetic.

"To the trip? Hmm"—Cayenne taps their lower lip in consideration with an orange-painted nail—"because of my extreme overabundance of charm and beauty? Because I appealed to your long-suppressed sense of abandon by offering you a weekend in paradise?"

"Because you said you liked me." He lets his thumbs sweep lightly over Cayenne's chest and onto the pale expanse of their throat. The skin there is so fine he can see the blue of veins, the pulse gratifyingly swift. At least he isn't alone in this, out on the cliff's edge of his honesty. "I kept reading that bit over and over. Out of all the things you wrote, that's what did it. That was all it took." The corner of his mouth curls up. "Not much of a challenge after all, am I?"

Cayenne blinks and swallows thickly. "Ravi—"

"I'm..." He has to draw in a fortifying breath to continue. "I'm actually very easy to break." *So please don't*, goes unsaid.

*

CAYENNE HEARS IT quite clearly, regardless. An ache swells underneath their breastbone. They feel...a lot of things, a mess of it, really, too tangled to parse. Far easier to wrap their arms around Ravi's neck, to whisper against his lips before they take them in a bruising kiss.

"I'll be careful with you." Another big promise, tasting of copper and regret, another one they know they can't keep. But it seems to be the right thing to say, because Ravi melts into them, and in the next moment he lifts Cayenne off their feet.

They give an undignified squeak as they are easily hefted up and carried, Ravi's capable hands spanning the breadth of their thighs. Cayenne clings to him like a limpet as he finally, *finally* carries them to bed. In the space of a blink, they're pressed back into the crisp white sheets and getting the air kissed right out of their lungs. They've wanted to be here under him for so long, for what feels like forever, it's almost surreal to have it happening now.

Any hesitation Ravi had previously has vanished, and in its place a passion so ardent it's nearly frenzied. It seems when their shining knight makes up his mind, he gives of himself entirely. The intoxicating weight of him atop them, the eager sounds that escape his throat as he strips off their fishnet top. *Merde*, but they could certainly get used to this.

"What do you want, my sweet?" they ask as they hurriedly unlace their sandals and kick them carelessly across the room, causing a crash they both ignore. With a practiced glide, they unzip his tight jeans and get a hand on him, and oh, that's *nice*.

Ravi gasps and bucks against them, his eyes now nearly black with arousal. Cayenne licks their lips. "Just tell me how you would like me." Words Cayenne has said many times before; a little unsettled how shaky they come now. They'll do just about anything to keep them here in this bed. If he changes his mind now, they had promised there was no turning back the clock to try again.

They aren't sure why they said they'd be careful with him. It's not something they can follow through with, no matter how much they might want to. Time travel carries with it endless advantages, but the one thing it can't do is let Cayenne change their own past. They can't change what happened, who they are, what they did. What they *will* do.

But introspection is definitely *not* their style. Might as well get what they can before August comes. Get as much of this delicious man as he'll allow them to take. They shove away any misgivings and push Ravi's purple-stained shirt off his shoulders.

Ravi crushes their lips together before answering brokenly, "I want anything you want," his mouth feverish hot on Cayenne's neck. Lips and tongue and teeth at their nipples, their flat belly, the scrape of beard against their hips, hands fumbling for the skintight edge of their shorts and peeling them off, down over long legs.

Oh, well, if he is *offering*. Cayenne goes loose and pliant, a reed bending to the wind.

He's *good* at this. Better than Cayenne had assumed, this poor repressed knight, surely snatching moments of pleasure from unpracticed, unsatisfying unions, but... Cayenne gasps, back arching. *Much* better.

Ravi licks a long, slow stripe up their cock before taking it in his mouth, and Cayenne's heels dig into the mattress. The heat of his tongue teases the underside, taking his time, and *merde*, if this is what he had meant earlier by "savoring the moment," Cayenne can definitely see the appeal.

They let their hands fall where they want, tunneling into Ravi's thick black hair, holding him tightly in place. He makes such a sweet little sound, a low aroused moan. When Cayenne twists their fingers tighter, pulling sharply, they are *quite* interested at the full-bodied shudder that courses through the man against them. Very interesting indeed.

"That's *so* good, sweetheart," they say, experimentally, and Ravi shivers, his skin pebbling. Ah, some pieces fall into place. Ravi looks up at Cayenne, his black lashes impossibly thick, cheeks hollowing. With gilded features and disheveled hair, he looks like he belongs in a harem, something out of a dream.

How was I to know? comes a wild, unwelcome thought. *How could I have known that under those fancy, buttoned-up suits and that cold, impenetrable demeanor,* this *person has been there the whole time?*

Well, Cayenne *had* intended to give Ravi perfect happiness. And maybe what Ravi needs to be happy is for someone to grasp greedily at his hair, to thrust up into his willing mouth. Perhaps he needs a generous volunteer to pull him up the bed demandingly into a scorching kiss, for someone to lean in close to his ear and whisper, "Good boy." And, if at that praise Ravi gasps, his whole face now flushed dark, goes boneless and pliable beneath their hands, well then, if so, that is not such a great hardship, now is it?

"I want you to fuck me, sweetheart. Can you do that for me?"

Ravi nods, eyes glazed over. Cayenne gives him a sultry grin and pushes at his shoulders. Ravi obediently gets up and rummages through the pocket of his duffel. Cayenne watches, noting that his hands are shaking. Fair enough; they feel a little unsteady themself.

Before crawling back in bed Ravi drops the shirt, still clinging on only by its cuffs, and kicks off his jeans. And okay. Yes. Well. Well, well. He'd definitely be the main attraction of that harem. Well-defined but still graceful, smooth skin decorated by a handful of interesting scars. Cayenne has slept with a lot of artists, but for the first time, they wish they had some of that talent themself. He's made to be carved in marble or cast in bronze.

They beckon to him from their ample throne of pillows. He slinks up the bed on his hands and knees, hungry gaze flickering over Cayenne like a starving man eyeing a feast through a window.

"You are so gorgeous," he stresses, not the way Cayenne would have said it, with flirtatious intent, but with his usual matter-of-fact cadence; just voicing another truth. It's disquieting, like he's seeing under their skin to something they've tried to keep hidden, parts of themself they've buried, and Cayenne squirms at the sincerity and pulls him down on top of them for a deep, filthy kiss.

Ravi takes one of those long, centering breaths he often

favors before lavishing some attention on Cayenne's pink little nipples, causing their spine to arch in response. He licks and bites alternately, paying attention to what Cayenne likes and adapting to suit. He runs his hands up and down their flanks before busying with the little bottle he'd fished out of his bag.

Cayenne pushes back into the pillows and luxuriates in the anticipation. A powerful hand pushes their thigh up and back. Cayenne hums with approval, spreading wide. Ravi's slick fingers are slow and careful until Cayenne twists impatiently. Ravi glances up, checking their comfort. It's all Cayenne can do to not just impale themself on those too-gentle fingers.

One side of Ravi's lips curls up as he watches Cayenne's face intently, and he crooks his fingers. Firmly. Cayenne swears, the French tripping from their lips.

"O-*kay*," they quaver, planting the ball of a foot on Ravi's chest and nudging him backwards. "On your back, I think."

Ravi nods, the swell of his throat bobbing as he swallows hard. He slicks on a condom as they switch places, his chest rising and falling rapidly. Looks like his breathing exercises aren't working anymore. Cayenne slings a leg across his hips, curves down to thoroughly explore his mouth with their tongue, grabs rough into his hair to hold him in place.

Ravi actually *whimpers*, a lovely sound, hands coming up to grasp Cayenne's slim hips while they grind down onto him. They only have the patience for a few seconds of teasing, before leaning back and giving Ravi's cock a few pumps with their hand before sinking down on him with one smooth slide.

They breathe in sharply, adjusting quickly and impatiently. Humming with pleasure, they draw themself up into a long lean line, arms folded straight up over their head, knowing they look like sin itself, and start up a fast, punishing rhythm, thighs working hard. It's *good*. Worth all the effort it took to get here. They arch back just so, finding the angle they like best, taking what they want, and only then glance down at the man thrusting up into them.

They can read Ravi's face so easily, every expression bared, maskless. As they move above him, he looks up with wonder, with reverence, like he's beholding an amazing feral creature, golden and glittering, makeup surely now more closely resembling warpaint. His admiring gaze hits like a punch to the gut. Unfair.

"So good, my darling, you *delicious* thing, just like that," they croon, watching with satisfaction as Ravi squeezes his eyes shut, jaw tensing prettily. A little praise absolutely *destroys* this boy, keeps him pliable. "Come on, sweetheart, let me see you."

Ravi hisses under his breath, hands clenching tight, pulling Cayenne forward on every thrust, and *oh*, that is *particularly* nice, catching them just *so*. Their skin prickles, goosebumps chasing up their arms. Reaching back, they brace their hands on Ravi's thighs and ride him, head thrown back. They're no longer in full control of the words that spill out, a stream of consciousness in a mess of English and French, "Yes, like that, *baise-moi comme*, Ravi, so fucking good, *ça fait du bien*, good boy, c'mon..."

And that does it, Ravi bucking up wild and savage beneath them, *perfection*, and crying out his climax into the back of his bitten fist. He arches up into Cayenne as they take themself in hand and finally, truly make a mess of him.

They fall panting to the mattress, enormously satisfied, and stare dazed up at the lazily spinning fan. At some point one or both of them ripped down most of the mosquito netting, and the fabric is piled up around them. Cayenne sprawls half on top of Ravi, limbs a graceless knot. Ravi slides a hand up Cayenne's forearm hesitantly, like he's not sure how the touch will be received, if he's allowed to ask for it.

Lacing their fingers together, Cayenne kisses the back of Ravi's hand and props up on an elbow to better admire their handiwork. Stains of violet all over, skin sparkling like he's burnished brass, and now striped with white. It is a *very* good look. Perhaps they are an artist after all.

"You want to do that again?" they ask, throat raw.

Ravi's sleepy eyelids flash open. "Right now?"

Cayenne laughs, nosing along his jaw and nibbling at an earlobe. "Right *then*, in fact. Just the last few seconds." They lift their eyebrows at Ravi's perplexed frown and smile at him, as if they offered this sort of thing all the time. "There are *some* benefits to sleeping with a chronomancer." They hold their palm up, an offering. "I did say I wouldn't leave you behind, *mon chéri*."

Ravi meets their eyes, gaze searching. And takes their hand.

Chapter Fourteen

JUDGING BY THE pale slant of the equatorial sunlight spilling across their eyes, they are awake at a truly unholy hour of the morning. They shift onto their side to settle in for a nice long lie-in and stretch a hand over to Ravi. Their fingers find nothing.

Cayenne's eyes flash open, a jolt of apprehension banishing any chance of sleeping in like the sweeping of cobwebs. They push themself up from the chaotic nest of pillows, duvets, and errant mosquito netting.

They'd be very chagrined to admit to the relief of seeing Ravi still there, though it takes a moment for it to click what on earth he's doing down on the floor. Push-ups at dawn, *mon Dieu.* It would be utterly *tragic* if the man didn't make the whole affair look so damned appealing. In a pair of gray joggers and nothing else, clean again from their shared, hasty scrub before finally falling asleep last night. Such a shame they are just going to have to find a new way to dishevel him today.

A Cheshire cat grin spreads across their face as they nestle back against the headboard to watch the show. After a moment Ravi shifts off his palms and moves into sit-ups, noticing his audience belatedly. "Oh! You're up. Morning." The hint of shyness behind his words is simply adorable.

"Mm," is all Cayenne says, letting the slow crawl of their gaze speak for them.

"I didn't mean to wake you," Ravi says apologetically, still doing his crunches, not even having the decency to be out of breath.

"I would have thought you got enough exercise last night, *oui*? Perhaps I need to *really* put you through your paces next time, hmm?" They stretch out with feline grace, kicking the covers off one leg to show a tantalizing amount of hip. The tips of Ravi's ears darken, his version of blushing. Some pieces of glitter still stick to his skin like faint, far-off stars.

"You definitely did." He clears his throat. "I do this every morning."

"*Every* morning? Ye gods, darling."

He cants his head, conceding, "Almost every. There have been extenuating circumstances before." Cayenne watches the planes of his muscles shift as he raises up into each rep. Could they perhaps convince him to come back to bed? This kind of show would be much, much better up close and personal.

Reaching some predetermined number, Ravi springs to his feet and moves over to the dresser. "Do you jog?"

Cayenne recoils as if asked whether they supported the eating of infants. "*Do I jog?*"

Ravi's eyes crease with amusement as he pulls on a tee and sneakers. Ravi has a way of smiling without smiling, like sunlight hidden behind clouds, unseen but for a hint of brightness. "I'll be back soon."

Cayenne sighs, concluding their chances at a little morning sex are quickly dwindling down to naught. "What breakfast would you like, my dear? I'll ring room service now so it will be ready when you get back."

Ravi shrugs. "I'll just have a coffee and a protein bar."

"*No.* Absolutely not." Cayenne sits up, incensed. "It's meant to be a vacation, you...you *madman*. Do your para-military calisthenics routine if you *must*, but afterward you will eat something delicious and nourishing, and I will go to truly obscene lengths to guarantee that." They cross their arms firmly.

"I'm good with the bar and the coffee."

"Truly. Obscene. Lengths."

Ravi gives them a long, considering look. "Okay."

"I mean it! A protein bar, honestly. I won't have it."

"I said okay." Ravi shrugs again, with the slightest hint of an agreeable side-to-side head wobble. It's the first time Cayenne has ever seen him perform such an overtly Indian gesture, on any side of the timeline. They wonder how long it took him to train himself out of it, and what it means that they're seeing it now. "Order something French and extravagant, then. I'll do my best to choke it down," he says, and he winks. Actually winks. Cayenne is so taken aback they can't even make the salacious jest that comes immediately to mind. "No beef or gluten. I'll be back in maybe half an hour."

All Cayenne can manage is an agreeable hum, watching as Ravi leaves the bungalow.

*

AFTER BREAKFAST, CAYENNE does manage to coax Ravi back into bed. It takes a very cunning plan: an elaborate strategy wherein Cayenne slides a foot up the inside of Ravi's thigh while he sips his coffee. After a second of spluttering, Ravi puts down the mug and proceeds to crawl on the bed over Cayenne like a big cat stalking its prey. Well, perhaps it's not the most elegant of plans after all, but it works well enough.

After a thorough session of making out, by unspoken agreement letting their arousal simmer for the time being, Cayenne stretches out on their stomach with Ravi's comfortable weight draped across their back. Ravi murmurs something into their skin. "Hmm? What's that, darling?"

Ravi lifts his face. "You have freckles on your shoulders." He traces them with his fingertips, as if pointing out constellations. "No scars? I can't find any."

"Oh, perhaps you should check me over very, *very* carefully. Just to be sure." Cayenne suppresses a shiver at the light touch of Ravi's mouth on the crest of their shoulder, tongue following the path his fingers have laid. "What's the scar on your back from?" Might as well learn a little something of interest while they deflect questions. The freckles annoy them. They only noticed they had overlooked them when it was already too late to fix. "The bullet wound. Or aren't I allowed to ask about *any* of the lovely marks you are decorated with?" Without warning, Ravi bites down reproachfully. They hiss with surprise, then arch up into it with a little moan. "Mm. More of that, *s'il te plaît.*"

With a throaty chuckle, Ravi obliges, peppering biting kisses along the span of their back, the scratch of his facial hair raising a trail of goosebumps. "Just a graze. Friendly fire from a London agent. There was a shadow creature stealing peoples' memories. Damn hard to track. Took six of us to bring it down."

"Hm, harrowing. The ones on your forearms?"

"You saw those? Barely even there anymore. Constance got some kind of poultice on them that seemed to heal them up almost good as new."

"But of course I saw them. I have been making *quite* a study of your lovely body, after all. What terrible beast caused them?"

"A giant praying mantis thing made out of crystal. Wrecked my car too."

"*Que c'est intéressant*! And what about those little bites? The ones adorning your *exceptionally* toned calves."

Another warm laugh against their spine. "My most recent acquisition. It was a tiny little teddy bear."

Cayenne clucks their tongue and twists around to face Ravi. "Really? *That's* what you're going with?" This time they get to see that laugh up close, and their heart skips an unsettling beat.

"The others are totally believable, but not a little teddy bear? It's true, though not as cute as it sounds. Lucy made it out of blood accidentally when we met her, before she learned some control over her somamancy. An ankle-high teddy bear made of blood with giant fucking fangs."

Cayenne sticks their tongue out in exaggerated disgust, then lays a hand on the center of the man's chest. "And this one?"

Ravi goes still, teeth catching his lower lip in hesitation. He peers deeply into their eyes. It's almost too much, having the weight of that singular focus centered on them. It's the same look he has when lining up a shot through a sniper scope; every twitch and blink accounted for, even his breaths measured with intent.

Eventually, he sighs heavily and moves to lie back on the mattress, tucking one hand behind his head and the other coming to rest on his chest, near the scars. Cayenne takes the implied invitation to drape across his side, propping their head up on one hand while the other is free to trace invisible patterns across Ravi's ribs in a silent encouragement to speak.

Ravi doesn't for a long moment. "Do you know what *bagh nakh* are?" He doesn't look at Cayenne, dark eyes instead turned up, absently watching the slow turn of the ceiling fan.

"Can't say as I do, darling."

"A long time ago, before the British came and decided it was too uncivilized, *bagh nakh* were a traditional dueling weapon among the highest castes. They're…" Here he searches for words and holds his hand up in a tensed claw. "They're like brass knuckles, but they go on the inside, over the palm. They have four curved blades, like tiger claws. I was learning basic fighting forms then in between schooling. Mostly simple stuff—how to roll and block, that sort of thing—and I watched my mom and my uncle train almost every day. They were incredible. You can't even imagine it, the way they moved. Maybe it's because they were twins, but they always knew exactly where to be. When I did have blades training back then, it was with dulled edges, of course. But not them. They sparred with the real things. And I *begged*. I begged to be taught. But I was too young, they said."

Cayenne doesn't like where this is going. They don't think they want to hear it at all. "How young, exactly?" they ask softly, too softly. Ravi continues right over them, still watching the ceiling.

"So, one day, *finally*, Uncle Nirav agrees to teach me something. He says my first real spar with a real opponent should be in keeping with tradition. With the first weapon *he* learned. He helps me put them on—they're too big, but he helps me wrap my hands so they fit—and shows me the correct stances. The *chuvadu*. I do pretty good for a while. I'm quick for my age, but he's going easy on me. And he keeps telling me, keep your guard up, keep your guard up, but I'm, you know, I'm trying to remember where my feet should go, so I keep dropping my hands. I...I can't do it. So," Ravi gestures carelessly at his chest, "this happens.

"Mom was watching from the sides, and she was pretty pissed. She storms in and starts yelling at Uncle Nirav. He tells her something, I don't quite remember what exactly. Something about the way she taught him everything he knows. He goes over to me and helps me up, and tells me, 'You gotta learn to keep your guard up. And stay calm, even when you've been hurt. It's just pain. Keep that shit on lockdown, kid.' And he was right. It was a good lesson. I always remembered to keep my guard up after that.

"But yeah, I definitely was not allowed to train with edged weapons after that for a couple of years," he says with a chuckle, scratching through his beard. "I wasn't allowed a real blade again until I was twelve."

And it is there, sudden and furious, an ugly thing clawing inside their own chest: *hatred*. Their hatred for The Trust surges up fresh and vibrant, like a new grown thing. Whatever good deeds the order might do, all the lives they might save, all the monsters they may stop, don't matter a whit to Cayenne. Everyone on the payroll can go hang, as far as they are concerned. They treated this boy so poorly, shaped him ruthlessly into a tool, then practically discarded him when he didn't fit their plans. This good, sweet, open-hearted, noble boy, *their* boy, these brutes hurt him and then taught him that he couldn't live his life honestly, couldn't be happy. They kept him in a cage where he had to lie about himself, and the greatest lie of all was that he deserved it, that he wasn't good enough for more.

Cayenne *aches* for the ability to stop time altogether, just so they could stomp around the room and rail against these complete *fools,* lay the blame squarely and solely at their feet, for their inability to see that no one could ask for a better, more perfect hero. *How fucking dare they.* How *dare* they do this to Ravi.

If it was up to them, The Trust would burn to the ground.

Cayenne has already done far, far worse.

But they can't do anything about that right now; can't go forward, no going back.

Guilt is for other people.

Instead, they bend their head down and press a long, lingering kiss to the raised lines of the scar. Ravi slides his fingers through their locks as he hums with pleasure. They can do this; press their lips to every rib, they can trail their tongue along the narrow path of fine, dark hair leading down his stomach to the dip of navel, they can set their teeth to the soft skin aside his hip; this they can do, like an offering, like a gift, or reparations.

*

RAVI PUSHES HIMSELF up to his elbows, watching Cay-enne tease him, gifting slow lingering kisses to his thighs, ghosting fingertips everywhere except where Ravi wants it. "Do you, um," he tries to ask, "do you do that trick often?"

Cayenne's laugh rumbles against his skin. "Oh, you sweet thing, I haven't done anything yet, *tu vas voir*."

"No, I meant…" Ravi flushes, trying to corral his words in the correct order while his body is much more interested in responding to Cayenne's featherlight touch. "I meant last night. Not just the sex. That was…well. It was great. I meant the time thing."

Saying he'd never experienced anything like that feels trite. *Of course*, he hadn't. Could anyone be *accustomed* to be-ing sent back to experience the same intense orgasm multi-ple times in a row, the memory of the previous one still thrumming brightly in the mind, adding and compounding to the shattering impact of the next one?

He's only sorry that the quick, frequent time shifts started to cause a headache, or he's not sure when he would have asked to stop. If ever. Cayenne had explained that his brain wasn't made for so much fiddling with, kissing him on both temples as if in apology before they both finally slept.

Cayenne pauses to rest their chin on Ravi's stomach. It's sharp, naturally, all those fine-boned fashion model angles, but Ravi doesn't shift. "By myself, sure, *quelquefois*. If you're asking if I just go around telling everyone I fuck that I am a time traveler capable of resetting my consciousness to an earlier state in my timeline, and oh, would you like a sample? Then I would have to say, no, not very often, darling." An ocean's worth of sarcasm laps at the edge of Cayenne's words.

Ravi rolls his eyes. "Just 'no' would have worked."

"We both have our reasons to want to stay off the radar," they add, voice dropping low. "If I get found out by the wrong people, I am surely bound for a dissection table. Or worse, a leash."

Ravi falls quiet for a long second. "Then I'm glad you think I'm one of the right people."

Cayenne's gaze darts away from his, their hands going tight for a split second before they relax into a seductive smile and ask archly, "So, it was great. Just great, hm?"

Ravi covers his face with his hands. "Look, I don't have your way with words. Better than great. You know."

"*Do* I know?" Cayenne teases, finally setting the flat of their tongue to work, Ravi jerking in shock despite all the buildup.

"*Yes*," he grits out, gathering fistfuls of the bedcovers

and trying to stay still.

Cayenne speaks between licks and laps, an unsteady rhythm that quickly drives him mad. "I *see*, better than great. Was it…pretty okay? Not bad, maybe? Somewhat adequate?" A pause while they easily suck his entire cock down their throat for a single second, then continue with the interrogation. "Perhaps it was mostly decent? Would you say passable?"

Ravi's muscles shake from the assault. "You are such a fucking brat," he hisses.

At this, Cayenne laughs loud and genuine, holding the base of Ravi's cock loosely with rainbow-painted fingers. "Aw, has the big, strong, secret agent finally met his greatest match, and it is a limited *vocabulary*?" Their smile looks more fond than it does mischievous. "Tell me something nice, and I'll be nice to you, hero."

Fuck. *"Vah sabase achchha tha jise mainne kabhee mahasoos kiya hai,"* he praises, the Hindi biting its way out of his throat. *That was the best I've ever felt.*

Cayenne stares, swallowing. "That's cheating," they say hoarsely, but it must be good enough, because they duck their head and finally, finally have a little mercy on him.

Chapter Fifteen

AS TEMPTING AS it is to stay in bed all day, eventually they rouse themselves and get dressed, deciding to hit the beach. It's another perfect day in the Seychelles, and knowing that the waters are now safer, Cayenne is willing to be convinced to join Ravi for a dip. They agree to walk a way down the coast, where the beach leads to a more secluded cove and they'll be less likely to run into other guests.

Cayenne plans to lounge under an umbrella and sip one of those nice minty rum drinks. Perhaps their beau could be wheedled into trying something fruity and heavily alcoholic. The kind of drinks that come in those little tiki face glasses.

Cayenne tilts their floppy hat back at a jaunty angle as they set out. Admittedly, they felt a bit weird picking it up today, turning the straw hat over in their hands while remembering how distraught Elissa had been yesterday over her injured best friend. For the teeniest, *tiniest* second, they wondered if they should give it back, then scoffed at themself. This is what came of associating with pathologically selfless heroic types; it was *catching*. Cayenne firmly planted the very fine hat on their head and left the bungalow without another thought about it. She *said* it was fair and square.

Ravi leans into them as they walk, just a little. It's a pleasant thing to press back, their arms brushing as they move. Passing by the more popular sunning area as they go, they stroll past a dozen or so folks draped across cushioned loungers, laughing and chatting under thick teak umbrellas. Since they're passing the bar anyway, Cayenne orders drinks. Ravi waits indulgently in the shadow of some palms a few yards away. He looks comfortable in this climate, clad in a loose linen shirt rolled up to the elbows, standing at ease instead of his usual stiff vigilance. He actually looks relaxed. No doubt Cayenne can take most of the credit on *that* front.

While the bartender mixes up their drinks, she asks, "Did I see you at the club last night? You served up all those fancy moves, right?"

Cayenne leans their elbows on the bar, chin in hand, gracing her with a brilliant smile. "*Oui, c'est moi!* Aren't you sweet? It was a lovely time."

"You guys make a really cute couple." She inclines her head toward Ravi, dreadlocks swaying.

Cayenne blinks at her. They glance askance at the man himself. Ravi notices and shoots over a small smile from behind his sunglasses. They can't help but smile back.

"We're not a couple," they tell her flatly.

She grins as she muddles the mint. "Then I've lost a bet. The two of you couldn't look away from each other the whole time."

The strangest thing happens; a blush takes over Cayenne's cheeks, which is baffling. There's no reason for it. Maybe they could blame their flushed face on the heat of the sun. Why the hell are they even having this conversation?

She slides the finished drinks over. One even has one of those little umbrellas in it. "Here ya go. Tell your not-boyfriend that he has some sick Bollywood moves."

They snatch the drinks off the bar, don't leave a tip, and march back to Ravi.

They hand him his fruity concoction wordlessly, shaking off their weird mood. "One very manly cocktail named after a sexual innuendo." They take a sip of their mojito. It's so perfectly made and well-balanced that it almost makes up for the bartender being so nosy.

"Something happen?" Ravi asks. Always so irritatingly perceptive.

"Not in the least." They grin up at him, pushing their half-moon sunglasses back up their nose. "Come on, let's get a secluded little spot we can hide away in." They wink.

Ravi's mouth slides up in that crooked smile Cayenne is growing very fond of, and they head off. "We're going to pass by one of the glyphs on the way. I want to check it out. Make sure it's still intact."

Cayenne gives a little Gallic shrug. "All the same to me, darling."

"What are you thinking for lunch?" Ravi asks as they walk, taking a small testing sip of his drink. His face brightens. "This isn't too bad."

"High praise indeed," Cayenne teases. "*Do* you eat actual food for lunch? Or just protein shakes or pellets or whatever?"

Ravi laughs loudly, a rare and precious thing. "Some people don't eat much in the morning. It's not that strange."

"Hmm. The little eastside bistro was *très* cute."

"Sure, that sounds..." Ravi's eyes narrow as they approach the small grove of palms. His pace quickens.

The sand has been churned up all the way to the dirt. Ravi squats and sifts through a handful of earth. He checks the area, dark brows drawn together in mingled frustration and confusion. "It looks like it's been kicked up. But only here. Someone destroyed it on purpose."

Cayenne sighs, placing a hand at their hip. "Let me guess; we're going to have to tramp around the whole beach *again* and check *every* glyph."

Ravi stands, looking grim. "Yup." He starts smoothing the sand back down with his foot. "First we have to redraw this one."

Cayenne groans.

A scream rings out, a weak frightened sound. Both their heads whip toward it. Ravi automatically reaches his gun hand under his left arm, grabs nothing, and swears. He throws his drink down and says, "Come on!" as he starts to dash in the direction of the scream.

Cayenne reluctantly drops their glass and follows, yelling out ahead, "We couldn't have just *one day*, could we?"

They are *so* done with this supernatural bullshit getting in the way of their vacation. How are they to get a thorough seduction going with all this nonsense taking up so much time? They fantasize briefly about rewinding time all the way back to the flight booking and picking a different island, stretching their ability to send back their consciousness nearly to its limits. But that would mean losing everything they've experienced here, only memories left, and they…they aren't willing to do that.

Pushing through some bushes, Cayenne breaks into the secluded cove only a second behind Ravi, but it takes a few more to absorb the scene before them.

Uwe screams as he is inexorably drawn closer to the shallow water from the beach. He claws at the sand, two thick, black whips wrapped around his bare ankle. The other ends of the whips disappear below the surface of the water, but the waves in the cove are low and the ocean crystal clear. The shape of the manta ray monster looms just under the surface, dragging Uwe another yard closer through the sand. He sees the two of them almost instantly and cries out wildly for help.

Ravi thrusts Cayenne behind him, stepping in front of them protectively. That's *so* cute. Also unnecessary, but cute, nonetheless.

"Stay out of its range," Ravi orders, and rushes in.

Things happen very quickly.

Ravi swiftly crosses the space and slides to Uwe as he struggles against the tentacles. He grabs the tentacles and tries to rip them off. Cayenne glances around frantically for any weapons, but there's nothing but bare, clean beach. "Fuck," they growl and check the vegetation behind them for driftwood or anything, but spot nothing. "Fuck!" They could rewind now, but without any useful information to take back to the past, doing so is worthless. Better to wait and see how to take this thing down.

Ravi manages to peel one tentacle off Uwe's ankle. The flexible muscle twists and curls in the open air before wrapping tight around Ravi's wrist instead. He leaps to his feet, planting them firmly in the wet sand, and keeping tension with his trapped arm, he starts using the other to reel the monster in closer. He strains, teeth bared, and the beast's head breaks through the surface. Ravi leans back, then darts forward to pick up the slackened section of tentacle. He winds it around his forearm and draws the creature even closer.

Damn, that's sexy.

Cayenne starts moving toward Uwe, staying out of the range of the whips.

A third of the creature is above water, its bulk scraping noisily across the sand. Ravi moves in close, waves lapping at his shoes, free hand dealing a flurry of quick strikes to its eyes, and *ugh,* it has three of them. The beast keens, a deep reverberating moan emanating from within it like whale song.

Apparently, the monster decides it's now more interested in fending off its attacker than in its original prey. The other tentacle finally lets go of Uwe. Cayenne, waiting for this moment, darts in to grab the man's hands and drag him further up the beach to safety. It's a little irksome to think how insufferable Ravi is going to be about this later.

"What is that thing?" Uwe cries, scrambling further away. "It tried to kill me!"

"Yes, yes." Cayenne pats him perfunctorily on the shoulder. "You're fine."

The monster keens again, its anger coming through despite any cross-species language barriers. It snaps its other tentacle around Ravi's ankle and yanks him roughly off his feet. He hits the sand heavily. The creature thrashes its slimy wings, water spraying, and heaves its massive body off the sand. It starts sliding back into the water, dragging Ravi half into the ocean.

"Ravi!" Cayenne jumps forward, heart in their throat.

This is going to be fine. Cayenne can just rewind a bit if things go south. No reason to lose their head.

Still, they bolt close. They slip their hands under Ravi's shoulder blades and get a good grip on his arms.

"Cay," Ravi yells, coughing water, "don't! Stay back!"

"Don't be stupid," they snarl. A shadow briefly cuts off the sun, then one of those titanic wings rises out of the water and slams down on them both. Cayenne catches only a glancing blow, but it's enough to knock them back. Dazed, they push themself up, spitting seawater and sand, just in time to see the monster pull Ravi completely under. It sinks down, swimming swiftly as a torpedo. And it's gone. He's gone.

Cayenne stands up and stares.

It happened too fast.

Okay. This is fine. They take a deep breath and think. Out of the corner of their eye, they see Uwe rise to his feet and start walking toward them, but they ignore him. They need to *think*, damn it.

What they need is a weapon. This fucking creature is too big, and they can't fight it in the water. This is no problem. Ravi is gone, but he *wouldn't* be. It was fine.

"Well, *that's* not happening," Cayenne states firmly, and winds back their tattoo.

*

THEY'RE RIGHT BACK at the bar, Cayenne holding the tiki drink out for Ravi. First things first: they take a long, thirsty sip of the mojito before dropping both glasses unceremoniously to the ground. Ravi jumps back, avoiding the spill. "Hey, what's—"

"So!" they interrupt. "Bad news, my sweet. The glyph has been disturbed, and the monster thing is about to attack our good friend Uwe."

Ravi blinks, and in the space of it his shoulders square up and his expression goes eagle-sharp. "I need my gun."

Cayenne's eyebrows go up. "You brought a gun with you to a tropical vacation?" Ravi gives them an incredulous look. "Ah, look who I'm talking to. *Bien sûr*, you brought a gun."

"When is the attack? Is there time to run back and get it?"

"Oh, sweetheart." They smile, wrapping their arms around him. "I've got nothing but time."

They intend to only give him a little peck, but the memory of him being dragged beneath the waves rises unbidden, and they surge into the kiss, Ravi grunting with surprise at their sudden urgency. That wasn't going to happen. And neither was this, so, might as well say something foolish.

"You're not allowed to die until I'm done with you, *ravageur*." Then they muss up his swept-back hair until it falls haphazardly around his eyes, blow him a kiss, and jump back.

*

BACK EVEN FURTHER, in their bungalow, holding Elissa's straw hat in their hands. They fling it aside and stride through their bungalow door and burst into Ravi's.

With an alarmed noise, Ravi leans out of the open bathroom, beard trimmer in hand. His alert stance relaxes when he sees Cayenne. "So, we're not knocking anymore, is that it?"

Cute. Cayenne claps their hands together briskly. "Okay, here's the deal, darling. In about twenty minutes the big ray monster thing is going to attack Uwe down at the secluded beach. Where *we* were supposed to actually *enjoy* ourselves for one whole day without this monster attack nonsense, but alas." By this time Ravi has emerged from the bathroom and stands in front of Cayenne, arms over his chest. "You fought it, and it did not go so great. So! You told me you need your gun. Now I am telling *you*: bring your gun."

Ravi's arms drop. "Twenty minutes?"

Cayenne nods.

Ravi nods decisively back, grabs his duffel, and pulls out a Glock in a compact clip-on holster. With economical, practiced movements he checks the barrel, the ammo cartridge, and the safety before clipping the whole assembly on the back of his pants and flipping his shirt to hide it.

"Okay, let's go," he says. Cayenne takes a moment to appreciate how cool and collected Ravi has been each rewind. It makes things *much* easier. They gesture to the door with an exaggerated flourish.

"We could always just not go," they offer, already knowing what his answer would be. It had occurred to them to not tell Ravi about any of this; perhaps lead him off in a different direction, or better yet, keep him distracted inside the bungalow all day. But they remembered Ravi's impassioned pronouncement earlier, wondering how he could live knowing he didn't help someone when they needed him. The silly thing would be absolutely useless with guilt when he found out, and that would ruin their vacation as well as any monster attack.

Predictably, Ravi just gives them a flat look at the offer. They demonstrate a little half-shrug as if to say "well, I tried," and they're off.

It's clear Ravi is making an effort to not break into a run as they walk casually past the sunbathers. Cayenne strolls easily by his side.

"How'd the glyph get wrecked?" Ravi asks, voice lowered.

"No idea." Cayenne's brow creases in thought. It *was* odd. "Just…be careful, darling. Last time that…that *thing* dragged you down. It was over so fast."

Ravi reaches out and quickly squeezes Cayenne's hand. "I'm sorry."

Cayenne looks at him in horror. "Don't *apologize*."

"What about Uwe?" They pass the bar, the bartender looking up quizzically at their hurried pace. "Did he make it out okay?"

Cayenne gapes at him, utterly appalled. "Did *he* make it out okay? *You* are the one who *drowned*!"

Ravi has the *audacity* to shrug. "As long as it helps someone. He got out, right?"

Cayenne throws their hands up and nods, unable to untangle their roiling emotions. This noble *idiot*.

Ravi glances over, sees their face, and slows his pace just the tiniest fraction. "Hey. It's okay. If it happens again, you can just go back and warn me again." A weak smile, head tilted. "Unless you get bored. I know this is taking up a lot of your attention and effort."

Cayenne spins on him, stung. Ravi's eyebrows fly up and he holds up his hands, calming. "Sorry, sorry. I was just trying to make a joke. I'm not great at those. You just seem really tense."

Cayenne forcibly relaxes, resuming their quick walk. "Imagine that," they drawl.

They push through the brush several minutes earlier than they had the first time. Uwe is a bit further up the beach than when Cayenne first saw him, still struggling against the tentacles. It's actually a bit impressive; must be a strong guy, or maybe just lucky with his footing. Again, he spots the pair of them coming through the foliage nearly instantly, yelling out for help.

Ravi quickly assesses the situation, drawing his gun.

"Stay out of its range," he shouts over his shoulder, running closer. Cayenne skirts around upland like last time, ready to grab Uwe when the thing lets go of his ankle.

Ravi holds up his gun and takes careful aim. A shot rings out, and *merde,* that's loud. Cayenne glances nervously at the main beach. Hopefully, this will all be wrapped up before resort security comes to investigate.

The bullet nearly tears one tentacle in half, and the monster rears up out of the water with that haunting moan. The torn tentacle falls uselessly to the ground, dissolving into a disgusting goo that disappears into the sand in seconds. Uwe kicks at the tight grip of the remaining tentacle, and Cayenne grabs his hand. "What is this thing?" Uwe cries out. "It is trying to kill me!"

"Uh-huh, yeah," Cayenne says, distracted, keeping a watchful eye on Ravi. He fires two more shots into the central bulk of the creature. It cries again, flapping hard against the sand, heaving itself back, pulling both Uwe and Cayenne several feet closer to the water. Cayenne tries bracing their heels, but the thing is *strong.* Ravi steps right up to the monster and fires another shot straight into its third eye.

That seems to be enough for it. With a furious, ululating whale song roar, it releases Uwe and throws itself back in the water. It sinks down under the surface and speeds away.

Cayenne hastily helps Uwe to his feet, then runs over

to Ravi. He watches the dark shape swim out to the horizon, his expression flinty. "It got away," he growls.

"Well," Cayenne says brightly. "At least nobody got drowned this time, my dear."

Ravi sighs, finally lowering his gun. "We should check on Uwe. Make sure he hasn't been bit." They start to turn around when multiple shouts ring out.

"Freeze!"

"*Putain de bordel de merde,*" Cayenne swears filthily. "*Really?*"

Four security personnel quickly move into semicircle formation around them. All of them aim tasers at Ravi, and one of them has an assault rifle slung across his chest. This resort's security is rather more attentive than Cayenne had assumed they'd be. Uwe hunkers back down on the sand, staying still as he looks up at security in alarm.

"Drop the gun!"

Ravi's eyes dart around rapidly as he absorbs the situation. His gaze catches on Cayenne, then with a sour grimace he drops his gun. It lands on the sand with a thump. He puts his hands up and chews at his lip.

Merde, Cayenne can easily imagine what he must be thinking. He's trying to figure out how to get through this without The Trust knowing about it and is coming up with no viable solutions.

"You too, Red, hands up! We're going to have to book you too." One of the guards keys the radio on his shoulder, calling for the local police in *sotto voce* creole.

Booking means mugshots. Fingerprints. A paper trail.

Cayenne stomps their foot. All that work for nothing. "*For fuck's sake!*" they howl, and rewind back yet *again*.

*

BACK IN THE bungalow. They drop the hat and let themself through Ravi's door. This time they march straight over to him, grab the trimmer out of his hand, and slap a palm over his mouth. "*O-kay*. Third time's the charm, *oui*? Just listen, my sweet. That *fucking* ray is going to be attacking Uwe in twenty minutes on the secluded beach. If you don't have a weapon, it *will* drown you, but if you shoot it with your gun we shall be mobbed by security, and the monster is going to escape *anyway*. So! Do you perhaps have any other deadly goodies tucked away? Something quiet, preferably?" They remove their hand and step back.

Ravi blinks, then does the same thing he has done so far in every rewind, which is to square his shoulders with steely-eyed focus. If Cayenne weren't so irritated, it would be quite alluring. "No. Just the gun." He glances around the room with a thoughtful twist of his lips. "Nothing weaponizable here. Unarmed combat didn't work?"

"Nope."

Ravi sighs with irritation. "I guess neither *kalaripayattu* nor Krav Maga were designed with giant aquatic foes in mind." He digs through his duffel and readies his gun. At Cayenne's expression, he explains, "Just in case. I'd rather have it on me than not. I won't use it unless I need to."

That will have to do. Cayenne takes a moment, tapping their hand to their mouth in contemplation. An idea strikes them. "Follow me," they tell Ravi, turning on their heel and heading down the dock. He's quick to join them as they stride toward the main sunning area.

Cayenne points an insistent finger at Ravi. "I want a *fucking* massage after this. With hot stones. And cucumber water."

Ravi smirks. "I think you've earned it."

"Fucking right I have," they mutter.

"Do you know why the glyphs didn't work?"

"Ah, yes. The glyph nearest there had been kicked up."

"So...someone wanted to draw that thing in, maybe?" Ravi looks up at the sky as if searching for answers there. "Wish the rest of the team were here. They would have figured this out ten times over by now. I'm only good at hitting things."

"*And* that thing you do with your tongue, darling," Cayenne teases, knocking a shoulder into his. His ears darken as he shoots them a pleased, sideways glance. They congratulate themself on forestalling some kind of maudlin inferiority complex. Has no one ever flirted with this boy before? He has no defenses against it. It's almost too easy to distract him.

When nearing the busy loungers, instead of passing by, Cayenne breezes right through the first row of beach chairs and grabs one of the big teak umbrellas, picking one that is still tied closed. They lift it up out of its stand, balance it on their shoulder, and walk off with it. They get a few strange looks but no one stops them, bless their incurious hearts.

Ravi steps in and places a hand on the umbrella shaft. "That's heavy. I can carry it."

They give him a coquettish moue. "*Such* a gentleman." They let him take it and situate it comfortably across his shoulders before they make a beeline down the coast.

"What are we doing with this?"

"All shall soon be revealed," they say with a playful waggle of their brows. Arriving at the grove of trees, Ravi frowns at the churned-up ground. "Here." They motion for the umbrella, and Ravi hands it over. As they recalled, two palm trees are spaced just right for what they have in mind. Cayenne braces the umbrella behind one tree and in front of the other and sets their feet against the sand.

"Ah. I see what you're doing. Let me help." Ravi moves

in next to them and wraps his hands around the bottom part of the pole. "On three?"

"*Trois*." They heave forward in tandem. For a long second nothing happens except a slight bend in the wood, but then the end of the umbrella creaks, splits with a loud crack, and shears off.

A weak, scared scream sounds from the cove. Ravi startles, head turning. "It's okay," Cayenne tells him. "We've got thirty seconds or so." Cayenne kicks at the broken bits of the umbrella and picks up the pole. It now comes to a satisfyingly spiky end. They hand it to Ravi. "*Voilà*. Now you have a spear, hero. Let's see how that does."

Ravi takes it, brown eyes looking deeply into theirs. He slides a hand through Cayenne's hair, thumb stroking the sensitive curve of their ear, and pulls them in for a sharp, brief kiss. Then he dashes off through the brush.

Cayenne lays a hand to their stomach, quelling a very inconvenient fluttering before following.

Ravi, already halfway there, quickly closes the distance, spear hefted in both hands. "Stay out of its range," he shouts back at Cayenne.

"Get it up on the beach first!" they shout back, moving up above Uwe. Uwe scrambles against the sand, and again Cayenne offers him a hand.

Ravi nods once, quickly assessing the situation before

moving toward the tentacles. Again, he manages to peel one off Uwe's ankle, and again gets roped around the forearm. This time, when he starts reeling the beast up out of the surf, feet dug deep into the sand, he uses the spear to brace himself firmly in place. He wraps the loose tentacle around his arm as if gathering up a rope, jaw set with determination, muscles straining with effort.

Honestly, it's almost worth all this time jumping just to get to see Ravi do that again.

"Stab the other one!" Cayenne yells out helpfully. "Can you sever the other tentacle?"

With an enormous amount of effort, Ravi heaves the thing up another foot out of the water, inching closer to the tentacle that still has a grip on Uwe. He hoists the spear and jabs it down onto the tentacle once, twice, thrice before it snaps straight through. The creature howls an angry, mournful moan, thrashing furiously, kicking up sand and seawater.

Cayenne yanks Uwe up the beach and to safety. Uwe kicks off the clinging tentacle, which quickly dissolves into goo. "What is that thing? It tried to kill me!"

"Not now, Uwe," Cayenne snaps. They smack their hands together to dust off sand, and move in a little closer, keeping a careful watch over Ravi. The spear seems to help, levering the monster closer. It's almost fully out of the water, only its back tail end swinging furiously for purchase. Ravi darts in close, readying the spear for a strike.

"Don't go for the eyes," they suggest, voice raised. "If you stab its eyes, it'll try to get away."

Ravi shouts back, "Anywhere I *should* aim?"

"No idea, darling. Might I suggest you start stabbing and see what happens?"

Ravi laughs, a fierce, wild sound. "Now *that* I can do." And he starts in with a whirlwind of strikes, moving easily forward and back, switching between flat thwacks with the pole and vicious punctures to the creature's slimy flesh. Instead of blood, it leaks a clear, glittery viscous fluid.

Cayenne enjoys teasing Ravi about his tough-guy demeanor, but actually seeing him fight is...something else. He fights like...well, like someone who's been training his entire life. On the other side of the timeline, Cayenne saw him fighting monsters with the rest of his team, mostly focused on backing up Val—who was the *real* heavy-hitter of the group—and almost always with a firearm. They only got to see him take center stage like this once before, and Cayenne didn't get to appreciate it properly at the time. Like his dancing, it's a melding of styles; various martial arts, fencing, and plain, dirty street fighting all mixed into one unrelenting force. It's a true pleasure to watch him work.

He deserves a little cheerleading, they decide. "You're

doing *magnifique*, my dear!" His face, stony with concentration, shifts into a barely there smile.

With a massive thrust and a war cry, Ravi buries the spearpoint straight down into the monster's head. Cartilage crunches, the wings flap with increasing feebleness, and the monster wails a long, keening whale-howl. Ravi keeps both hands on the spear, driving it deep through into the sand.

A few seconds feel like an eternity as the reverberating cry ceases, the creature finally going still. They both wait, holding their breath until the slimy form begins to bubble and collapse in on itself.

Ravi lets go of the spear and shakes off the rapidly disappearing tentacle, checking that it isn't turning into acid or anything. He glances quickly around, relaxing as he sees Cayenne and Uwe alive and well.

Cayenne runs forward and leaps into his arms. Surprised, Ravi staggers back, breathing hard and sweating. Cayenne runs both hands over Ravi, checking him over before setting their palms on either side of his face. "You're not hurt? This time it worked?"

Ravi grins broadly at them. "Yeah, *semma*, I'm good. You were amazing."

Affronted, Cayenne slaps lightly at his chest. "Me? I didn't do anything. *You* killed it, hero."

Ravi smiles so widely that his eyes crease at the corners.

"Yeah, you're right, you had no part in this. Could have easily done it without you."

"Okay, okay," they concede, rolling their eyes, dropping back onto their feet. Ravi moves over to Uwe, still sitting on the sand wide-eyed and dazed. He offers a hand and pulls him to his feet.

"You okay?"

"I...I think so," Uwe answers tremulously. "This was the creature I have seen from the dock. What was it? It is... dissolving."

Ravi looks over his shoulder. There's not much left of the monster, the gentle waves breaking it apart.

Cayenne wanders close to Ravi and stands off to the side with one hip canted. They give a careless shrug. "It's definitely dead, is what it is."

Uwe shakes his head in disbelief. "You were very impressive, fighting that thing." He glances up admiringly first at Ravi, then at Cayenne. "And you, so clever! You must have a head for strategy." He sways a little bit, and Ravi braces against his arm. "Sorry. I am a little dizzy." He looks at the inside of his wrist, going a touch pale. "Oh. It must have bitten me when it first grabbed me. I was right in the water when it came at me, and I managed to run up the beach before it grabbed me with those...those things."

Ravi takes his arm and inspects the bite, face grim. He

breathes out with relief. "It's just a scrape. Really small. You probably didn't get much venom. We can escort you to the resort doctor."

Uwe shakes his head, dark hair brushing his shoulders. "No, no, I do not think I want to explain this."

Ravi bites his lip, conflicted. "Well...your pupils look okay. Cayenne, how did you say Taylor looked?"

"Considerably more fucked up. He looks fine to me."

"I really just want to sleep it off," Uwe insists, rubbing at his bite.

Ravi breathes out and nods. "Okay. If you're sure. Can we walk you to your bungalow?"

"No, no, you have already done so much. You have both saved my life! I cannot think of how to thank you enough." He looks at them with a slight seductive tilt to his head. "I can find my way there myself. Unless...I can join you in yours?"

Cayenne grins at the amusing way Ravi's jaw drops. Did he really not see this coming? Uwe looks at them like he thinks they both hung the moon.

They can't help but tease. "What a sweet offer! How about it, hero? To the victor go the spoils, *non*?"

Ravi just levels a flat, unimpressed look at them before turning back to Uwe. "You're *sure* you can get back okay?"

Uwe nods, taking the tacit rejection gracefully. "Yes,

yes. I am feeling better already." He smiles shyly. "I will have to think of how to properly thank you both later."

"Good." Ravi moves over to Cayenne and takes them by the shoulder. He pushes them back up the beach the way they came. Cayenne blinks with surprise. "You get some rest. We'll see you later." He sets a hand in the small of Cayenne's back, urging them into a quickened walk back to the brush line. Bemused, Cayenne lets themself be led away.

"*Au revoir*, Uwe!" They wave cheerily over their shoulder, stepping back through the palm trees. "What on earth are you in such a hurry for, darling? I would have bet on you mother-henning that man all the way to the hospital."

"Nope," Ravi says shortly. "Got other plans."

Cayenne looks at him, worried despite themself. "Are you angry, my dear?"

Ravi exhales harshly, grabs Cayenne, and pushes them up against a tree. He crowds in close, hips aligning, and, *oh. Oh.* How was he even walking around with that thing?

"I'm not angry," he growls against their lips. "And if you don't want me to take you back to the bungalow and fuck your brains out, you'd better tell me now."

Lust blooms fast and abrupt in Cayenne's belly, curling through them like a drop of ink in water. "Ah…no objections here." They aren't sure if this is coming from the adrenaline of the fight or from Uwe's offer, but either way, they are *very* pleased to reap the benefits. It has been a thoroughly annoying afternoon, and they deserve a treat.

Chapter Sixteen

AS SOON AS they make it through the door, Ravi removes his gun and checks it before stowing it away. "Get your clothes off," he tells them gruffly, "and put your hands on the headboard."

Ooh, fierce. They *like* seeing this side of him. It's unanticipated, certainly, but utterly delicious. Well, they're nothing if not adaptable. They start skinning out of their clothes, pulling the shirt over their head. "Mm, as you wish, *mon tigre*."

Ravi unbuttons his shirt, watching them with the singular laser focus that makes them feel naked already. A frisson courses up their spine, and they make a show of shimmying out of their shorts. Ravi's lips curl up just the smallest bit at the performance as he lets his linen shirt fall to the bamboo floor.

Cayenne eases onto the bed on their knees, takes hold of the headboard as asked—or ordered—and casts a sultry look over their shoulder. On full display; long limbs, lithe muscle, pert round ass. They grin, a masterpiece and they know it. "Now what, handsome?"

"Keep them there," Ravi says huskily, stepping out of his pants and boxers in one smooth motion. When freed, his cock bobs up, nearly smacking his stomach. Cayenne licks their lips.

"Nothing else?" they wheedle, "Just keep my hands here?" A small plastic bottle and a square of foil are thrown on the bed. "Not that this isn't *scintillating*, my dear, but—" Ravi moves onto the bed and presses up against their body, cock tight against their ass. Cayenne sucks in a breath, an immediate visceral response as Ravi takes their hips firmly in his hands and grinds slow against them. "Oh," Cayenne squeaks.

Ravi leans forward and bites the edge of their ear over the cartilage. "Keep. Your hands. There." Then he reaches his own hand slowly over Cayenne's flat abdomen, blunt nails scraping. He flicks hard against a nipple and rests that hand right over their heart. He keeps it there, and Cayenne is sure he must be able to feel the damn thing about to beat its way through the ribcage.

"If you take your hands away from the headboard, I'm going to stop." His voice rasps low, and the whole time he keeps up that slow, intense grind, not going anywhere, not taking things further, just…very much *there*. Incredibly *present*.

"Ah," Cayenne gasps a little, "wouldn't it be easier if you tied me here, sweetheart? I've got some *very* nice silk rope in my bag."

A low, hot chuckle caresses the nape of their neck. "Of course, you do." He bites hard over the vertebrae, and Cayenne's back arches into a taut curve as the sharp pleasure of it scythes through them. Ravi still has his hand over Cayenne's chest, and for some reason this feels like the most intimate thing he's doing to them, somehow even more than rubbing his dick right up against their ass. It doesn't make sense. They can't decide if they want him to move it away or keep it pressed there, feeling their heartbeat, the whole time.

Ravi skims his tongue across their shoulders in a discernible pattern. It takes a second for Cayenne to realize he's tracing their freckles, brought out by the sun. "Who would it be easier for? Me or you?" He thrusts hard, brushing *almost* where they want it. Cayenne squirms back, trying to get more contact. "I want to see if you can do as you're told, for once."

A dry little shell of a laugh escapes Cayenne as they drop their head between their straining arms. Their hands clench against the wood; they want badly to turn and touch and take what they want. This would be *much* easier if their wrists were tied up. That was fun. They could writhe around and pout and have their legs bent in interesting, athletic angles. Being tied didn't take any of their control away, paradoxically, while *this*, having this be *their* responsibility, this was...

"You're trying to torture me," they accuse, forcing just enough of a tease into their tone to keep it light. They can't remember the last time they were this hard. They *ache*, and they've barely even *done* anything. It makes no sense. "After all the nice things I've done today."

"Is that what you think?" Ravi asks, and that hand over their hammering heart finally slides down to cup their cock. Not stroking it, just holding, gauging their arousal. It's maddening. "Keep your hands where they are or I'm going to stop."

"You're...you're bluffing," they manage with hitching breaths, trying to push into that touch but being held still securely at the hip.

"Do you think?" Ravi asks lightly, as if truly curious.

Cayenne exhales shakily. No, they do not think he is bluffing. Pretense isn't his style. They dig their fingernails into the headboard.

"I think you are a truly mean and wicked man, is what I think."

"Hmm," is Ravi's only response, and Cayenne nearly whines as his hand disappears, leaving them cold and aching. There's a click, and Ravi leans back just far enough to run his fingers, now slick and dripping, down through Cayenne's crease. They gasp and buck sharply against him.

"This okay?" Ravi checks, voice soft.

"*Yes.*"

"If you want me to stop, you can just let go, and I will."

How is this man even real? Simultaneously ripping Cayenne's defenses down to shreds and at the *same time* telling them he'll respect any boundaries they want him to; stripping away their control and giving them all of it too. How the fuck does that even work?

They're breathing like they have been running for miles. "I don't want you to *stop*, you evil brute. I want *more.*" By now they are very thoroughly slick, and they hear the tearing of the condom packet; hopefully, Ravi will get with the program soon and get on with fucking them. Like yesterday. Cayenne is an exposed nerve, a tangle of straining anticipation.

But he just returns to the intense, infuriating pressure he was inflicting on them before, now moving easier through the slick, sliding across sensitive flesh. Cayenne's knuckles turn white; they're gripping the headboard so hard they wouldn't be surprised if it splinters. The anticipation is *killing* them.

"Are you going to *do* anything, or just hump me all day?" they hiss, biting off the end of each word, trying to twist back against him.

An especially long, slow grind has their teeth on edge. "Maybe."

Cayenne growls, moving their hips back in a circle, trying to get that cock somewhere *useful* until Ravi's grip holds them still.

Ravi murmurs in amusement, "Call me crazy, but I don't think you're particularly good at waiting."

"*Fuck. You.*"

"Maybe later," Ravi says pleasantly, one hand skating up to grab a fistful of their hair, pulling their face around for a deep, scorching kiss. Their entire body is pulled taut and aching between the two points of contact. When Ravi releases them from the kiss, they bang their forehead on the bedframe and start cursing a long string of French, calling Ravi the filthiest insults they can think of.

He must catch a word or two of it because he has the

nerve to laugh, a deep rumble in his chest. "Funny story. I actually *am* a bastard." He drives hard against Cayenne, the force of it juxtaposed by the soft circles his fingers trace on their hips, still not giving Cayenne what they want. Their thighs start to burn, and they think they could come from nothing more than an errant breeze. Their hands shake, threatening to slip. The tease is intolerable. But Ravi only rubs, inexorably; the head of his cock *just* nearly catches the edge, but never does, never *goes anywhere*, and Cayenne's head spins like they are drunk, or drugged, nearly out of their head.

"Please," they finally say, ragged, shaky, "please, *s'il te plaît*, Ravi. If you don't fuck me right this instant, I will not be held responsible for my actions. I have had a *very* trying day."

Ravi places a kiss, slow and reverent, between Cayenne's shoulder blades, reaches down, and guides himself in. Cayenne's eyes roll so far back in their head they faintly worry they're going to get stuck that way. And then they can't think of anything at all.

"I can't," they whisper. They don't even know what they're saying, what they can't do, but Ravi must understand, because he stretches over and covers Cayenne's trembling hands with his own, holding them tight to the headboard as he grinds his cock into them. It's a relief so intense that they moan out, "Ah, *merci*!"

His hands press warm over theirs, protective. Intensely intimate, like his hand over their heart. It's too much.

It's over embarrassingly quick. Maybe two dozen thrusts and that's it, they're gone.

Cayenne's only peripherally aware of Ravi following them over the edge a minute later, his forehead bowed against their spine, hips working, his mouth shaping a whisper of their name against their skin.

Seconds or hours later they end up on their back next to Ravi, chest heaving like they've run a marathon. Which is ridiculous, they hadn't moved practically at all. How had staying still in one place been so difficult?

Cayenne turns to Ravi, both on their sides facing one another. "I hope you don't mind if I don't rewind us this time. I think once is all I can take." Their legs actually *shake*. "Who the hell taught you *that*?" Highly doubtful The Trust teaches their agents ropeless bondage...though it *does* possess some interesting possibilities for interrogations, now they consider it. Better than their other methods by far.

Ravi gives them a sidelong look, biting his lower lip. "I've never done anything quite like that before."

Cayenne goggles at him. "You *haven't*? Well, you're a natural." They run a hand over their face, skin pebbled all over with sweat. Ravi leans in to kiss them, and Cayenne eases into it, scooting closer and deepening it. When they pull back, they wince as an unpleasant thought occurs.

"You okay?" Concerned, Ravi cups their cheek in his palm.

"*Oui*, sweetheart. I was just, ah, *think*ing that" — they take a fortifying breath — "I *might* need to apologize."

Ravi leans back a fraction and narrows his eyes in suspicion. "Who are you and what have you done with Cayenne?" He's only half-joking.

They roll their eyes. "Very droll, pet. Seriously."

A cute little wrinkle appears between Ravi's eyes. "What for?"

"For…" Cayenne squirms. "For jumping back without you. I *did* say I would try to avoid that." They try to explain all in a rush. "But, you see, I can't bring you back with me unless we're touching, unless I have a lot of time to prepare of course, and you were gone, so—"

"Cayenne, no." Ravi interrupts, stroking his thumb along their lower lip. "That's completely cool with me, you don't need to apologize. You weren't trying to avoid an argument. This was an emergency. I don't want you to promise me anything that…that *hobbles* you."

Cayenne considers this and offers him a small half-smile. "So, leaving you behind is okay if it's for a good reason?"

"Well, I am automatically suspicious of your wording there, and who gets to decide what a good reason is, but...yeah."

Cayenne breathes a little sigh of relief. "I thought you might be cross with me."

"Are you kidding?" Ravi asks incredulously. "You were amazing! You saved that guy's life!"

Cayenne shakes their head vehemently. "You did the heavy lifting. And if I *was* saving anyone, it was *you*, not him."

Ravi smiles, eyes creasing at the corners. He's truly lovely. Unbelievable they didn't see that when they first met him. "And here I am, alive because of *you*." Uncomfortable, Cayenne scoffs, looking away. "It's true." He takes Cayenne's slender hand in his own and places it over his chest. His heart thuds steadily. "That's only beating because of choices you made."

Cayenne's nose wrinkles up with their little grunt of protest. "This is getting sappy."

"Oh no, how horrible for you," Ravi deadpans, "to hear that your actions had a positive impact on others." Cayenne's hand snakes away and pinches his nipple. "Ow!" he laughs, pulling away. Saucily Cayenne swings off the bed, testing their legs' stability first.

"I'm going to take a shower," they pronounce archly,

"and *you* are going to order a room service luncheon. I'm *absolutely* ravenous."

Ravi pulls over his watch from the nightstand. "Almost dinner, now."

"How the time *does* fly." Cayenne winks and stretches their arms over their head. Ravi watches with interest. They do so enjoy having his eyes on them; he makes such an appreciative audience. "Order me something sweet."

*

SUNSET POURS IN through the full-length windows, along with the cooling evening breeze, bringing with it the sound of soft waves and gently swaying palms.

Cayenne leans over and points with their chopsticks. "That looks good."

"It's spicy," Ravi warns. "I got extra Thai chilis." He watches Cayenne try a mouthful of his papaya salad, half expecting that despite their name, they have the spice tolerance of your average pale redhead, but they chew their mouthful with evident delight.

"Ooh, that's good."

Okay, Ravi is legitimately impressed. This stuff is *spicy*. "Have some more," he suggests, pushing the dish over, a little fascinated. "Help yourself."

They're both cross-legged on the expansive king bed,

dishes of food Ravi more or less randomly picked off the room service menu scattered around them on the duvet. He feels a little like one of his tutors is going to walk in any minute and scold him for eating on the bed.

"Here, my dear, want some yakitori?"

"Sure." He grabs a skewer. They share food, offering tidbits to each other and drinking Moscato: the "something sweet" Cayenne had requested. Ravi also ordered a couple of desserts for good measure. He doesn't have much of a sweet tooth, but Cayenne does.

Cayenne is already on their second glass of Moscato while Ravi is still working on the first. "You keep doing that," they tell him, after savoring a sip. "That thing where your forehead gets that *adorable* little crease in the middle, my dear. You're going to give your perfect face wrinkles if you keep it up."

Ravi rubs his forehead with the back of his hand. "Am I?"

"Mm. Is something troubling you, my sexy samosa?" Cayenne punctuates their question by plucking up a literal veggie samosa in their chopsticks and nibbling off the crisp end with a suggestive smile. It's silly and cute and Ravi tries not to break into a foolish smile.

"I guess I'm still wondering how the warding glyph got destroyed."

Cayenne shrugs. "It could have been an accident. Does it matter now? The beast is dead, so even if someone wanted to draw it in, or whatever the plan was, they are out of luck now, aren't they?"

"Yeah." Ravi frowns. "I suppose."

"So!" Cayenne says brightly, and Ravi is struck by a pang of guilt. He doesn't know how to relax, is the problem. Always expecting danger, always prepared for an attack. He's grateful when Cayenne changes the subject, swinging the conversation easily away from monster stuff. "You weren't tempted by Uwe's offer? Not even a little?"

Ravi watches them carefully, but they seem to be utterly at ease with whatever the answer might be. "Not really," he answers. "Were you?"

Cayenne shrugs breezily, clearing off a swatch of the bed to lounge on their back. They hold their wineglass at a precarious angle off the edge of the bed, centimeters away from spilling. "Not particularly, but if *you* were game, I would have been happy to oblige you, darling. It's meant to be *your* vacation, a little escape from the world. And if you want to enjoy a threesome on your vacation, I have no objections."

Ravi glances away. He takes a breath, then starts gathering up dishes. "You done with these?"

"*Oui, chéri.*"

He busies himself carting leftovers to the fridge. It takes a couple of trips; he ordered a lot. A fight like he's been in today always leaves him feeling he could eat a horse.

When he returns to the bed Cayenne frowns at him. "You have that wrinkle again. Where did you go just now?"

Ravi sits back against the headboard, puzzled. "To the fridge?"

Cayenne rolls their green eyes and *tsk*s. They clamber over to Ravi, barely keeping their wine in its glass. They plop their fiery head in his lap, looking at him upside down. "So literal." They reach up and tap him between the eyes. "Where did you go *here*." Their hand falls to rest atop Ravi's thigh and squeezes gently. "Is it about the threesome thing?"

Ravi sighs, letting his head knock back against the headboard before answering. "It would take me a long time to be comfortable with something like that."

Cayenne makes a dismissive sound. "Ah, it was only an idle thought from an unrepentant slut, darling. It is forgotten."

Ravi smiles, sliding his fingers into their hair and stroking gently. Cayenne hums with pleasure and shuts their eyes, looking for all the world like a pampered housecat.

"I actually did have a boyfriend once," he ventures. One of Cayenne's eyes pops open.

"Is that *so*?" They stretch the words out as if this is very juicy gossip they can't wait to hear. "Now this, I did not know."

"You didn't?"

Cayenne gives him a look. "I'm a time traveler, sweet thing, not psychic."

So, there *are* things about him that are still secret. That's comforting to know.

"I thought I'd give it a try. It was the first time I wasn't being watched by my family. Well, not true. I didn't hear from them for a few months when I was training in Israel. But it's harder now in Atlanta, than it was in London."

"Ah," Cayenne says, "London. That's why the night-club?"

"Yeah, that's why. We only dated for four months. And only two of them were any good," he adds with a short laugh, still carding his fingers through Cayenne's hair, admiring the coppery sheen. "Near the end, he kept asking me to try a three-way with his friend. Turns out he just wanted to start dating that guy instead. So."

"What a complete and utter asshole."

A surprised laugh slips out of Ravi at Cayenne's intensity. "Nah. Luke was an okay guy. I put him in a tough position. He was an intelligence agent, so we had reasons to meet up every so often. But he wanted us to see each other more. Coffee, movies. Going out with groups of friends. Normal people stuff."

"Normal people stuff," Cayenne repeats with vitriol, picking up their head to take a big swig of Moscato. Ravi snags the bottle from the nightstand and offers to top up their glass.

"Yeah," he says as he pours. "Normal people stuff. I tried. But you know. Couldn't hack it." He decides to pour himself another glass too. Why not. At first, it was too sweet for his palate, but it's growing on him. "He was out, and I was essentially asking him to go back in."

Cayenne blinks up curiously. "In? In what?"

"Oh, you know." Ravi looks away, heart skipping a beat. "The closet."

"Ah, of course." Cayenne bites their lip so hard they are surely going to leave a mark. Then they blink with surprise. "Wait. You say he was an agent in The Trust?"

"Yeah, an intel agent. I'm field."

"Yes, but...he was out and The Trust knew?"

It takes a second before Ravi understands the question.

"Oh! Ha. Yeah. Agents and independent contractors are free to live their personal lives however they choose. Barring fraternization with known evil entities, of course. They're—*we're* not a prejudiced organization. We combat supernatural threats all over the world. It's...it's just family stuff, with me." And Chosen stuff and Abhiramnew stuff and tradition stuff and Indian stuff and bloodline and legacy stuff, but Ravi is absolutely not going to whine to Cayenne about *any* of that. "I made him sneak around. It wasn't fair to him. It was hard for him to lie about something like that."

Cayenne pushes up and spins around, nearly straddling Ravi's thighs. "Ravi, I could not give less of a *flying fuck* about whatever-his-name-was; was it hard for *you*?" Their voice crackles slightly at the edges like a lit firework.

It's...a big question. Every time Ravi tries to grab an edge of an answer, the sheer scope of it is too much, and he can't manage to wrangle any words together. They just fall uselessly from his grasp.

So instead, he says, "In Chennai, fucking a guy was one thing. That's easy. As long as you're *careful*; blackmailers still do a very brisk business there. I had to pick men I knew were going to be safe. That's why I usually stuck with older guys. But anything more than a sneaky fuck or two was out of the question." He licks his lips, which have gone dry. "I thought maybe when I left, I'd have a chance for something different. But no matter where I go, I take it with me."

Cayenne presses their lips to his, slowly and sweetly. "You aren't the problem, dearest. I promise you that."

Ravi shivers a little, at that. "You know," he says softly,

"you can tell me things if you want to."

Cayenne goes stiff in his arms. "Like what?" they ask warily.

"I don't know. Nothing in particular. Anything you like. I like to listen to you talk. Fortunately," he mutters playfully, intending to be heard, trying to set them at ease.

Cayenne obligingly laughs and slaps his shoulder. "Are you saying I talk too much?"

"I'm saying you have a nice voice, and I like to hear it."

Cayenne goes quiet, biting their lip with pleasure. Then they lean back, taking another long drink. That's the third glass almost gone. "I don't think I've heard enough about your romantic exploits."

"Such as they are," Ravi drawls wryly.

"So, this asshole Luke wasn't the first guy you were with, no? *Mon Dieu, please* tell me he wasn't, that would be simply *trop de tragique* for me to handle."

"He wasn't."

"Good. So, there were other men?"

"Yeah." This is starting to feel like an interrogation. "You going to tell me about any of *your* exes?"

Cayenne's tone goes light and teasing. "I *might* paint you a picture with very broad strokes. But I did ask first, *mon beau*. No women at all for you?"

"No. Not all of us are made as lucky as you. Why all the

questions today?"

Cayenne's expression is clearly a mask of carelessness worn over something else, but Ravi can't figure out over what, and doesn't want to pry. He'll take whatever Cayenne is willing to give. They shrug and drink their wine. "You're interesting." They slide off his lap and sit next to him.

"Hmm." Doubtful. Ravi takes another sip. No way he's going to be able to catch up to Cayenne, but it won't hurt to start building up his tolerance if he's going to be doing this kind of thing more often. "I suppose you do something with your tattoo to avoid hangovers?"

"Who's worried about hangovers, darling? I've hardly had *one* little bottle. Are you worried you won't be able to rise with the sun and carry water pails up mountains, or whatever you do?"

Ravi laughs. "I'm sorry, is my morning routine somehow bothering you?"

"Well," Cayenne murmurs into their wine. "It might be nice if you stuck around a *little* bit. I don't get many opportunities to give snuggling a try. One never knows, I might even like it."

"Oh." Ravi considers that unexpectedly sweet sentiment. And yeah, that...that sounds nice. "I could give it a try. I guess it's mostly that I'm used to making myself scarce, afterward."

"*Darling.*" Cayenne casts him a sultry look, lids low-ered, voice gone smokey at the edges. "Who would *possibly* want to kick *you* out of bed?"

"Well," he explains, "I usually had to leave before their wife came home."

After a pause, Cayenne pinches the bridge of their nose, and their foot starts bouncing from where it's draped over the opposite knee as if they were overflowing with nervous energy with nowhere to channel it.

"I suppose that will teach me," they mutter. "This is what asking questions gets me. *Putain l'enfer,*" they swear, accent thickening considerably. "Give me the rest of that bottle, sweetheart." Obligingly Ravi passes it over, a little surprised and amused when Cayenne starts drinking straight from it.

"This is nice," Ravi says, putting a hand on Cayenne's leg, tracing small strokes with his thumb.

"It *is*?" Cayenne asks incredulously.

"Yeah, I think so." He smiles. "Let's do this tomorrow."

"Do what, exactly?"

Ravi gestures around the room, at the two of them sit-ting side by side. "Just...this. Stay in, eat leftovers. Talk. Watch a movie. Not worrying about monsters or anything else. Like normal people."

Cayenne looks at him keenly for a long moment, then

their face softens in a genuine smile. "Like normal people."
They snuggle in alongside Ravi, wine bottle tucked up by
their legs. Ravi moves his arm around their shoulders, and
they rest their heads together. "Okay."

They gaze out at the view, sunset fading to blue.

Chapter Seventeen

THEY DOZE A bit, the events of the day finally settling in on them both like a heavy blanket. After a couple of hours Ravi wakes with a start, twitching for his gun. Cayenne makes a little muffled sound of sleepy protest, and he remembers there's *supposed* to be a warm body next to him.

He stretches down to his toes while looking over at Cayenne. In repose they look as beautiful as they ever do. In slumber their features are soft, relaxed, without the usual artifice and flirtation, like a mask fallen away and something else revealed underneath. He realizes with chagrin that he's already spent way more than his fair share of time watching Cayenne sleep on the plane and hopes it's not becoming a creepy habit.

Then their eyes flicker open, flashing that shocking, otherworldly green. He briefly wonders what Lucy had been thinking of when she designed them for Cayenne. Emeralds? Grass-covered hills? Sunlight shining through leaves?

Cayenne yawns, covering the pink of their mouth with the back of their tattooed hand. They smile and it pins him in place like it always does. "See, this *is* nice. I thought it might be. Don't you feel deliciously decadent, skipping your little exercises?" They stretch languidly over him, layering their hands on his chest and propping their chin atop them.

Ravi touches their cheek fondly. "It's only been a few hours, Cay."

Cayenne's eyes flutter a bit, then they tilt their head back to check the windows. "That's so odd. I feel quite rested, considering the *harrowing* day we've had." They drop their face into Ravi's chest and nuzzle there, like a cat rubbing its scent. A warmth spreads under Ravi's skin; not lust but a slow, comfortable glow, like drinking hot coffee on a cold morning. He closes his arms around Cayenne, wishing he was the kind of person who could get used to this.

"Me too. I think we slept about four hours. That's a

pretty good nap."

"I've never taken a nap with anyone before. If you're not counting post-coital passing out as a nap, that is."

"Hm. Hard to say where the line is, there."

"I suppose that's true enough." Cayenne drops a quick kiss to the middle of his chest and hops up to their feet. "Well! I'm feeling quite *energetic*. Fancy a midnight visit to the pier? Now we know for sure that the water is safe, I think I'd like to *enjoy* the moonlight."

Ravi sits up at the edge of the bed, running a hand through his hair. "You want to go right now?"

"I like the ocean considerably more at night. The beastly sun isn't glaring up from it and trying to give me skin cancer." They pout, and Ravi chuckles.

"Sure, why not. Might take a swim too."

Cayenne grins at him, arms akimbo. "That's the spirit! It's good to see you embracing some spontaneity, hero. Shall we enjoy our swim *au naturel*?" Their smile takes on a sly edge.

Shaking his head, Ravi laughs. "No."

With a dramatic flourish Cayenne drapes themself across Ravi's lap, like a swooning heroine from a Harlequin romance. "Why ever not, you cruel man? It's the middle of the night, we will have the dock *all* to ourselves." They peck a kiss to his chin, the bridge of his nose, his eyebrow, "I ask for so little" — their voice breaks audibly around a suppressed laugh — "and all I want is for you to *enjoy* yourself, and also to get you naked in public. Is that *such* a terrible — "

"Okay, okay!" Ravi laughs so hard his shoulders shake. He tries to contain a lapful of squirming, flailing redhead from dragging them both off the bed. "*Thik hai*, fine. Once we're in the water, *maybe* I'll consider it."

"I'll take it," Cayenne says pluckily, sneaking a kiss to the tip of Ravi's nose.

*

IT'S A PERFECT night for night swimming; the moon nearly full, lambently glinting off the water in shifting patterns. The rounded pier at the end of the shared dock is one of several jutting out from the land in irregular spokes, giving each bungalow an unimpeded view of the ocean. There are three bungalows to a dock, but the third one adjacent to theirs had been vacated that day, so the pair have the entire pier all to themselves.

It is, he has to admit, a pretty romantic atmosphere. All railings and pergolas have been strung with solar fairy lights, now pleasantly dimmed at this late hour. Cayenne and Ravi walk arm in arm to the edge, an open space for divers and swimmers. Ravi glances around nervously.

"Why someone who looks like *you* should be so modest absolutely boggles the mind, darling." Cayenne settles at the edge, long pale legs dangling in the water. They pat the dock next to them, inviting Ravi to sit with them. "No one is here, sweet thing."

Ravi looks around once more to confirm Cayenne's assurance before folding cross-legged beside them. "You're a bad influence."

"Oh, *sweetheart*, you're just now figuring that out?" Cayenne says with their fox-sly grin, leaning in. Ravi moves in for a kiss when Cayenne jumps, jerking their feet out of the water. "*Aïe!*"

Ravi's every muscle is instantly tense. "What? You okay?" His hand flies to the small of Cayenne's back and he looks them over.

Cayenne pouts, rubbing their leg with an irritated whine. "Something bit me!" They crane their neck to look over the pier's edge into the dark water. They raise their left hand, tattoo up, and lay their fingers on it. "Ouch. I'm just going to skip back a teensy little bit, my dear. You don't mind, do you?"

Ravi huffs with disbelief. "For this? Do you avoid mosquito bites like this too?"

Well, *mais oui*, darling, I hate being itchy." They flash him a grin. It falters at the edges before falling completely.

"Actually," they say, swaying into Ravi's side, "I feel a little strange."

In a blink Ravi is on his feet, pulling Cayenne up with him. Cayenne staggers, blinking heavily, letting Ravi drag them away from the edge. "Cayenne, let me see that bite." But he doesn't really need to. Instincts triggered, senses thrumming, a surge of adrenaline keeps Ravi sharp and alert. He hears the lap of the waves under the dock. Feels the soft breeze. Smells the salt of the air mingled with Cayenne's spicy cologne.

"I'm, ah. I'm feeling pretty dizzy here," they mumble against his chest. Ravi's eyes dart, looking intently for any movement or shadows, perhaps a tentacle slithering up from the water. The faint glow of the solar lights illuminates the two of them far better than it does the darkened ocean, leaving them exposed in the open. A bad spot to be caught in for an attack.

"It's okay," he tells Cayenne, pitching his tone low and soothing. "We're going to stay away from the edge, and get you back to the bungalow, okay?" He starts inching them back toward the narrow entry dock but pauses. No safer there than here, surrounded on either side by water. *Fuck.* He looks around for anything he could use as a weapon. Nothing. Still no sign from the water, no movement, no sound other than the gentle lapping of waves. But the tiny hairs of his neck are each standing on end. He knows with a bone-deep certainty that they are being watched.

"Okay," Cayenne says agreeably, grabbing onto Ravi's tank for balance. "Ravi?"

"I'm here." He chafes their arms, foolishly, as if they were cold instead of drugged.

"I can't shift. I can't rewind like this, I'm…" They swallow heavily, and in the clear moonlight their skin is so pale it's nearly blue. "*Qu'est-ce qui se passe?* Is the thing not…not dead?" Dazed, they blink in confusion.

"I just need you to walk with me, Cayenne. Can you do that?" There's no other option but to move. All he's got to do is keep Cayenne safe, to get them somewhere defensible. He can do this. He's *good* at this.

"*Je peux marcher, ravageur,*" Cayenne says, sounding annoyed. They push away from him, trying to stand on their own.

The hairs on the back of Ravi's neck rise anew and he spins around, keeping Cayenne behind him. To his surprise there's nothing there. Then he hears it.

A slow, deliberate scrape, underneath the dock, near the edge. The scrape is joined by another, then another, the unhurried drag of fingernails on wood. And Ravi realizes he's made a costly mistake.

Ravi whirls around and grabs Cayenne's face between

his hands. "Cay. Can you walk on your own? Can you make it back to the bungalow?"

Cayenne blinks up at him, and Ravi hates the fear there. It doesn't belong there, on that face made for smiles and sidelong glances. "I think so," Cayenne whispers, and Ravi wants to kiss them just for that, the bravery in it.

"I need you to go get my gun. From my bag. Can you do that?"

"I can try," they say in a small voice.

"I *know* you can do this." He presses a quick, fervent kiss to their forehead and pushes them toward the bungalows, setting their hands on the railing for support. They stumble a little, usually the picture of grace, and mutter something in an unfamiliar language. But they manage it, step by step.

Then Ravi, setting his bare feet down loud and deliberate with each step, hopefully drawing attention away from Cayenne, strides back over to the edge of the pier, hands gathered into loose fists, thumbs out.

"Hey!" He shouts over the water. He waits, ears pricked for any hints. "Come and fucking get some."

It's *fast*. He expects the strike to come up from the edge, but at the last instant feels the disturbance in the air and spins on his heel a half-turn to the side. The blow whips past where his head had been a split second before. Ravi grabs the arm, one hand at the wrist and one at the elbow, and twists while shoving forward. A brutally efficient move. A human arm would have easily snapped.

Instead, there's a laugh, and the attacker steps back out of his range. Uwe, black hair dripping, wearing the same wrap pants he had when they first met, shirtless and barefoot. His hands are elongated strangely, nails sharp talons. He holds himself easily, loose-limbed, swaying minutely in place like a mongoose. He smiles, watching Ravi raise his arms and step back into a defensive stance.

"Are not you a *meal*," Uwe says with delight, that strange accent heightened by a new predatory rasp. "You know, I thought you might be a hunter when I first saw you. Live as long as I have, and you get a knack for picking them out of a crowd. You all have that same stink; desperate for approval, so eager to be heroes."

Ravi flicks his eyes quickly to the side, checking to see how far Cayenne has gone. Out of view. Good. Hopefully staying out of Uwe's attention.

"Then I saw you laying down the wards, and I knew for sure. I owe you my gratitude, by the way." Uwe cuts a mocking little bow. "For killing the Warden. Those pesky little killjoys are forever trying to drag my kin back through the Veil."

The two slowly circle one another, Ravi's eyes

snapping to Uwe's shoulders, the feet, and eyes. All the while his mind races; the fight with the ray had been over quickly, and it had only attacked Ravi when it couldn't avoid him. It had wanted Uwe with a singular focus he had *fucking* missed. And he realizes, wanting to kick himself, he hadn't seen a mouth anywhere on it.

"Don't worry," Uwe says pleasantly, "it doesn't have to be painful." And grins, too widely for a human mouth, and inside is all needle teeth and blackness.

"What are you?" Ravi demands. How long would Cayenne be? Were they okay? What if they passed out, were alone and exposed? He forcibly drags his focus back to the present moment, *keep your shit together, kid*. Good thing Uwe is a talker; it'll buy Cayenne more time.

Uwe's feral grin widens horribly. "You do not know a nix when you see one? Some hunter you are. You are a bit dim without your pretty little matchstick, hmm?" The nix chuckles darkly. "I thought that might be the case. I do not think he is coming back, Ravi the hunter. One little bite is not much venom, but it is just enough to keep him confused, enough to keep him from giving you all those clever little clues. What a boon he was to you on the beach, yes?"

"They," Ravi growls, sliding back on the ball of his foot. Uwe's stance steadily changes, little hints of an incoming attack. He tries desperately to remember what Nate had said about nix from the long list of possible foes, but all he can think about is Cayenne giving him bedroom eyes while Nate's voice was in his ear, distracting him from the call.

The nix ignores him. "You have no idea how maddening it has been, just getting a little taste and then having that blasted Warden interrupt me *every* time. I have been kept from my meal for *days* now, so I am very, *very* hungry."

It lunges forward, a flash in the moonlight, and Ravi is ready for it.

He turns away one swipe with a palm, sidesteps a gouging claw to the throat, deflects a blow to his femoral artery with his forearm. He is about to go on the offensive before he catches the goading look in the nix's eyes and realizes with alarm that he's only being tested. This thing is stronger and faster than he is, and it's baiting him.

Uwe makes a few more lightning quick jabs, getting a feel for Ravi's defenses, seeking weaknesses. Finally, they break apart, Ravi taking deep, centering breaths and keeping his stance low and guarded.

"Well, are not you a hearty one. I am going to enjoy you. Why the Courts even care if a few of you humans go missing is beyond me. There are millions of you. We are not supposed to cross over to feed anymore, but you are *so* tasty. Well worth the trip." It springs suddenly forward. Ravi spins left under its arm, ducking low and striking a hard blow to the kidney, if this thing has a kidney. The nix staggers forward in surprise, then turns about with a laugh. "Especially the two of you, oh, I am going to keep you alive in your room for *days*, such a feast I shall have. You smell just filled to the *brim* with life. You will not even notice it is gone. Not at first."

This time it's ready for his sidestep. It feints back, drawing him in close enough to slash its claws across his shoulder. Ravi hisses through the bloom of pain, then ignores it, hopping back on the balls of his feet, keeping his distance. He runs through the mental catalogue of his myriad martial arts, calculating his disadvantages. Too many.

"Little hunter. This would have been easier if you would have taken me home with you earlier. You might not have even noticed— Just a blissful sleep. But I can make up for lost time." Uwe crouches low and leaps like a wolf. He catches Ravi in the gut. They both go tumbling back across the deck and smash into the railing with a loud crack.

Ravi erupts into a flurry of jabs, focusing on pressure points and vulnerable spots while fending off Uwe's teeth. Hissing and snarling, the nix is now wholly dedicated to getting its razor teeth into him, and every ounce of focus Ravi possesses is bent on preventing it. He manages to land a lucky blow on the nix's jaw. While it blinks back, he swings around over it, knees on its chest. He grabs it by its long hair and smashes its head into the dock as hard as he can. He gets three slams in before Uwe kicks him off.

The nix staggers to its feet, chuckling through bloody needle teeth. "Someone taught you well, human."

This fucking thing talks too much. He closes the distance in a rush, catching it by surprise, but instead of launching into the attack it expects, he simply heaves it into the water with a splash. Instantly he spins around and sprints for the dock, hoping he's bought a few seconds to get to the bungalow and find Cayenne.

But Cayenne is there, dragging the duffel bag behind them. Legs shaky, the whites of their eyes startlingly glassy, but they're here. Ravi grabs their arms and pulls them into the middle of the pier, the point furthest from the water.

Cayenne stumbles and falls to their knees, muttering words in a jumble of languages. Ravi keeps his head on a swivel, expecting another attack any second, but kneels to join Cayenne. They shake their head as if to clear it and switch to English. "M'sorry, I couldn't find it, so I brought the whole thing... I couldn't..."

"It's okay, Cay," he says, pressing a hasty kiss to their temple. "You did good." He digs through his duffel and grabs his gun, immediately feeling more confident. His mother had always said that guns were a coward's weapon, but Ravi can live with that if it means he can keep them both safe.

Uwe's voice rises from below the dock. Ravi jumps to his feet, finger poised beside the trigger. "Oh, here is your little matchstick! What a shame he can't help you."

Ravi readies his aim. "Come on up, Uwe. We've reconsidered your offer."

A gurgling laugh rings out near the edge of the pier. Moving lightly, quietly, Ravi edges forward on his toes, ready for an attack.

But instead of a body, a splash of seawater is raked up directly into his eyes, the nix still tucked safely underneath the dock. Ravi swears, blinking furiously, eyes stinging. He immediately backs up from the edge, but a set of claws whip up and grab his ankle, yanking him forward. Luckily his backward step causes his balance to shift back rather than forward, or he would have gone straight into the depths. Slim chance he would have made it out of there again.

He lands flat on his back, skull smacking the boards. Stars burst behind his eyes, and he feels the thump of feet next to him, water dripping onto him. On instinct he rolls away, catching a graze across the ribs that he fervently hopes is from claws and not poisoned teeth. He scrambles to his feet and brings up the gun, his vision not yet cleared.

The nix rushes on him just as he can see again, too fucking close for a shot. It barrels sideways into his arm, wrenches the gun from his grasp with inhuman strength, and flings it into the ocean.

Ravi growls in frustration, driving the heel of his hand hard up into the nix's face. Cartilage cracks and it reels back, no longer grinning but snarling, eyes narrowed in fury.

Then Cayenne swings the duffel bag into the side of the nix's head with all their might. The nix staggers back, hissing. Ravi's things scatter over the dock, the bag falling mostly empty beside Cayenne.

"I'm *not* a matchstick," Cayenne yells, their French accent incredibly thick, "I am a *monsoon*!"

Ravi takes the opportunity to step next to Cayenne, a united front. Cayenne leans into him for just a moment, their body moving into an unfamiliar fighting stance.

The nix shakes off the blow and smiles. "I am impressed by your spirit, little humans. You know, I could take you back with me to Faerie," it offers with a needle-sharp smile, tone seductive. "Two pretty things like you, I would take *such* good care of you. I would only eat a little bit at a time, and the things I could show you! I promise you will not even miss it here."

As it speaks, Ravi keeps one eye on it while crouching down to his duffel. He dips a hand into an inner pocket and pulls out one long, hand-forged iron nail.

I'm going to owe Constance an apology. He rises up and

throws himself at the nix like an arrow from a bow, putting himself in striking range. He swings an empty-handed feint at its ribs. It steps back, then curls toward him with teeth bared. Ravi slams his other fist, nail out, right into its eye.

The nix reels back with a horrific screech, clawing at its eye. Following up with a roundhouse kick to the face, Ravi drives the nail deep enough to bury it there completely. The scream is abruptly sliced short, and the nix drops like a puppet with its strings cut.

Heart pounding, Ravi watches carefully, bouncing on his feet, until he's sure that it's dead. The nix's body begins to dissolve with a sickening hiss, like the Warden's had.

The second he's certain it's down, Ravi goes to Cayenne, joining them where they've fallen to their knees. He slides a hand over the back of their neck. "It's dead. You okay?"

Cayenne nods, pulling Ravi close enough to lean their foreheads together. They stay like that for a long moment, breath heaving. "Ça va?" Cayenne rasps. "You're all right?"

"Yeah, I'm all right."

"I...I couldn't *do* anything, I—"

Ravi shushes them, pulling them into a hug, ignoring the sting of his shoulder. "You did plenty. You did *great*. You're a fucking monsoon, Cay."

Cayenne pulls back and gives him a weak smile. Their

pupils are enormous, only a thin line of green left. "Did you notice…I was dressed like one. *J'étais,* I was…at the club?"

Ravi grins. "Is *that* what that outfit was?"

Cayenne folds onto his lap, shivering. "You inspired me."

Ravi pats their shoulder and pulls them to their feet. "Here, let's get you back. Can you hang on to the railing for a minute?"

Abruptly, Cayenne's face twists like they've bitten into a nettle. "I can do whatever the fuck I want to do, thank you very much, you errand boy." Cayenne sniffs haughtily, mood swinging wildly. Or maybe hallucinating, no way for Ravi to be sure.

"I'll only be a minute." He makes sure Cayenne is propped up against the wooden post of the pergola before gathering up as many of his things as he can and shoving them back in the bag. He looks mournfully over the edge at where his gun disappeared, and sighs. It's going to be hell to requisition another one.

The nix has been reduced to a filmy sludge across the boards, one long black nail sticking up from the mess. Ravi leaves it there.

He throws Cayenne's arm over his shoulder to lead them back to the bungalow.

"Ooh," murmurs Cayenne, "why, 'allo, handsome.

Where are we going?"

"C'mon."

*

BY THE TIME they get back to the bungalow, Cayenne seems a little more present. Ravi eases them down onto the couch and throws his bag in the corner before heading to the bathroom. Complete first-aid kits thankfully come standard in all these beachside hotels. He finds it under the sink and when he comes back out, Cayenne is folded over, resting their head on their knees.

Ravi grabs the ottoman and drags it over in front of them. He plops down and unzips the kit. "Give me your foot."

Cayenne groans in protest. "*Non.*"

Ravi sighs. "C'mon, don't be a brat." Cayenne pouts and swings their foot up into Ravi's lap. They sink back into the couch cushions, eyes closed. "Thank you." He gives the bite a thorough inspection. The tooth marks are small and crowded together, not bleeding. The skin around the bite seems normal, no swelling or redness. He does his best with some antibiotic ointment and an extra-large bandage. Constance would know better. She'd likely have five different ways to heal this with leaves and moss she found in her pockets.

Fuck, Constance *did* know better. Without the nails, he would have lost that fight.

Cayenne rouses a little, blinking and looking at him. "You are thinking *very* loudly, my dear."

"I thought you said you weren't psychic." Ravi strokes a thumb over the arch of Cayenne's foot before lowering it to the ground. "Are you hurt anywhere else?"

Cayenne gives themself a once-over. "I...do not think so. And I do not feel so...out of it. Still dizzy. I'm not sure *when* I am?"

"It's June 2016. You're in the Seychelles."

"Yes, yes, I know that," Cayenne says flippantly, but their shoulders relax a fraction. Then they sit up straight, eyes wide. "You're bleeding!"

Ravi takes inventory. Grazed knuckles, a pair of shallow lacerations on his ribs. The worst is a series of jagged rakes to his shoulder, bleeding lazily. Two of his fingernails split from smashing that thing's head into the dock. He feels a multitude of what will soon become bruises, but apart from that he is relatively unscathed. Not bad; he's come away with worse tangling with foes with the rest of the team.

"I got very lucky," he tells Cayenne.

"I don't feel lucky from where I am," Cayenne grouses.

"Yeah, well." Ravi shakes his head, jaw tense. He tears

open an alcohol wipe and starts cleaning out the gashes on his shoulder, the sting helping to keep him focused. "That nix thing tricked us. Uwe maneuvered us so we'd kill his enemy for him. He drew in the ray where he knew we'd be, made a big show over being helpless. He bit his own arm to sell the story, and I *knew* he didn't look affected. I just didn't fucking think." He opens a new wipe and uses it to pick splinters out of his knuckles. "Harry would have figured it out right away. Nate would likely have known what the nix was as soon as he saw it. There were probably all sorts of clues I missed. Constance could have used magic to *talk* to that Warden thing, which was only trying to keep the nix from eating people, and *I killed it*. Val could have smashed Uwe in two seconds, and this whole thing would have gone down much differently."

Cayenne leans forward and flicks Ravi right between the eyes.

"Ow!" Ravi leans back, rubbing the spot. "What was that for?"

Cayenne grabs the first-aid kit with one hand and yanks Ravi onto the couch with the other. They straddle his hips, a little unsteadily, unrolling a handful of gauze. "That was for being an idiot." They grasp his chin in their hand, staring him straight in the eye. "*You did a good job.*" They let go and start wrapping his shoulder. "*Bordel de merde.*

Whoever raised you really did a number on *you*."

Ravi can't really muster up anything to say to that, so he lets Cayenne tend to him.

It takes a few minutes to finish. Afterwards Cayenne curls into him, shivering. Ravi holds them, concerned. "Should we get you to a…" He stops, feeling foolish.

"A hospital?" Cayenne laughs once, harshly. "I shall be fine. I'm just…I just can't *shift* like this." They shiver again, and when they raise their head Ravi can see the slightest sheen of unshed tears. "You can't know what it's like. It's like…you know those butterflies, the ones they pin down and put in a frame?"

"Yeah," says Ravi softly. "I know the ones."

"What if something happens," they breathe whisper-quiet against Ravi's neck. "What if something happens and I can't do anything, if I'm *helpless*, I *can't*—"

"I've got you." Ravi strokes their hair in what he hopes is a comforting manner. "Cayenne. I'm here. Nothing's going to happen to you, okay?" Cayenne sniffs. "Let's move to the bed. Hang on." Cayenne grunts and wraps their arms around his neck. It's a little awkward, a strain on his shoulder, but he heaves them both up. He wraps Cayenne's legs around his waist and carries them over to the bed. He sets Cayenne down with care, and they startle and look around wildly when their back hits the sheets.

"When is it?" they ask, a little frantic.

"It's June 2016. You're in the Seychelles." He keeps his voice mellow and reassuring.

"Ah, yes. Your vacation." Cayenne smiles, hair fanning over the pillow. Ravi eases in next to them, suddenly exhausted and shaky as the last of the adrenaline leaves his system.

"Did you kill a monster with a pen? Or did I hallucinate that?"

Ravi smiles weakly. "Ha, well. An iron nail. Lucky stab."

Cayenne's pupils are blown wide with the venom, skin still icy pale. "That is *unbelievably* hot." They grin, trembling at the edges, but it's still a relief to see it there. "I am absolutely going to give you the world's best blowjob."

Ravi's ears go hot. "You should probably get some rest." Cayenne squirms close, laying their head on his chest. Ravi wraps his arm around them and tugs them in tight.

"I thought you got all hot and bothered after a fight?"

"Yeah, sometimes, if the conditions are right," he laughs, "but right now I'm kind of focused on something else."

"Oh? *Quoi?*"

"Making sure you feel safe."

The silence stretches on so long that Ravi assumes

Cayenne has fallen asleep. Then Cayenne tilts their head up, eyes *haunted*.

"I'm…I'm not a good person, Ravi." Something in their tone sends a chill through him.

He shakes his head, frowning. "Cayenne, don't—"

"I have something I need to tell you."

"*Don't.* You're drugged. You…you shouldn't tell me anything right now that you wouldn't otherwise."

Cayenne growls and bangs their head against Ravi's collarbone. "You are so frustratingly noble. I could just scream, I really could."

"I wish you'd stop saying that. I'm really not. Just…please, Cay. Get some sleep." He slips a finger under their chin, tilts their face up, and gives them a hard kiss. He doesn't move from it until he feels Cayenne's tension unspool, finally easing into a comfortable drape over him. He places one hand on their head and the other on their back and strokes gently. "I've got you."

Chapter Eighteen

DAWN LIGHT SPILLS into the room, stretching in ribbons across the floor and over the overturned mess of the sheets, making Cayenne's skin glow golden. Ravi brushes a lock of hair away from their forehead, trying not to stir them from their sprawled slumber across his chest.

"Mm," Cayenne murmurs, evidently awake. "That feels nice."

He presses a kiss to their forehead. "I didn't wake you?"

"No." They nestle themself impossibly closer within the circle of Ravi's arms. "Can't you sleep in, sweet thing? I could sing you a lullaby," they tease, with a soft nuzzle to the underside of Ravi's jaw.

He cranes his neck to give Cayenne better access, still stroking through their hair. "How do you feel?"

"Hmm. Let's see." They sit up just enough to start ticking off points on their fingers, nail polish starting to chip. "I'm not dizzy, *grâce à Dieu*. I woke up a little bit ago and was able to rewind with no trouble—just a minute or two, darling, relax—that stupid bite on my ankle *still* hurts, I am *very* annoyed that I didn't get to properly appreciate you kicking a monster in the face to death, and even *more* annoyed that our *entire* getaway has been overshadowed by supernatural faerie monster *bullshit*—honestly, I could scream." They spread their hands and smile beatifically. "Aside from that, I feel fine."

"Good," Ravi says. "I know it was scary for you."

Cayenne gives him a reproachful look. "Here I am, trying my best to keep things trivial and entertaining, and you just have to go and be oh-so-serious, don't you?"

One corner of his mouth curls up, involuntarily. "Sorry. It's a habit."

Cayenne sighs, running their hands lightly over his shoulder. "And you? Feeling worse for wear, *mon grande*?"

"Little sore, little bruised. I'm fine. Don't even think I'll get an interesting scar out of it."

Cayenne laughs. "A true shame." They pick up one of

his hands and turn it over, the torn skin already scabbing over. Cayenne presses a light, lingering kiss to the back of his knuckles. Ravi's heart skips in his chest at the mischievous look in their eyes. "So, if *hypothetically* speaking, I wanted to *thoroughly* ravish you, you are well enough for such a thing? I am *fairly* sure last night I promised you the world's best blowjob."

This time his heart completely flops over. "I, uh." He clears his throat, suddenly very dry. "I think so." Cayenne starts nibbling along his neck. "I'm fine. I've had worse from family sparring sessions."

Cayenne stops, sits up, and says crisply, "Your family sounds like utter shit."

Ravi laughs once, more of a soft bark than anything of amusement. "That's fair." Shadowing their eyes, Cayenne rubs the bridge of their nose briefly before burrowing back into Ravi's neck, lips teasing. "You never talk about *your* family," Ravi murmurs, low enough that Cayenne can pretend they don't hear him if they choose.

Cayenne's lips stop their slow crawl across his throat. A sigh sends warm breath brushing his skin. "Family. *C'est chiant*. The very concept is…extremely overrated." For a moment, the only sounds in the room are the distant lapping of the waves, the wind soughing through the palms.

Cayenne shakes their head, expression veiled. "Enough

of sad things, yes? We are here to *enjoy* ourselves, are we not?" They pull him into a hard, demanding kiss. It's an obvious bid to change the subject, but Ravi responds, nonetheless. "So...enjoy me, Ravi," they whisper breathily in his ear, punctuating it with a nibble of his earlobe.

They both have pasts they don't want to talk about. He wants to hear anything Cayenne wants to tell him—can't even deny that he's curious—but knows he has no right to pry. He'll take whatever scraps he can get. So, he lets Cayenne change the subject, lets the mood build and build like a growing electrical charge. They kiss for what feels like hours, until Cayenne is surely feeling the burn of his beard, face reddened. They rock their body against his, languid and unhurried, grinding into his thigh.

They trail a hand down from his throat, over his scars, his navel, detouring across the jut of his hip. When they drag the hand back up, they scrape with their fingernails, just on this side of too hard. Ravi hisses, goosebumps shivering up through him.

"Mm," Cayenne hums approvingly, "so *responsive*, my dear. I never have to wonder if you enjoy what I'm doing to you. Fortunate, since you're such a quiet thing in bed, aren't you?"

Ravi's face blazes hot. "Complaints?"

Cayenne's laugh buzzes against Ravi's chest, where

they nibble lightly at the swell of his pectorals. "I can talk enough for the both of us, you *sweet* shy thing, you." Their wandering hand cups his testicles, rolling them gently. Ravi nearly jerks off the bed, his pulse a sudden whoosh in his ears as every drop of blood heads south. "See, look at that. Just one little touch and I've got you right where I want you." They sink their teeth into his nipple, then give it a soft flick of their tongue.

"Cay," Ravi breathes, begging for something, anything.

Cayenne looks up at him through their eyelashes, that shadowed sultry green. "Why don't you let me take care of you, for once, hmm?" They sink down, teasing kisses until they finally swallow him down with a pleased moan. Ravi tries taking long, even breaths, but each one gets caught in his lungs. His breath hitches on every stroke of Cayenne's slick tongue, leaving him oxygen-starved and light-headed.

Cayenne is both skilled—no real surprise, considering they could go back in time to practice any talent they please as many times as it takes to become an expert—and enthusiastic, which is what really turns Ravi's head. Every time Cayenne makes one of those little sounds of pleasure, or they grind their cock against his leg as if unable to help themself, he's driven wild with wanting for it to happen again.

He's so close when Cayenne slides off him with a gasp,

their face flushed and lips swollen as they grin up at him. "You're holding yourself so *tensely*, my dear beautiful boy. You're undoing all my hard work to relax you."

Ravi just pants, control hanging by a thread, hands fisted in the sheets. Cayenne slants a knowing brow, then untangles both of Ravi's hands from their desperate grip and guides them into their tousled ginger locks. Ravi gulps, fingers tightening of their own volition. Cayenne gives him a saucy wink, and licks a long, wet line from balls to tip.

"You can fuck my mouth, if you want," they say, lush lips brushing against sensitive skin.

Ravi bites his lip, unmoving.

Cayenne easily corrects, "*I* want you to. Can you do that for me, darling?"

Ravi exhales shakily and nods.

"Good boy," they whisper, tongue lapping at the head, tasting him with evident relish. Then they slide their lips over him and it's…

It might be the world's best blowjob.

Ravi comes hard enough that the cuts on his knuckles split open again, hands clenched tightly in Cayenne's hair. His entire body arches like a bow being drawn and fired. He slams his hips up so forcefully he's sure *this* time it's going to be too much for Cayenne, but they just keep effortlessly moving with him, groaning their enjoyment. When he finally comes back down to earth he'd swear he's turned to liquid, every muscle a puddle.

Cayenne pulls back, licking their lips with satisfaction. "You may hold your applause," they say, voice ruined, "until after Act II."

Ravi tries and fails to catch his breath, not following. "Huh?"

And Cayenne grins at him, bright and happy and genuine, and sends them both spinning back along the timestream, just far enough that Ravi is again caught right on the edge of ecstasy, at the point of no return, and this time he shouts with surprise as he comes down Cayenne's throat.

When he comes back to himself, he sits up, grabs Cayenne by the shoulders, and pulls them into a deep, biting kiss, sinking his teeth into their lower lip. Cayenne crawls into his lap, their thighs trapping his hips, hands scratching marks down his back.

"Fuck me," Ravi growls into their mouth.

Cayenne goes still, but their voice comes as easy and casual as ever. "Would you like me to?"

Ravi bites his lip and nods. He has to bury his face in Cayenne's neck, cheeks on fire, before he lifts his chin and says raggedly, "Yeah, I would. I like...I like both."

Cayenne makes a light, delighted sound. "What a

happy coincidence, *mon cher*, so do I! My tastes are, hmm, shall we say, varied and eclectic." They lean across him to snag supplies off the nightstand. "How would you like me, my sweet?"

Breath stumbling, Ravi swallows. "You pick."

"Ooh. I am absolutely paralyzed with *so* many ideas right now." They bite hard at his neck, and Ravi gasps through it, not caring if it will leave a mark. "While I would be thrilled to bend you over, say, the back of the couch, I think for this time I want to see your lovely face while I'm fucking you."

Ravi's stomach immediately swoops at the words, like he's missed a step on the stairs, falling hard before catching his footing. His spent dick gives a valiant twitch, and he bites his lip and nods.

"Aren't you *cute*." Cayenne beams and catches him in a sweet, wandering kiss. They ease Ravi back into a nest of pillows. He lets himself be maneuvered as they like, a pillow tucked under his hips and Cayenne's expressive artist hands smoothing his thighs wide, their eyes greedily traveling over him. Ravi fights against a blush, wishing the curtains were drawn to cut some of the illuminating sunlight; but then he wouldn't get the pleasure of seeing Cayenne kneeling there between his legs, the light shining through their hair and lining their skin like an illustration from a stained-glass window. *Fuck*, but they're unfairly beautiful. Even knowing it's manufactured doesn't help.

"You're a *picture* and no mistake, sweetheart," Cayenne croons, thoughts obviously in line with his own. "I can hardly wait to have you." Ravi has to cover his eyes with an arm, embarrassment prickling over him, and he mumbles a protest that Cayenne ignores. "Let me just... *There* we go. How's that, pet?"

As Cayenne's slick slender fingers move inside him, spreading and stroking, he nods and breathes carefully through it; it's been a while since he let someone do this for him.

For once Cayenne has fallen utterly silent, so Ravi moves his arm and looks up. Cayenne's eyes rove all over him as if trying to memorize the sight of him, their reddened mouth open and panting. Then they glance up at his face, and the hunger Ravi sees there is such a turn-on that it's not long before his dick is back in the game. Cayenne's chest heaves as they pull their hand back. They take Ravi's thigh in one hand and slide on a condom with the other.

"Yes?" they ask, licking their lips.

"Yes," Ravi says.

He pushes back as Cayenne drives in. They're a tight fit; larger than their slight frame would suggest, and Ravi forces himself to breathe, to relax. A jolt of pleasure lances sharply as Cayenne fully eases in, a shocked little moan crawling up the back of their throat.

Ravi throws his head back, mouth falling open. Cayenne shifts up onto their knees, drawing Ravi's leg up over their shoulder and hanging on to it for leverage. They rock into him with a slow, grinding rhythm that quickly has Ravi shaking, desperately wanting more.

Acting on instinct alone he writhes, hands grasping wildly at their hips to spur them on, get them even closer. Cayenne chuckles, finding their voice again. It's low and husky, but they manage to keep up a string of mingled praise and teasing without faltering.

"*Merde*, but you are an eager thing, aren't you? I *pride* myself on my wanton nature, but look at *you*, sweet thing. Just give you the opportunity and you can match me, aha, stroke for stroke. Guess it's true what they say about you buttoned-down types." They fold Ravi's leg up so high his knee is nearly by his ear and lean over him with one hand propped on the headboard. "And aren't you delightfully *bendy*!" They rock into him with a variety of strokes, a goddamn sampler platter, some long, some short, some circling and teasing, until Ravi can't possibly predict what's coming next and it's absolutely a form of torture.

Their voice is breathy, faintly shaky. "Look at you, I wish you could see yourself right now. Under those fancy bespoke suits, you're *greedy* for it, aren't you?"

Body open wide, Ravi covers his face with his hands. "Stop. Talking," he pleads.

"Oh, I thought you *liked* it when I talk. '*You have such a nice voice, Cayenne,*'" they say with a mocking grin. They let go of the headboard to sit back up, and Ravi seizes his opportunity. In a flash he pulls Cayenne down on top of him and wraps his thighs around their waist, his heels digging into the back of their legs, effectively trapping them in place, buried deep.

With an amused huff, they push themself back up with hands planted on either side of Ravi's face. They're about to say something, almost inevitably something snarky, but whatever they see there a few bare inches away from Ravi's face freezes the words on their tongue. Cayenne looks at Ravi like they're seeing him for the first time.

No one has ever looked at Ravi this way before. Terrifying and thrilling both, scales balanced.

He lets his hands fall away from their shoulders and rest, palms up, on the bed. Without breaking eye contact, Cayenne lowers their weight to their elbows and lays their hands overtop his, palm to palm. Their fingers tangle together.

When they start moving, more slowly now, hips rocking in tandem, Ravi feels every inch of his body as an open nerve. The only thing more unbearable than Cayenne's constant stream of dirty talk is *this;* this silent, unwavering focus. Ravi wishes he could hide his face. Every little thought and emotion must be written plainly across it, in big, bold letters.

This time when they come, it's not a wild, explosive show, the hard clap of flesh and sultry moans. It's a shocked, quiet gasp, forehead to forehead, fingers interlaced tight. They pant, breath mingling together. When Ravi rocks down on Cayenne with a plaintive sound, they reach a hand down between them, wrap it around his cock, and still buried deep inside him they draw out an orgasm that feels like it comes all the way up from his toes, from the ground itself. Momentum swells as it rises, a building thunderhead, and when it finally crashes over him it's exactly like the first storm of the season. Rain on parched earth.

Staring, they breathe each other's air, and separate slowly, untangling limbs. The last thing to pull apart are their hands, clasped so tightly they're beginning to cramp.

They look up at the ceiling, catching their breath. After a moment, Cayenne places a palm on Ravi's stomach. He covers their hand with his own.

"How am I supposed to go back?" he asks softly. "Just get off the plane tomorrow and…life as normal." And he knows he's doing it again, pulling off his armor and inviting

Cayenne to strike, but can't stop himself. Being around Cayenne shakes him up, truth rattling and tumbling out.

"Well," Cayenne says, voice shaking, before they clear their throat and try again. "We don't actually have to."

Ravi looks over. "What?"

"I could take us back. To the first day. We could stay here as long as you want."

Ravi stares. "That's not going to scramble my brain?"

"*Non, non*...probably not." They muster up a wink. "A headache, maybe a touch of nausea, but it should be fine. I, ah, haven't actually...brought someone back with me before, that span of time. So, I'm not one *hundred* perce—"

"I'll do it."

Cayenne bites their lip, looking away as a pink flush creeps up their chest and into their face. "This evening, then."

"Cayenne?"

Cayenne doesn't look over. They shut their eyes tightly and draw in a deep breath. "Yes?"

"Will you take my picture?"

Cayenne's eyes flash open, and they sit up. "Will I take... Whatever for, darling? I mean, certainly, if you like."

Ravi had been giving this a lot of thought, in the back of his mind. "I know you can't have pictures of yourself out in the world. I get that. So"—he slides up the headboard and rests his head back—"so, I can't have a picture of *you*, but I can have a picture of *me*. Looking...happy. And I'll be able to look at it and know that you were there with me, that you...you were the one who made me look that way."

Cayenne blinks several times quickly, covering their mouth with their hand, and turns away. They sit on the edge of the bed with both feet touching the floor. For a long moment they don't say anything, back still turned. "I don't know, Ravi," they finally say, gravely. "It's against the resort rules."

Ravi laughs, one of the rare loud ones that Cayenne so easily extracts from him. "I know how you hate breaking rules."

Cayenne stands up and turns with a flirty grin. "Well, this shameless lawbreaker is fully at your beck and call, my dear. Where's your phone?"

After a stop at the sink to clean up, Cayenne fishes Ravi's red phone from his bag. When Cayenne takes the shot, they look at it for a long second. "Not bad, if I say so myself, *mon chéri*. Okay if I text this to mine?" Ravi nods, trusting Cayenne to keep it secret, then holds out his hand.

Cayenne quickly sends it through to their own number, then hands the phone over and scoots next to Ravi at the headboard, their shoulders touching.

Ravi looks at himself and blinks. He hardly recognizes

the person looking back at him. His hair is absolutely crazy, and he automatically starts smoothing it back. Even his short-cropped beard is mussed and disordered. But the biggest change is his face. It's not the same one he sees every day in the mirror. This is someone he's never seen before. He's showing the camera a secretive smile, nose scrunched, the set of his jaw easy and relaxed. The edge of the frame just catches the top of his bare shoulders. His eyes are drawn to something or somebody just over the camera lens.

He clears his throat and sets his phone aside. "Nice shot. Thanks."

Something strange happens to Cayenne's expression; a slight manic twist to their lips, their eyes darkening.

"I paid the flight crew to spy on you and report what you did," Cayenne blurts, raking a hand fiercely through their hair.

Ravi gapes at the sudden tonal shift. "You…did?"

Cayenne points a finger at him accusingly. "You didn't take my picture or grab some fingerprints or go through my things or—" They cut themself off, clearly frustrated. "Why didn't you?"

"Why didn't I take any—"

"And!" Cayenne interrupts, voice rising an octave. "You…you could have asked me *anything* you wanted when I was under the effects of that venom. Gotten all sorts of secrets out of me. Why didn't you?"

"I..."

"The Trust would be *wild* to get their hot little hands on me. Aren't you a *loyal* little agent, obedient to a fault? *Why didn't you?*"

Ravi just shakes his head.

"No answer? Nothing? *T'expliquer!*"

He doesn't have an answer. Not even for himself. "I don't get it. Did you...did you *want* me to try to gather intel on you?" His voice also rises, angry and confused.

"No!"

"Then why are you mad at me?"

"*I don't know!*" And with that they launch themself at Ravi, a crazed, graceless kiss that Ravi surges up into, teeth bumping and hands greedily grasping. It goes on for a long time, messy and uncoordinated.

Cayenne breaks the kiss and rests their forehead against his, gasping for breath. They shut their eyes and visibly collect themself. When their eyes open, they offer him an apologetic smile. "Normally I would have just rewound myself a little bit there, have a redo, but..." They sigh. "I am unused to only having one try."

Ravi reaches up and cups their chin. "It doesn't make you feel trapped, does it? Like on the plane, or with the venom?"

Cayenne waves a hand airily. "No sweetheart, it is not the same. Leave it to you to—" They break off with a groan of frustration. "I tell you I spied on you, and you ask me *that,* making sure that *I'm*...fuck." They stop and take a deep breath. "*Désolé, mon chéri,* you must forgive my little..."

"Tantrums?" Ravi offers helpfully, with a teasing smirk.

Cayenne mock-shoves him, then leans in swiftly to give him a quick peck. "Now! What shall we do with the rest of our day? I believe there was talk about a movie, some lounging about?"

Chapter Nineteen

THE PAIR MANAGE to achieve some quality lounging, eating leftovers and drinking a mostly full, slightly flat bottle of Moscato, bickering over what to watch. Cayenne eventually suggests the first Terminator movie, as James keeps making references to it along with a multitude of other popular time travel movies, and Cayenne is sick of not being in on the joke. Aside from popular Bolly- and Tollywood fare, there are only a few dozen movies that Ravi has seen *ever*. *The Terminator* isn't one of them, so they dial it up and settle in. They both get a kick out of it for different reasons; Cayenne laughs frequently at explanations of time travel, and Ravi enjoys the action scenes. If either of them happens to find the star-crossed tragedy of Sarah Connor and Kyle to be incredibly romantic, they both keep it to themselves.

The whole while Cayenne rests their head on Ravi's shoulder, and they feel, if only for a little while, something like normal people.

Evening crests as they head to the lobby, Cayenne explaining that it'll likely be less of a strain on Ravi if they're in the same place they will be rewinding back to.

"You know what I am most looking forward to?" Ravi asks them.

"Oh, I can imagine," they say with a flirtatious hip bump.

Ravi shakes his head with a feral smirk. "I'm looking forward to the look on Uwe's face."

Cayenne claps their hands together in delight. "Oh, yes! This time I will get to be fully cognizant to watch you work your particularly violent brand of magic. Oh, *oui*, that *will* be fun, *mon tigre*." Their grin morphs into a pout. "I wanted to give you a relaxing vacation, darling, a little escape. Such a *shame* it was taken up by so much monster nonsense. Though I *suppose* it is nice to know you can be relied upon to dish out your heroics at a moment's notice."

"Ours," says Ravi.

"*Quoi*?"

"*Our* heroics."

Cayenne slaps his shoulder. "You bite your tongue."

Ravi tries unsuccessfully to smother a grin as they enter the lobby. A few folks talk amongst themselves or lounge at the coffee bar. Cayenne takes Ravi by the hand and guides him to a spot by the door. They glance around speculatively, lips pursed. Then they nod once, satisfied with something only they can perceive.

"You ready, my dear?"

Ravi takes a deep breath, quelling nerves. "Yeah."

"Come here." They wrap Ravi in their arms, completely encircling him in an embrace right there in the lobby. Cayenne smiles that foxy grin and catches him in a kiss. No hue and cry from the handful of people scattered in the lobby, not even a murmur of reproach. No one cares. It's a luxury Ravi has never been afforded before, and he loses himself kissing back, eyes shut, hands at rest on Cayenne's slim hips. A strange sensation rises up through him, stronger and more disorienting than the small time skips Cayenne has taken him on before. There's a lurch in his gut, like a car coming to a sudden stop.

He blinks, suddenly standing apart from Cayenne with a dizziness that fades as quickly as it arises. Cayenne watches him, looking very pleased with themself. "There, you look none the worse for wear, my dear. Come now, let's not keep the nice lady waiting." Ravi blinks and sees there is a lady standing next to them. In fact, it's the same young lady who checked them in days ago. Same silk scarf at her neck, hair in the same artful bun, waiting a polite distance away. All the other people who had been in the lobby when they started kissing are gone. Sunlight no longer paints the room with the low orange of sunset but has the clear quality of morning. Ravi's bag is slung across his shoulder, and when he checks his hands, the skin of his knuckles is whole and healed.

"Gentlemen," she says, inviting them to the desk. "We are very happy to welcome you to the Seychelles!" Ravi lets Cayenne lead him by the hand.

"*Bonjour*, miss! We've a reservation for two beachside bungalows. Though"—here they give Ravi a glance that is both sly and inquiring—"we've discussed on the way over that we think we will only need one, if that will not be a problem." Cayenne shoots Ravi a wink.

In answer, he squeezes their hand and says, "Yeah. One is fine."

*

IT TAKES BUT a matter of moments to dispatch Uwe, the nix, as soon as he introduces himself, and after that there are no further incidents, the Warden presumably resuming its post at the Veil between worlds.

The days and nights blend easily into each other, many more dinners and dances, more walks on the beach, more hikes to the jungle vista, even a few couples' massages at Cayenne's insistence. And lots and lots of time spent in bed. And on the counter. The couch. The shower, up against a wall, a couple of times the floor, and once, memorably, outdoors hidden behind some palm trees.

Ravi buys a sun hat for Cayenne from the gift shop, who complains that it's not nearly as nice as Elissa's but wears it anyway. Sometimes they fight—in truth, very often they fight—but they always make up so enthusiastically that Ravi worries he's developing a Pavlovian response to Cayenne being irritated with him. They talk. They learn to better navigate the hills and valleys of each other's more delicate subjects, which paths to take and which pitfalls to avoid. Ravi, through practice and perseverance, learns just a little how to live in the now. He'll never be great at it, but it's a lesson he's grateful Cayenne wants to teach him.

Even so, he can't shake the growing disquiet of abandoning his duties, of shirking his responsibilities, so one fine day he sighs, and tells Cayenne he has to go home.

On the flight back Cayenne nervously tries out what Ravi had suggested during their first flight and gets incredibly drunk instead of taking the sleeping pills. They pop a bottle of champagne and proceed to mimosa themself into a handsy, giggly state that works decently well as a distraction.

A few hours out from Atlanta, Ravi's game console gets plucked from his hands, replaced by a lapful of restless redhead. "Ravi, darling, I'm *bored*."

"I hadn't saved that," Ravi mutters.

Cayenne rubs their face against the rasp of his cheek. "Mm, so soft and scratchy. Can I invite you to the club?"

Ravi hangs on to Cayenne's waist as they start to tip off their precarious perch on his lap. He shakes his head with a crooked smile. "What club? What are you talking about?"

"Ohh, *you* know," Cayenne sing-songs, "the Mile High Club, of course. *Faisons-le, mon cher.*"

Ravi kisses Cayenne's cheek, avoiding their lips when they try to turn it into a full-fledged make-out. "*You* are very drunk. Cute, but drunk."

Cayenne looks mortally offended. "You think I'd be any, how d'you say, a *smidgen* less interested sober? Darling, have you met me?" They drop kiss after kiss on Ravi, anywhere they can reach, until Ravi puts his hands up in defense and holds their face still between them.

"I...literally cannot say no to you," he says with some alarm. So, he drags Cayenne to the jet's sleeping cabin. And it's the closest they come to saying goodbye.

When they land, disembark, and step onto the concourse, Cayenne turns to him with a bright, plastered-on smile. "I absolutely *hate* goodbyes, darling, unpleasant things that they are. So, I'll just say now... I'll be seeing you." They wink, tap him on the nose, and disappear around the corner.

Literally disappear. Ravi skids around after them, swearing under his breath when he finds only an empty hallway.

*

HE GOES HOME. Or what passes for home. To the Trust-issued apartment he has been assigned while stationed in Atlanta. He sits on a black synthetic leather couch he didn't pick out and looks around at the bland hotel art he didn't choose and thinks about the sound of the ocean.

He reassembles his Trust-issued phone, sliding the battery back in and setting it to charge. On his personal phone he starts composing a text to Nate, thanking him for his help with the monster intel, before realizing none of that happened.

Fucking time travel.

Instead, he texts Constance to tell her, *I'm back in town. Thanks for the iron nails. They came in handy*. She sends back a blurry picture of her thumb, then a one-and-a-half second voice message of her cursing, then finally, *Always happye to lend mine hande, witch-hunter.*

He takes out his third phone, the candy-red color standing out brightly in the monochrome room, when the Trust phone, now charged, flashes and buzzes.

A message from his Aunt Padme. Ravi sighs, shoulders slumping. A politely worded request to take lunch with her tomorrow. He knows better than to think it isn't mandatory. He'd hoped for a little more time to adjust. Not just the effects of jet lag, he feels…it's like waking up from a dream, the kind that leaves you confused and disoriented, unsure which side of reality your feet are on. But he is—as Cayenne eloquently put it—a loyal little agent. Always has been. Always will be.

*

RAVI RESUMES HIS daily routine, rising early to exercise, then breakfast with coffee and a microwaved masala dosa he eats about half of. Then he dons his armor. Not his literal bulletproof vest, though that would help him feel better, but one of his best suits, the one with the South Asian cut of the collars and cuffs. Long-sleeved shirt buttoned up to the chin, waistcoat, slim-lapel jacket, tie, pocket square, cufflinks, watch; each item fixed into place like loading a bullet into a magazine. He checks the mirror carefully before leaving, inspecting his appearance for any flaws or tells. But he looks like he always does. He's fine.

He enters the restaurant with shoulders squared, taking a few long, settling breaths. He's a few minutes early, which to Aunt Padme is nearly as bad as being late. Sure enough, when he approaches her table, she raises one elegant eyebrow and remarks, "Cutting it close today, are we?" She indicates the empty chair with a slight wave.

"Sorry, ma'am." He slides into his seat, back straight. He's glad he went for a formal look, as her outfit is a sublime Indo-Western fusion that perfectly marries business suit and sari. She keeps him waiting for a moment, taking a long sip of her tea.

"You look tired." She possesses an imposing voice with an accent colored by British education, and beautiful eyes that glint like ice chips.

"I'm fine."

She sniffs delicately, a habit she's had as long as he's known her, and likely has had her whole life. She manages to say a lot with only a sniff. This one conveys that her high expectations had yet again, sadly not been met. "Which one of them is it?"

This is an unusual deviation. He keeps his face still through his confusion. "Ma'am?"

She sighs deeply with disappointment. "Surely not the witch. Just tell me it's not that grubby little private eye with the horrible fashion sense. Honestly, Ravi."

He freezes, mind racing furiously. What did she know? What had she seen? Should he call her bluff? Had he left signs, was there a trail? "I don't know—"

"Please do not insult me by pretending ignorance." Her words slice down with scalpel precision. "I don't necessarily object to you—" She pauses with a hint of distaste, "—*fraternizing* with the hired help, though it is a disappointment, I must admit. I just want to know: which one is it?"

He lowers his chin so she can't spot the pulse racing in his throat. "Valiance," he manages. Guilt and disgust rise sharp and sour into his mouth at his relief that his aunt had followed the clues he must have left—*sloppy*, should have been more *careful*—and come to the wrong conclusion. He swallows it all down, crushing it low, the action made easier by long years of practice.

"Ah!" Aunt Padme perks up the smallest fraction. "Well. If you were going to dally, she is the most acceptable option, despite her not being human. A fine warrior, by all accounts. One could hardly blame you. But"—she sets her teacup down, the china clicking—"the time to dally is over. You are twenty-five. It has been nearly eight years, Ravi."

He licks his lips. "Nothing from the networks?" He hopes to put her on the defensive, make her answer for the failure of the intelligence channels in finally finding answers to the question of where Durga's favor would manifest. But he knows it's a vain hope before he even speaks.

"The networks are not your concern. Your concern should be *our* concern, The Trust's concern. Our *family's* concern. We need the new Chosen, Ravi. It is only a matter of time before there rises a serious threat only the Chosen can match. We need their abilities, and we need them to be under *our* guidance."

"With respect, ma'am." She looks at him archly, surprised at his interruption. He's pretty surprised himself. "It's not like my...my *eggs* are going to dry up. I've got time."

She shakes her head forbiddingly, unimpressed. "This is not a matter for levity, Ravi. It takes a long time to raise the Chosen to their full potential. Surely you remember some of that, after all the time we fruitlessly invested in you."

He takes a deep breath, keeping his hands flat and still on the table. "But—"

"Enough." Her voice has the ringing peal of finality, a bell that can't be unrung. "I have been very patient while you play soldier. It is long past time to assure your legacy. Our *family's* legacy. Durga's Chosen has been born to the Abhiramnews for generations, for centuries; we will *not* lose that." She picks up a silver spoon and stirs honey into her cup. "Your mother was able to get away with flaunting tradition because she was the Chosen. You do not have that luxury. You need to put away your toys and marry—and marry someone *suitable*—and have babies. Your mother broke with tradition, refused marriage and wasted her bloodline, and look where that got us," she says with a dismissive wave in Ravi's direction and a tired sigh.

He concentrates on the feel of the cloth under his palms, thinking about the sound of the wind through palm trees.

"I have arranged a dinner for you with Jessika Eaton. She's of good stock, from the local branch. Her father is a senator."

"I remember Jessika," Ravi says numbly. She's not any sort of monster-hunter, but one of the more public figures of the younger generations of The Trust. A successful media publisher focusing on digital content. They'd known each other as kids, and in recent years he's run into her several times at Trust functions. Seemed like every time he turned around, Jessika was always there.

"Excellent. You're meeting her in three weeks."

Three weeks. He thought he'd have more time. A lot more. Years. He hadn't planned on this barreling toward him so soon. Sand falling through the hourglass.

What would Cayenne do, were they in his place?

Maybe, if he was clever, he could find a way around this. He had a little time to do his research, to plan. To buy some more time.

"Yes, ma'am," he says, knowing it is exactly what his aunt wishes to hear.

She smiles warmly and pats his hand. "Good lad. Now. Enough of that. To business." She draws herself up with all the poise of a general. "Any new developments with McAllister's team?"

"No, ma'am. Status unchanged on all counts."

"How is the new one settling in?"

"Dr. Corbin is doing very well. He's adapting quickly to the situation. His knowledge has already helped a great deal."

She nods in approval. "And the time traveler?"

His heart stops before he realizes she's talking about Constance. "She is also adapting well."

His aunt brushes away his words impatiently. "*Bandar kya jaane adrak ka svaad?*" It's a favorite idiom of hers. *What does a monkey know of the taste of ginger?* "I am not inquiring how the peasant girl is enjoying modern conveniences, Ravi. I need to know if she has figured out how to replicate the magic that sent her forward into our time. Or learned how to return to her own."

He shakes his head. "No, ma'am. I don't think she's

concerned with that. She's singularly focused on hunting the demon that came through with her. Still no new leads there."

"Hm. And what of this James? Nothing more from him after the incident with the young somamancer?"

"Nothing."

Aunt Padme laces her fingers together. "Ravi. We need this person. We need intelligence on him. Better yet, we need you to bring him in. Recruitment, ideally. Think how much it would mean for us, if we could understand his ability, his technology. Think how much we would set right if we had the ability to travel through time. How many evils we would thwart. How many lives we would save." She is so earnest, her strength of purpose and dedication making him sit a little taller in his chair. Sometimes it's inspiring just to be near her. She doesn't rule solely with an iron fist, but with this, her unwavering sense of duty. "It's an ability too powerful to be in the hands of those who would misuse it."

He licks his lips. "I understand."

"Good." She takes a sip of her tea. "Once you have started a family, you will of course be removed from field work. *However...*" He can't help but raise his brows at her conspiratorial tone. "If you find any leads on this time traveler, or any time anomalies Shaw may yet cause, then those must take precedence. I'm sure Miss Eaton would understand any delay necessary."

He blinks. This is…unusual. The first time anything has been deemed more important than his usefulness as breeding stock. The first time he can see a real, tangible way out of the trap of an arranged marriage.

And all he has to do is get his hands on a time traveler.

Epilogue

THAT NIGHT HE finally plucks up his nerve and sends a text on the red phone.

RAVI: *Just making sure you sobered up ok :)*

Cayenne's response comes within the minute.

CAYENNE: *Aren't you a SWEETHEART! I am fine, darling. Apologies for the less than tender goodbye but I thought you might prefer a LACK of public displays of affection.*

Ravi: You thought right. Thanks. I know subtlety is not

your preferred style.

CAYENNE: *But of course, darling! Any free time in July? What do you say to another getaway to COLDER climes this time? Snuggle in front of a WARM fire in our own cabin, yes? It'll give you a break from the OPPRESSIVE summer heat!*

RAVI: *I'll let you know. My schedule might have some changes pretty soon.*

Not sure if I'll be able to get away. Trust stuff.

I like the heat.

He adds a sun emoji, then hits send before he thinks better of it.

CAYENNE: *C'est TRAGIQUE! Your Trust, they are the absolute WORST! (frowny face emoji)*

Alas, I am a DELICATE ginger flower, darling, so I would prefer to not have to slather on so MUCH sunscreen—unless YOU are doing the slathering, of course!

Ravi smiles at the kissy-face Cayenne tacks on.

CAYENNE: *Well, if you CAN get away, DO let me know,*

dearest!

Ravi bites his lip. "Dearest" is a new one.

RAVI: *Trying to get me somewhere secluded?*

If I can get away, somewhere snowy it is.

Ttyl

Cayenne sends a string of alternating kisses and chili peppers, so long it wraps around the screen. Ravi stares at it for a while, welcome warmth spilling through him, near overflowing with it. He's a bit startled when his personal phone vibrates in his pocket. He fishes it out, swaps it for the red phone, and swipes into a call with Harry.

"Hey, agent guy!" she says before he can even get out a greeting. "Back in town?"

"Harry. Yeah, back in town."

"Kill any fun monsters while you were away?"

"Actually, yeah," he admits with a wry little huff.

Harry snorts. "Fuck, I was kidding. Take a vacation sometime, dude. Anyhoo, there's another poker night happening in about an hour. You in this time? I bet you could clean up, you're like Mr. Poker Face. Free advice, Nate can't bluff for shit and Constance cheats."

Ravi considers. Maybe he could—

His red phone buzzes in his pocket; another text from Cayenne. "No thanks. I'm… I've got plans."

"Fair enough, more winnings for me. So." Ravi straightens up at her business-like shift in tone. "You been hearing any rumblings about some new vampires moving into the city?"

Ravi frowns. "Nothing on my end."

"It might be nothing, but I've been putting together some clues from the different hunter forums, and I dunno. Looks a little sketch."

"Hm. I'll see what I can dig up."

"Same here. I'll keep you posted."

"Harry," he offers, "I just filed a status report with the upper brass. Wanted you to know."

She's quiet for slightly too long. "Are we still head of the class? Getting straight As?"

"Highest success rates in the region."

"Golly," she says with a hefty dose of sarcasm. "Just so you know, I've always appreciated that you laid your cards on the table from the get-go, with us. I'll bet that wasn't standard operating procedure, with a group of rando amateur monster-hunters."

"Yeah, with your credentials, I didn't think I'd be able to get away with the usual cover story. Flash you a badge from one of the alphabet agencies and keep you in the dark." He's never regretting the decision to tell Harry about The Trust, or at least, the outer circles of it, and that they were interested in working with her. Honesty is a rare novelty.

"Hm. You still in hot water about the Lucy thing?"

Ravi shrugs even though she can't see it. "Not exactly."

When it's clear nothing more is forthcoming, Harry just changes the subject, forging ahead. "Cool, great. Well, thanks for letting me know." She's good at boundaries. Ravi likes that about her. She never pries. Keeps things professional. "Hey. Rav. You know that if you, like, need anything...you can ask, right?"

Ravi blinks, surprised. A little baffled. "Sure." That's probably an insufficient response. "Thanks," he adds.

He can make out a tiny, resigned sigh on Harry's end. "Okay, good. Guess we'll see you the next time there's a job."

After an exchange of goodbyes, Ravi hurriedly checks his scarlet phone, eager to see what else Cayenne has written.

CAYENNE: *For once I hope you are wearing pants, my sweet.* (winky face, gift emoji)

I sent you a PRESENT, just a little reminder that freedom is just a KISS away!

Ravi only has a second to puzzle over this before a knock raps at the door. Just in case, he grabs his 9mm and tucks it behind him before checking the peephole. He cracks open the door, and the delivery man tips his hat in a friendly fashion.

"Package for you, sir."

He takes it with a muttered thanks and shuts the door. The large, flat package is big enough that he has to move aside his half-eaten salad to set it on the minimalist coffee table to unwrap it.

He uncovers a framed poster of the Seychelles, one of those classy vintage designs. It showcases the white sand beach, a ribbon of turquoise ocean, palm trees leaning into the frame. Stippling the sky are several black parrots, wings wide in flight. Ravi picks it up, smiling broadly. As he tilts it to the light, something catches his eye. It's hard to see, but in the lower right corner hides a rich plum-colored lipstick mark.

Acknowledgements

My profound thanks to my Monster of the Week group for their unwavering support and helpful critiques. Amanda Schuckman and S.T. Pelletier, both my writing and my life have been enriched by knowing you in ways I can't even measure. Special shout-out to K.D. Bryan from the bottom of my drama-loving heart for the spice. This is your fault.

A big heartfelt hug to my partner for suffering ever-so-stoically as a writer's widower. I literally could not have done this without you.

And finally, a massive thanks to you, Mom, for gifting me your love for the written word, and for always believing in me. Please skip the sex scenes.

About the Author

Fox Beckman lives in the Twin Cities and enjoys crafting stories about swords, sorcery, and smooches; the queerer and spicier, the better. Especially stories about diverse nuanced characters creating found families, and monsters becoming lovers—or even lovers becoming monsters.

And for some reason, there's always a talking animal.

Email

fox@foxbeckman.com

Twitter

@foxbeckman

Website

www.foxbeckman.com

Connect with NineStar Press

WWW.NINESTARPRESS.COM

WWW.FACEBOOK.COM/NINESTARPRESS

WWW.FACEBOOK.COM/GROUPS/NINESTARNICHE

WWW.TWITTER.COM/NINESTARPRESS

WWW.INSTAGRAM.COM/NINESTARPRESS

Made in the USA
Monee, IL
14 March 2024

54436357R00184